"I've been look

Brady turned as a woman came down the hospital corridor toward him, and for an instant he thought he knew her. Then the idea fled. If he'd met this woman before, he wouldn't have forgotten the incident easily.

"You're looking for me?"

"Yes, I am," Jayne said as she glanced at his visitor's badge. "I was beginning to wonder if you might have backed out. Shall we?" She motioned to a door.

He reached out and pushed back the door with one hand, then stepped through.

"Here we are. This is Rocky, and this is Mandy." She inclined her head to two tiny bundles, one pink, one blue, and both squirming.

Brady realized that the "bundles" were babies.

Jayne touched his arm. "Sit down and get comfortable."

"I—I don't think . . ." he stammered.

"You don't get a choice tonight, Mr. Appleton. You're getting Rocky."

Appleton? Babies? He was *getting* Rocky? Before Brady knew what was happening, she had handed him the tiny blue bundle.

Dear Reader,

I hope you've noticed our new look and that you like it as much as we do. At last, Silhouette Intimate Moments, the most mainstream line in category romance, has a look as exciting as the stories themselves. And what stories we have for you this month!

Start off with the Award of Excellence title, Linda Howard's *Duncan's Bride*. This story of a gruff rancher who advertises for a wife puts a few unexpected spins on a traditional plot. Reese Duncan wants a woman who will cook and clean and bear his children. Madelyn Patterson is willing to do all that, but she wants something in return: love. Heather Graham Pozzessere's *Wedding Bell Blues* reunites Brendan O'Herlihy with his ex-wife, Kaitlin. As best man and maid of honor for a series of weddings, they are forced to confront each other—and the feelings that have never gone away. With *Lightning Strikes*, Kathleen Korbel brings her irrepressible humor and passion to a tale of a woman who sees the future and a man who won't have a future unless he listens closely and spends it with her! Finally, Mary Anne Wilson offers *Brady's Law*. Watch as a case of mistaken identity and a tiny baby named Rocky bring together two people who never should have met but can't seem to say goodbye once they've said hello.

In months to come, watch for Emilie Richards to provide a sequel to her "sisters" stories, Lee Magner to follow *Sutter's Wife* with *The Dragon's Lair*, and favorites like Marilyn Pappano and Paula Detmer Riggs to offer new books—and all of it will be happening only in Silhouette Intimate Moments. Join us for the excitement.

Leslie J. Wainger
Senior Editor and Editorial Coordinator

MARY ANNE WILSON

Brady's Law

SILHOUETTE·INTIMATE·MOMENTS®

Published by Silhouette Books New York

America's Publisher of Contemporary Romance

SILHOUETTE BOOKS
300 East 42nd St., New York, N.Y. 10017

ISBN: 0-373-07350-X

First Silhouette Books printing September 1990

Books by Mary Anne Wilson

Silhouette Intimate Moments

Hot-Blooded #230
Home Fires #267
Liar's Moon #292
Straight from the Heart #304
Dream Chasers #334
Brady's Law #350

MARY ANNE WILSON

fell in love with reading at age ten when she discovered *Pride and Prejudice*. A year later she knew she had to be a writer when she found herself writing a new ending for *A Tale of Two Cities*. A true romantic, she had Sydney Carton rescued, and he lived happily ever after.

Though she's a native of Canada, she now lives in California with her husband, children, a six-toed black cat, who believes he's Hungarian and five timid Dobermans, who welcome any and all strangers. And she's writing happy endings for her own books.

For Linda Wisdom
who managed to survive...

strange airports
Kamikaze Charlie
room keys that didn't work
and watching trains at midnight

Thanks!

Prologue

Y ou don't want to die, believe me."

Jayne Spencer heard the voice from a great distance, a deep, insistent male voice that seemed to echo somewhere inside her. And she wondered why he thought she wanted to die.

As she stood on a narrow ledge six stories above the full parking lot of Santa Barbara Memorial Hospital, she felt immortal, just as she had when she was a child. She and her sisters had climbed to the highest limb of the old elm tree in the backyard of their house and dared each other to jump. She had always thought that if she wished hard enough, she could really have flown. But she'd never had the courage to take that step and really let go. Not until now. Now she felt as if she could take that one step and fly away forever.

Gazing across a sea of red-tiled roofs, the city far below the hill where the new hospital had been built, down to the brilliant blue of the Pacific a few miles away, she lifted her chin and let the warm sun of July caress her skin. If she just wished hard enough, she could fly. She knew it.

Tendrils of disheveled ebony hair brushed across her cheeks, and she relished the gentle tickling sensation. The kiss of the warm breeze ran across her nerves in the most pleasant way. Even the gritty hardness of the ledge under her bare feet felt good to her.

She hadn't felt this alive since—

That voice cut into her thoughts. "Talk to me. Just talk to me. Stand very still. Don't move, and tell me what's wrong."

Jayne tried to block out the words and thought about drifting away, going higher and higher, soaring. Sara, her big sister, would understand. She would know Jayne could fly. She wouldn't want her to stay here, not now.

"Look at me. Now!" the voice commanded sharply. "Look at me, Jayne."

Her muscles tightened, and her bare toes curled against the cold ledge. That damn voice was keeping her anchored, and she hated it. The speaker didn't understand anything. She closed her eyes tightly, bit her bottom lip so hard she could taste the sharp metallic sting of blood on her tongue and concentrated on flying. She just had to close out the sound of the voice, to wish, to believe.

But it didn't work.

"Jayne," the voice said again.

"Let me go," she sighed, but the words were torn away by the breeze as soon as they were uttered. That was all she wanted. She certainly didn't want to stay at the hospital, not when she had a way out, a way to leave behind everything that had become unbearable to her. The operations, the pain, the recuperation . . . a life without Elliot.

When she was five, the idea of flying had been magical for her. Standing on the branch of the old elm, her arms outstretched, her face lifted to the sky, she'd almost taken that first step. If her mother hadn't yelled, she would have.

She wasn't going to let this voice stop her now.

"Jayne, come to me. Come back inside. Let's talk. Please."

"Leave me alone," she said as the breeze caught at her hospital gown and tangled it around her bare legs. "Just leave me alone and let me go."

"No, I won't. I can't."

Tears of frustration stung her eyes behind her closed lids. Why was he doing this? She was certain she didn't know him. He couldn't know her. What did he care if she soared above the city? Why couldn't he be like Sara had been and clap his hands and urge her on. "You can do it, Jayne, you can fly. I know you can," Sara had called to her from a lower branch.

But there was no encouragement in the man's voice, just a deep insistence. "Stay still. I'm here for you. I won't leave. Just talk to me." The voice seemed to surround her and began to sap her strength. "I'll try to help, to make things right again, I promise."

No, she knew the magnitude of that lie. The same words had come from her parents, even Sara, her other two sisters, her doctors, and the nurses.

Lies, all lies.

Slowly she opened her eyes and looked down at the dark blur of the parking lot cut into the steep hillside that was still raw from the construction of the hospital. "You can't," she said, the ground beginning to spin, shimmering with a fuzzy grayness. Just one step, one short step into the air. Now was the time to do it. One step. She slowly lifted her bare foot.

"Jayne, no!" The voice was there immediately. "Don't! I want you to come inside with me. Please, come inside."

"Who...who are you?" she asked, uncertainly putting her foot back on the cold granite of the ledge but not looking toward the source of the voice.

"I'm with the Santa Barbara Police Department. I want to help. Please, don't move. Just let me help you."

Without warning, the world came into sharp focus for Jayne. She saw a gathering crowd of people in the black asphalt parking lot, all looking up, and she could almost feel them collectively holding their breath. Two police cars with flashing lights and screaming sirens screeched into the lot, and people were running toward the building.

She didn't know what they were doing. Ever so slowly a mist seemed to be filtering into her mind, blurring her thoughts. Slowly the ground started to undulate, coming closer to her, making that one step so easy. So very easy. One step out into the air. Just one step.

Without warning, she sensed movement beside her, and at the same moment she heard that voice coming from just inches away. He was going to stop her. "No!" she screamed and frantically leaped forward into the air. But instead of soaring, she was jerked to a bone-jarring stop. A viselike hold on her wrist kept her dangling like a rag doll above the parking lot. Wind roared in her ears; the world swirled in a painful blur. Jayne fought frantically to be free, flailing her legs, swiping futilely with her free hand to try to break that unrelenting grip.

"Damn it, stop!" the voice yelled, not soft and encouraging now, but rough and angry. "The lifeline won't hold if you keep this up. You may want to die, but I don't!"

No, he had it all wrong, she thought as she went limp. She wanted something—no, she needed something—but it wasn't death. Then she felt herself being tugged upward and enveloped by fierce heat and strength.

Her clenched hands were pinned between her breasts and some strange man's chest. Where was Elliot? Why wasn't he here holding her? Hadn't he promised never to leave her, not to forsake her, through sickness and health, until death...

"Oh, God," she groaned, knowing everything in that moment.

"I understand," the voice said, rumbling against her face as fingers laced in her tangled hair to hold her tightly. "They told me about your husband. No one can blame you for wanting to get away from such pain."

With a gasp, she sagged, clung to the strength all around her and began to cry in great gulping sobs. Elliot was gone. Gone, and she couldn't fly away from the pain of her loss.

The next thing she knew, she was being lifted high in someone's arms.

"You're not going to die today, Jayne," the voice said. "Not while I'm here. You have your whole life ahead of you."

What life? she wanted to ask, but she couldn't get any words past the agony that was choking her.

Then the voice was there, filling her ears with softly whispered words she couldn't quite understand as she began a downward spiral into a long, black tunnel of blessed forgetfulness.

Chapter 1

Two years later

Brady Knight slept alone by choice.

He decided long ago that women were a pleasant diversion but not a necessity. He enjoyed having warmth and softness next to him, reaching out to find someone there in the deep shadows of the night. He simply didn't want the emotional commitment prolonged closeness bred. He didn't want the core of his life cluttered with emotional dependency, didn't want to spend his time trying to meet the needs of another person. He liked being alone.

He'd tried marriage once, a few years after he made detective with the Santa Barbara Police Department, and he had failed miserably. He wasn't good at being everything for another person, so he did what he knew he was good at—forming brief relationships that filled niches in his life from time to time.

Right now he wasn't involved with anyone or anything except seven current open cases that were nowhere near being marked "closed." One of them had kept him out until two o'clock in the morning, so when the phone rang and his hard-earned sleep was shattered, he muttered one single curse and forced himself to wake up.

He shifted his six-foot-three frame and felt the rough tweed of the couch against his bare back and legs. He remembered he'd fallen asleep there, unable to make it to his rumpled bed in the small bedroom not more than twenty feet away. The phone rang again on the end table, about a foot from his ear. With a repeat of his original curse, but with less sleepy grogginess, he groped above his head. Once he touched the cold plastic of the receiver, he gripped it and managed to get it to his ear.

"Yeah?" he muttered as he rested his forearm over his eyes.

"Thank God, Brady. I didn't think you were ever going to answer this thing. Are you awake?"

He recognized the voice of Jack Wills, his partner, even though the man was speaking barely above a whisper. "I am now, Jack. What the hell do you need?"

"*I need you* to come down to Waylan and Glenn as soon as you can. I've been working on a hunch, and I've stumbled onto something. I need you here. My car's just past the first alley north on Waylan. Park behind it, and I'll find you."

Before Brady could make heads or tails of what Jack was talking about, the dial tone droned in his ear. He hated the idea of having to get up and go out again, but he knew his partner wasn't a capricious man. This had to be important.

With real regret at the sleep snatched away from him, Brady pushed himself up with one hand and squinted over his shoulder through the shadows of the living room to the luminous digits of the clock by the phone. Four a.m.—

only two hours since he'd walked into his apartment, stripped down to his jockey shorts and lain down on the couch. Everything was a blank until Jack's call.

Double shifts were about seven hours too much for him anymore. He raked both hands through his unruly blond hair and tried to shake off the lingering tendrils of sleep. Had Jack mentioned going anywhere except home when they'd separated at the station? No, he didn't think so. But he remembered that Jack had files with him.

Then again, Jack was always taking his work home. Jack was the exact opposite of Brady. He was the sort of cop who started at point A to get to point D without even considering skipping B or C. Brady went on hunches, flying past the mundane to go with his instincts. But Jack would spend hours going over reports trying to find a needle in the haystack.

Procedure. Jack loved that word. Brady hated it and avoided it as much as he could.

Now it seemed Jack had gone into one of the most undesirable sections of the city and found *something*. Brady couldn't begin to guess what that something was. He scrubbed at his eyes with his knuckles, then stood in the silent room and ran both hands over his face. He took a deep breath, then shook his head sharply from side to side. The need to shed sleep as quickly as possible was part of police work, and he'd perfected it over his fifteen years on the force.

"You could keep decent hours if you came into the company," his father had said more than once before reluctantly accepting the fact that his only son wasn't cut out for land development and wanted to be a cop. "Nine to five, Brady, and the quality of people..."

Brady shook his head again, knowing he would never work "banker's hours" on this job. But he had no intention of sitting behind a desk making deals all day. And as far as he was concerned, the people his father dealt with were the same type he dealt with, just better dressed, better mannered, and drove better cars.

He thought about the drug dealer he had arrested a week ago in a new Porsche Carrera. Maybe not better cars, he conceded as he padded into the darkened bedroom and grabbed the first clean clothes he came to—jeans, sneakers, a cotton shirt in a loud Hawaiian print and a black sweatshirt. He dressed quickly, then headed for the door and picked up his gun from the table by the entrance. He snapped its small holster to the back waistband of his pants, tugged the sweatshirt over it, then pushed his badge into his pocket and left.

He drove quickly through the predawn streets in his black Camaro, and in less than ten minutes he was pulling west onto Waylan off of Glenn and parking behind Jack's old sedan. He stilled the low rumble of the Camaro's engine, then sat back in the bucket seat and fingered the leather-clad steering wheel. He watched the empty street and waited.

When Jack hadn't appeared after five minutes, Brady decided to go looking for him. Although it was the middle of October, the air wasn't particularly cool. It held the scent of the nearby ocean mingled with the unmistakable odor of age and decay from the neighborhood.

Only a few cars drove by, and he didn't see anyone on foot. This rundown business district was slated for renewal, but it was far from it right now. And it was a constant source of trouble—robberies, burglaries, assaults, drugs. He hunched his shoulders a bit and looked up and down the street, then walked around the back of the Camaro and onto the sidewalk.

Slowly he headed toward the corner and walked onto Glenn—a two-lane street with cracked pavement, trash in the gutters and massive amounts of graffiti on the walls of a scattering of small businesses and vacant buildings. Three men were huddled in front of an all-night convenience store two doors down. Jack was nowhere in sight.

Brady went west, passing the store and the men who never even looked at him, going past a few boarded up buildings, then crossing the mouth of an alley that ran between a closed Navy Surplus store and a two-story warehouse.

"Brady!"

The harsh whisper surprised him, and he stopped, then turned and took two steps back to the alleyway. He couldn't see anything at first; then he heard a rustling, and Jack emerged from the thick shadows just far enough for Brady to see him.

In a dark suit, the slender man almost blended with the night at his back. At forty-four Jack Wills was nine years older than Brady, and he only had two years until retirement. He wasn't a large man, six inches shorter than Brady, and a good thirty pounds lighter than Brady's a hundred and ninety.

Jack lifted a hand and took another step, then froze when a soft popping sound echoed in the alley, followed immediately by another. The instant Jack began to crumple, Brady understood what was happening. Adrenaline poured through him, and he lunged for Jack, grabbing him just before the slender man fell facedown on the ground. Brady jerked Jack back around the corner of the warehouse to relative safety on the street.

The feeling of sticky, hot blood under his hands barely registered as Brady propped Jack against the brick wall. Then he jerked his gun free of the holster and silently inched toward the corner of the warehouse. His heart pounded in his ears, and he literally held his breath as he cautiously peered around the edge of the building into almost impenetrable shadows. Nothing moved.

He gripped his gun with both hands, took a ragged breath, then broke from cover and aimed into the darkness. "Police," he yelled. "Freeze!" But the only answer was his own voice echoing back to him. He moved farther into the alley, his eyes darting back and forth, but whoever had been there was gone. He could sense he was alone.

Slowly lowering his gun, he waited for one more heartbeat just to be sure, then he turned and hurried back to the street. At the mouth of the alleyway, he turned and yelled at the men in front of the store. "Hey, you guys!" The three of them turned in the direction in unison. "Call 911. Tell them an officer's down. He needs assistance."

He turned back to Jack, dropped to his knees on the sidewalk by the unconscious man slumped against the wall and laid his gun on the cement. Reaching out, he tugged the limp man against his chest, and in the dim glow of the streetlights, he saw the damage. Two points of entry under Jack's right shoulder blade were bleeding freely. He could feel Jack's breathing, thready and uneven, and carefully eased his partner down onto the sidewalk.

"Hang on, buddy, just hang on," he whispered. "You're going to be all right. You'll make it."

Quickly Brady tugged his sweatshirt over his head and balled it up. He had to stop the blood, had to put pressure on the wounds until the ambulance got there. He used the sweatshirt as a makeshift compress, then darted a look back at the convenience store.

Instant rage burned past his fear when he realized the men hadn't moved. They were just staring at him. With a violent oath, he eased Jack onto his back so the sweatshirt was pressed between the wounds and the ground, then he reached for his gun. Scrambling to his feet, he took off at a dead run toward the store. The mèn moved back as he got to them and let him pass to go into the building.

A bell rang as Brady stepped into the cluttered liquor store. A large black man behind a counter turned toward him, then quickly raised his hands and shook his head sharply. "Hey, mister, take whatever you want. Just don't shoot me. I don't care nothing about this place or their money."

Brady looked down at his blood-smeared hand that held the gun. Very slowly he raised his other hand. "It's okay. Take it easy. This isn't what you think. I'm a cop." Carefully he eased his badge out of his pocket, flipped open the case and showed his shield. "I'm Detective Knight, Santa Barbara Police Department. Call 911. Tell them my partner's been shot. I need an ambulance and backup. Give them directions to get here."

Brady sat motionless on the beige chair in the waiting room at Santa Barbara Memorial and fervently wished he hadn't given up smoking two years ago. He wanted nothing more than to draw acrid smoke into his lungs and feel all the tension in him ease. During the hours since Jack had been brought in, while they waited to make a decision about surgery, Brady had stayed in the hospital, not sleeping or eating, maintaining himself only on gallons of bitter coffee.

When Jack had been taken for surgery three hours ago, Brady had paced the halls, contacted headquarters by phone and talked to the other officers who had dropped by to give their support. Right now, though, all he craved was a cigarette.

The sight of Jack's wife, Marcia, sitting across the room with her mother and father hovering over her only increased that urge. A tiny woman with blond hair skimmed back from a pale face, Marcia Wills stared dry-eyed at her hands clenched in her lap. Her parents stayed close, not touching her, yet trying to ease her pain and protect her. But they couldn't.

No one could help that kind of pain. God knows, he couldn't. He closed his eyes for a moment to block out the scene. Santa Barbara was a relatively small town, and in all the years he'd been on the force, he'd never had a partner shot. Now he couldn't get over his feeling of frustration and helplessness. "You've been damn lucky," his father was fond of saying. "You might as well put a gun to your head and play Russian roulette as be a cop."

Brady clenched his hands and wondered why words his father had said in the past would bother him so much now. He'd become adept at shutting them out, ignoring them, or simply walking away. Just the way his father did when he couldn't be bothered with something.

When Brady heard someone come into the room, he opened his eyes. He saw the surgeon, still dressed in surgical greens that were rumpled and stained, come through the door and walk toward Jack's wife. "Mrs. Wills?"

Marcia was on her feet before the doctor reached her, and her father and mother were at her side. Brady stayed where he was, his hands gripping the chair arms. The doctor had come in to tell them about the surgery before it had begun, to explain what he had to do. Now he looked like a pale version of his former self. Exhaustion had deepened the lines on his face and made his skin seem almost chalky. He pulled off his green cap, exposing gray hair clinging damply to his scalp. He wiped the cotton cap over his face, then crushed it in his hand before he spoke.

"Your husband made it through the operations. He's in recovery."

"Is he going to be all right?" Marcia asked in an unsteady voice.

The doctor shrugged. "We're optimistic, but we won't know anything for certain for at least twenty-four hours. We were worried about his lungs, that's why we waited before we operated. One wasn't damaged, but the other was pretty torn up. But your husband's strong. He was obviously in good physical condition before this happened."

Brady turned from the scene and stared out the curtainless window. The darkness over the city seemed to echo the emptiness deep in his being. He could hear the doctor speaking softly to Marcia. "We'll know more when he regains consciousness."

"I . . . I need to see him, please."

"Of course. He'll be in recovery for a while, then he'll be on a respirator, but in his own room. Go down the hall to the right, and the nurse will tell you when you can see him."

"Come on, baby," her mother was saying. "We'll be with you."

There was movement, then the doctor spoke again. "Detective Knight?"

Brady turned to find the doctor closer to him and the room empty. "At least he made it this far," Brady muttered as he sat forward, his forearms on his knees, his hands hanging limply between his legs.

"That's really encouraging," the doctor said, but his face looked grim. "Cops' families are a special breed, I guess. They handle this sort of thing better than most people could."

Brady wasn't so sure they were better at enduring the pain and uncertainty. Maybe they simply expected it. There wasn't the shock someone else would feel. No, that wasn't true. He was on the street all the time, and he still hadn't expected this. Shock was making him vaguely nauseous. The idea of Jack dying cut him deeply—too deeply. For a fleeting moment he wondered if a settled, routine existence would have been the better choice. He wondered if he should have done what he'd been born and raised to do—be the son of Alexander Knight and head A.K. Corporation.

Then he rejected that thought. He was who he was. He lived the way he wanted to. And this was all a part of that life, a part he could deal with. He had to.

"How about yours, Detective?" the doctor was asking.

Brady frowned at him. "My what?"

"Your family. How do they deal with your being with the Police Department?"

"They pretty much ignore it," he admitted.

My son is "in law," his mother would say if anyone asked. *He's making his own path in the world, determined to succeed on his own merit.* That made him sound ambitious instead of foolish for not taking what his father had been ready to hand him.

"Detective Knight?" the doctor asked. "Is something wrong?"

Nothing that some sleep, decent food, and good news wouldn't help, he thought as he stood. "Just worried," he murmured as he tugged at the rumpled Hawaiian shirt, making sure his gun and holster were hidden under the loose cotton before he held out his hand to the doctor. "Thanks for everything you're doing for my partner."

The man's grip was warm and sure, in some indescribable way comforting to Brady for that brief second of contact. "It's my job, Detective. Just like being a cop is yours."

"When can I see Jack? I need to talk to him, to get answers about what happened out there."

"There won't be any answers for a while. We have to get him out of recovery and into a room. Then his wife can go in for a few minutes. If everything looks okay, you can see him after that. But he's on a respirator and couldn't talk even if he was conscious." He glanced at his watch. "It's almost eleven. You look exhausted, too. Go home and get some sleep, then come back in the morning." Unexpectedly he patted Brady on the shoulder. "If we're very lucky, he'll be awake by then."

"No, I'll stay."

The doctor must have sensed that there was no use trying to talk Brady out of staying. With a sigh, he nodded. "All right. But it's after visiting hours." He motioned to the visitor's badge Brady still had on his shirt. "Keep that on so you won't be stopped in the halls. It might be a few hours before you can see Jack."

"I'll go down for coffee," Brady murmured.

"He's going to be on the fifth floor. Contact the nurse at the station there in about an hour or so."

"Thanks," Brady said and watched the man turn and leave.

He stared at the empty doorway and knew his decision to stay was the right one. His ability to sleep at his apartment would be next to nil, and writing up a report could wait forever, as far as he was concerned. He wouldn't really know what to put in it until he could talk to Jack, anyway.

He took one look around the empty waiting room and headed for the door, then walked out into the green-tiled corridor and along to the elevators. He knew the way down to the cafeteria by heart. Coffee. Maybe it would help dissipate the chill deep inside him.

An hour later the hot coffee hadn't helped Brady to warm up at all. He felt cold and alone. As he waited for the elevator, he glanced at his watch. Ten minutes after midnight. He would go up to the nurses' station on the fifth floor, ask about Jack and wait up there where people were moving around, where he could talk to someone if he wanted to.

When the elevator doors slid open, Brady stepped into the empty car and reached out unseeingly to push the floor button. As the doors slid shut, he leaned back against the cool wall.

Closing his eyes for just a moment, he tried to shake the guilt that seemed intent on falling on his shoulders. If only he had told Jack to wait for him at the car. If only he had been able to ask Jack what he'd been working on. He stood straight and shook his head sharply. He hated "what ifs" almost as much as he hated "might have beens," so he wouldn't consider them now.

When the elevator stopped and the doors opened, Brady took a deep breath, then stepped out into the corridor.

"Hello there. I've been looking for you," a soft, decidedly feminine voice said from somewhere to his left.

He turned as a woman came down the hall toward him, and for an instant he thought he knew her. Then the idea fled. If he'd met this woman before, he wouldn't have forgotten the incident easily.

Raven-black hair was skimmed back from a stunningly beautiful face with flawless skin and darkly lashed amber eyes. She wore a white cotton smock that covered her from her neck to her knees. The sleeves were gathered at her slender wrists, and dark slacks showed below the hem and were worn with black pumps.

His heart lurched. Maybe this woman had come to tell him that Jack was worse. It took him a moment to be able to ask, "You're looking for me?"

"Yes, I am," she said as she came within a foot of him and glanced at the visitor's badge. "I was beginning to wonder if you might have backed out. I hoped you hadn't, so I waited a few extra minutes. I was worried you couldn't handle it and wouldn't come. But you did, and that's good."

She spoke rapidly, in a low voice touched with a suggestion of huskiness. Her delicate perfume edged out the scents of the hospital, giving Brady a reprieve from them for a moment. She didn't act like the other hospital personnel he'd dealt with, and, oddly, he found he liked the sound of her voice. It was as soothing in its own way as the doctor's grip had been in the waiting room earlier.

She looked at his shirt, not quite scrunching up her nose at the loud colors. But the distaste was there in her eyes. "You'll need a sterile cover-up."

"If you say so," he said.

Her finely arched brows lifted slightly. "It's hospital regulations. You need to wear one of these." She tugged at her cotton smock. "No masks, but we have to be careful. I know they asked you this, but I want to make sure you don't have a cold or any communicable disease."

They could have asked him anything in the past hours and he wouldn't remember now. He'd spoken to so many nurses and doctors that one blended with another. Until this woman. "No, I'm healthy." He didn't want her to stop talking, not yet. If she did, he would have to face why he was here. He needed a diversion, and this woman, not quite tall enough to look him in the eye despite her heels, was definitely a diversion.

"Good. Wonderful. I know hospitals are depressing for some people, but they do so much good," she said as she glanced at her watch. Incredibly long, dark lashes swept low, feathering against her cheek for an instant. Then she looked at Brady again, a smile curling the corners of her lips, exposing a single dimple in her right cheek. "It's all in a person's attitude, I say. I don't think positive thinking hurts a thing, and who knows, it could very well help."

Amber eyes and dark hair. A provocative combination, Brady thought as he inhaled her perfume again. "No, it couldn't hurt," he murmured.

"Some people feel pretty awkward here," she said as she came closer and, without hesitating, reached out to him. Casually she touched him on the arm, and he barely had time to absorb the softness of her touch and the heat of her hand against his skin before she began to lead him down the corridor. "When they talked to you, they seemed to sense you were a bit reticent about it." She talked quickly as they walked, barely pausing long enough to take a breath. "After all, a man in your profession doesn't spend much time in hospitals, I would think."

She looked at him, flashing that smile again, and he felt its impact somewhere behind his breastbone. "I'm glad you're doing this. It will be good for you. There are rewards in this world, you know. Just doing the right thing brings rewards, but when you help someone, that's special. When you give your time to help healing…" She shrugged. "It can't hurt."

As they approached a pair of green doors, she stopped and let go of Brady. He regretted her releasing him almost as much as he had enjoyed hearing her talk. "Now for the ground rules. All you need to do is act on your instincts. Do whatever you feel is right."

He had the strangest idea that he was finding out first-hand what it was like to be caught up in a whirlwind.

"You can sing, if you feel comfortable with it," she added.

He was sure he hadn't heart her right. "What?"

"We had one man who used to whistle, and it worked beautifully. Follow your instincts. Your audience will be very nonjudgmental, I promise you that."

Was this a sick joke? He found himself beginning to take a step back but was immediately stopped by her asking, "Do you have children? Old Mrs. Ryan has ten children and fifteen grandchildren. What a sweetheart. But you know the old saying, you don't have to be able to make a car to drive it. I agree with that wholeheartedly."

He had the fleeting idea this woman must have escaped from the psychiatric ward, but he didn't have a chance to do anything before a nurse approached them. The nurse smiled at Brady and certainly didn't act as if she was on a retrieval mission for a psychiatric patient.

"So, she found you," she said to Brady, then looked at the woman in white. "Are you ready?"

"We will be a minute." She took a plastic package the nurse offered her. "Give us two minutes, Elaine." As the nurse nodded and walked back down the hall, the woman tore the plastic open. She shook out a white cotton cover-up and looked back to Brady with narrowed eyes. "I hope this is large enough to fit you." She shook it one last time. "The only way to tell is to try it. So, hold out your arms, and I'll help you with it."

No sleep, too much coffee, stress—the combination had to be affecting his reasoning process. Maybe this beautiful woman was talking in a completely rational manner and *he* was reacting irrationally. She seemed so sure of herself, so intent on getting everything right.

When she motioned for him to lift his arms, he did. She slipped the crisp cotton over them, then moved behind him. He could feel her doing up the back, and when her fingers accidentally brushed across the nape of his neck, he felt a shock go through him. But before he could figure out what had happened, the woman was facing him again, studying him critically. "There isn't a lot of extra room, but I think it will work, don't you, Mr....?"

"Brady," he supplied. "Just call me Brady."

"And you can call me Jayne." The name was soft and gentle, but plain in a way its owner could never be. She motioned to the doors. "Shall we?"

The thought of going through the doors stopped Brady cold. From nowhere he experienced a real need to touch Jayne, to hold on to her and let her voice wash over him. He wanted nothing more than to run the tip of his finger along her delicate jawline to the heat of her throat, then lower. To take the pins out of her hair and see just how long it was, how silky it would feel against his skin.

He shook his head once to clear it, trying to regain some degree of control. He felt close to the edge, disoriented. He knew rationally that he couldn't make a stranger his anchor, that he couldn't get lost in her and forget the reality behind that door. He turned from her, deliberately reached out and pushed back the door with one hand, then made himself step through.

The room in front of him was softly lit, with pale blue carpet underfoot and murals of forests and meadows under fluffy clouds on all four walls. A thatched cottage painted on the far wall incorporated the room's real windows, and through them the skyline of Santa Barbara could be seen. Santa Barbara through the windows of a fairy tale cottage, Brady thought as he glanced out at the midnight sky. Then he looked at the furnishings—four easy chairs that formed a half circle to face the windows.

When Brady glanced at Jayne by his side, the impulse to reach out to her came back with such renewed strength that he clenched his hands. He took a breath. "What is this?"

"I guess you could call it our 'relaxation space,' but some of us call it the Forest Room."

Just another waiting room, he thought cynically. A rose by any other name.

Jayne tilted her head to one side and studied him, frowning for the first time since he'd seen her. But the frown didn't diminish her beauty. The fine line between her eyes only enhanced the delicacy of her features. "They didn't tell me how long you'll be here. You can stay for a while, can't you?"

He wasn't going to leave until he got some answers. "I planned to stay for as long as it takes."

"Good."

He suddenly felt awkward and found himself trying to make small talk. "Do you like this shift? It's so late."

She shrugged her slender shoulders. "I'm a night person. I always have been. I'm up and going when most people have been in bed for hours. You know, watching old movies on television, ironing, gardening."

"Gardening at night?"

She smiled at him. "Patio gardening with the lights on. I love those little tomatoes. I have pots of them growing in a sun room by my kitchen. They're so easy to grow. Just soil, water, some sun."

Brady wondered if this woman ever gave one word answers. "I see," he said, even though he didn't see at all.

"Here we are," someone said from the doorway and Brady turned to see that the nurse had returned. "This is Rocky, and this is Mandy." She inclined her head to two tiny bundles she was holding, one pink, one blue, and both squirming.

As she came forward, Brady realized that the "bundles" were babies. Jayne touched his arm. "Sit down and get comfortable, Brady."

"I—I don't think..." he stammered. When Jayne gently pressed him toward a chair, he sank weakly into the softness and stared up at the nurse as she came closer.

"You don't get a choice tonight, Mr. Appleton," the nurse said. "Jayne asked for Mandy, so you're getting Rocky."

Appleton? Babies? He was *getting* Rocky? Before Brady knew what was happening, the nurse had handed him the tiny blue bundle.

Chapter 2

Brady stared down at the baby swaddled in the pastel blue blanket while the nurse talked to Jayne.

"She's doing a bit better," the nurse was saying. "Rocky still isn't able to suck, so he just needs holding tonight."

All Brady could see was a tiny face, more gnomelike than human, with wrinkled skin a strange shade of pink, a puckered mouth and eyes scrunched closed. There was no hair on the vaguely pointed head, just a pale fuzz and two nasty looking bruises that stood out vividly, one at each temple.

Since Brady didn't like children and had decided a long time ago that he would make a terrible father, he had never considered having any of his own. They always seemed like an alien species to him, little entities that he had no connection with, strange beings that had a place in other people's lives—never his.

Yet as he stared at the baby in his arms, he was shocked at the nudge of some strange sense of pride, the certainty that if he ever had a child, his wouldn't look like this. His would be more like the babies on television and in magazine pictures—round and pink and cooing. This feather-light creature in his arms didn't even look pleasant.

"You won't have to worry about feeding him, Brady," he heard Jayne saying. "He's still not able to suck, so they'll give him his nourishment when he goes back to the nursery. Just hold him. Poor little thing, he hasn't had much human contact. Not that the nurses don't try, you understand. But they're so busy that they don't have the luxury to just sit and cuddle the babies very often. And the babies need it desperately. When a baby doesn't get that human contact, it doesn't do well. It's called 'failure to thrive,' but it's really lack of love."

Brady felt as if he were drowning in uncharted waters, and this creature in his arms was pulling him down where there wouldn't be any air at all. He looked up at Jayne, who had sat in the chair next to him and was holding the pink bundle. She was speaking in a soft voice, words over words, all touched with a certain quality of gentleness obviously meant to soothe the baby she was cradling. For an instant Brady found himself wishing she would talk to him like that and gentle away the sharp edges of the past nineteen hours. Then he pushed aside the foolish idea.

He felt uneasy with the quixotic notions he'd developed since he'd been around this woman, and he craved fresh air, something to help clear up his distorted thought process.

But one thought he didn't want taken from him was the fact Jayne was beautiful, a woman he certainly wouldn't mind getting to know better, but not here. Not like this. He opened his mouth to tell her how mistaken she was, that he wasn't Appleton and he didn't know what was going on, but that he'd like to see her later. After he knew Jack would make it, he'd love to sit and let Jayne talk to him while he simply looked at her.

But the words died before they could be uttered when he saw her pick up a bottle the nurse must have left on a little table by her chair. The soft light in the room sparkled fleetingly off a simple gold band on her ring finger.

He exhaled in a rush. No wonder she looks so natural with the child, he thought as disappointment settled like a heavy lump in his chest. This was a day he would like to forget completely. "Listen, I don't know what—"

Jayne glanced up and cut him off with a rush of words. "You don't have children, do you? You never did tell me when I asked you before. At least, I don't think you did."

I didn't have a chance to, he thought and remembered his first idea was that she had to be slightly insane. Or was he the less than rational one? "No, I don't have children, but—"

"I bet you've never held a new baby, have you?"

"No, but—"

"It's difficult at first, especially with babies like Rocky. Poor thing, he's had such a rough time. I held him last night, and he didn't know how to act. He was really stiff and awkward." She glanced at the baby in Brady's uneasy hold and made a statement Brady recognized as a kind, but blatant lie. "You're doing great, Brady, just great. Maybe Rocky needs to bond with a man, to have a male figure in his life. I—"

"Jayne, listen to me, I—" A soft whimpering sound came from the child in his arms and Rocky began to jerk, going ramrod stiff. Brady froze.

"Talk to him," Jayne urged softly. "Just talk to him."

Brady looked down, and the baby's eyes—an indeterminate color—suddenly opened wide. Slightly crossed, they peered up at him, and in that split second Brady was struck by the fact that he was holding a delicate life in his hands. His eyes burned. Life and death. He felt bombarded by mortality tonight.

Quickly he looked back at Jayne, who was looking uneasily at the blue wrapped baby. He cleared his throat and spoke quickly before she could start talking again. "Jayne, I am not Mr. Appleton." Her huge amber eyes swept back to his face, and he added with deliberate bluntness, "I'm not supposed to be here."

She looked blank. "Pardon me?"

Rocky whimpered, relaxed for a fleeting second, then stiffened again. But Brady kept his gaze on Jayne. "I don't know what this is all about. I don't know what you're doing here with the babies, but I don't belong. And my name isn't Appleton."

"But you were on the elevator, and you had a visitor's badge...." As her voice trailed off, high color splashed across her delicately defined cheekbones. "Oh, my," she whispered. She closed her eyes for a fleeting moment, and the color in her face deepened even more when she looked back at Brady. She shook her head. "I'm sorry. I feel so foolish. I never thought you wouldn't be the man I was looking for. Mr. Appleton was overdue, and it's late, after visiting hours, so when I saw the badge I thought...I guess you don't look like a CPA, but I..."

She bit her full bottom lip and grimaced. "Then again, what's a CPA supposed to look like? Short, with glasses and pale skin? I don't know if I've ever met one, actually."

He had to smile at that. "You still haven't met one. I'm not a CPA, and I don't know what's going on here."

"No, you wouldn't," she whispered. "I'm so sorry."

Brady was beginning to feel as embarrassed for Jayne as she seemed to be about her mistake. "Just get that nurse back to take the baby, and I—"

"Elaine won't be back for ten or fifteen minutes. She's in the middle of things in the pediatric ward." She exhaled and put the bottle on the side table, then shifted the pink bundle to her shoulder and started to softly pat the tiny baby's back. "I guess Mr. Appleton decided not to come after all. He didn't sound really sure on the phone when he talked to the coordinator, but he should have called if he wasn't going to make it."

"Maybe he's wandering the halls somewhere looking for you," Brady said, trying to lighten her embarrassment with a bit of humor. "You could send out a search party."

Jayne shook her head, taking his suggestion with a degree of seriousness. "No, someone would have found him by now and brought him in here. I don't think he's coming at all, and that really makes me angry. He could have called to let us know. I mean, really, there *are* phones on every street corner."

While Jayne was speaking, Rocky began to squirm, and Brady glanced down at the puckered face. This child would never win a beautiful baby contest. And his head actually did look pointed. Brady looked back at Jayne. "I'm sorry Appleton stood you up." He spoke in a rush when Rocky began making strange noises, not unlike a fish gulping air, and stiffened again. "But I'm no good with children, and I've got things to do."

Jayne studied Brady intently from under a sweep of dark lashes. "Why didn't you tell me in the hallway you weren't Appleton?"

He almost said, *You didn't give me a chance to do more than take a breath,* but then he realized how sarcastic the statement would sound. And he didn't mean it that way at all. Her voice had been a buffer against his thoughts, against what he knew was waiting for him in Jack's room. "I was confused," he said, hedging, yet speaking a degree of truth.

She seemed to accept that without a need for elaboration. "Do you think you could possibly stay for a few minutes? Just until Elaine comes back. Fifteen minutes at the most. I can't manage both of the children myself."

All day he had craved solitude. He had fought the urge to go to the beach and never look back, but he'd stayed, waiting, worrying. And if he was entirely honest with himself, these past few minutes with Jayne had been the most peaceful of the entire time since Jack's phone call. Maybe it wouldn't hurt to stay here for a bit longer before he went to see Jack, especially since no one was going to let him see his partner for a while longer anyway. He didn't let the unsettling idea that he was putting off the inevitable do more than flit through his mind. He'd admitted enough truths to himself tonight to last a lifetime.

"I just need you to hold Rocky. That's all you have to do," Jayne was saying. "Since he can't eat on his own yet, he can't take a bottle. It's just holding that he needs, being close to someone, feeling some human warmth."

Brady wanted to look at his watch, but he was afraid to shift the baby enough to read it. He was sure it was past twelve-thirty. Fifteen more minutes would give the staff more time to get Jack settled, and fifteen more minutes would bring Jack that much closer to consciousness.

"Please, Mr.....er..."

"My name is Brady, Brady Knight." He exhaled. "All right, I can give you fifteen minutes, but that's it."

"Thank you." She settled back in the chair with a sigh and softly rubbed the baby's back in slow, lazy circles. "Mandy appreciates it, and so does Rocky."

"Where did he ever get the name Rocky?" Brady blurted out before he could stop the question.

"His real name's Albert, but I tend to give them nick-names. I thought Rocky seemed to fit him." The gentle-ness in her amber gaze as it rested on the squirming bundle in Brady's arms was as welcome as a cold drink on a hot day. He knew right then that her husband was a very lucky man for more reasons than just having a beautiful wife. "I think Rocky's a survivor. At least, I hope he is. When I first saw him, I didn't think he'd last. He's so tiny, and he's been so traumatized. But he's out of the incubator now, and he's breathing well. I'm starting to think his prog-nosis is better than anyone thought it would be." She stared at Rocky intently. "God, I hope it is," she whis-pered. "If he can just get his sucking reflex. It's a sign of lack of maturity in the nervous system, and if he doesn't learn soon..."

As her voice trailed off, Brady felt her concern, and it made him incredibly uncomfortable. He wasn't in any condition to deal with any more intense emotions tonight. He shifted, felt his gun biting into his back and changed the subject to something he wondered about since he first saw Jayne. "Are you a doctor?"

Jayne Spencer finally looked directly at the man across from her, a good assessing look she'd neglected until now. Up to this moment he had been a blurred combination to her: blue eyes, a loud shirt that looked as if it needed a good ironing, a voice that had struck her as oddly com-forting right from the first words he had uttered, and an impression of size and height.

Now she realized that the reality of the man matched her jumbled impressions. He really was tall, probably six inches over her own five foot ten, with a face she could only call rugged, square-jawed and shadowed with the rough beginnings of a beard. Tanned skin stretched tautly over high cheekbones, and sandy blond hair, sun-streaked and vaguely shaggy, emphasized his dark coloring. His lean, wiry build indicated that there wouldn't be an extra ounce of body fat under that rumpled Hawaiian shirt and well-worn jeans.

Although Jayne was terrible at guessing ages, she thought he looked somewhere in his thirties. What vaguely shocked her was her sudden regret that she hadn't had time to touch up her makeup or do more than skim her hair back from her face in a plain twist. That reaction, something she hadn't felt for a long time, made her feel even more foolish. She could feel heat in her face. Damn it, she wished she could control her blushing.

Her embarrassment deepened even more when she realized Brady had asked her something ages ago and she'd simply been staring at him. Now he was watching her, waiting, looking incredibly awkward as he tried to jiggle the tiny baby in his arms. His eyes, a startlingly clear blue under dark lashes, were narrowed by an intense squint that sent lines fanning from the corners. And they were aimed at her.

The man was expecting an answer, but she couldn't begin to remember what the question had been.

"I'm sorry. What did you ask me?"

"I asked you if you were a doctor," he repeated in that deep, rough voice that awoke something in her, something she couldn't put a label to beyond a nebulous "sense of trust."

"No, I'm a volunteer, just like the other 'holders' in the program." She saw the quizzical look on his face and realized he didn't know a thing about Loving Touch. Something that had been her lifeline meant nothing to this man—or to most people, for that matter. "This program, Loving Touch, was started to help the babies in the pediatric ward. Volunteers come to the hospital during feeding shifts and take turns holding the babies and feeding them and talking to them."

"Where are the mothers of these babies?"

She could feel her expression tighten. "Rocky's mother is only fourteen and in the hospital withdrawing from drugs. The same way Rocky's been going through withdrawal. He's three weeks old and undersized. He was born prematurely, with breathing problems and a full-scale addiction. He's been in intensive care ever since, and it's only now that he's able to be out of the incubator for any length of time. He's barely beginning to behave like a normal newborn."

Brady didn't look as shocked as most people did when they heard about the babies. "This program . . . ?"

"Loving Touch is trying to do something about the problem. The babies need to be held, to have human contact." She knew she was talking quickly, the way she always did when she was nervous or excited, but she wanted this man to understand how vital the program was to the children. "That's why Loving Touch was started. That's why we talked the hospital into supporting it, why we went out and got donations to have this room fixed up like this, and why we're so thankful when people volunteer to come and hold the babies for their feedings. That's why I'm so disappointed Mr. Appleton didn't come tonight. We have a hole in the scheduling now, all thanks to that man."

Brady sat stiffly with Rocky in his arms, and the baby stilled. "Shouldn't I be doing something for him?"

"Just hold him. Let him get used to being in someone's arms."

"Sure," Brady said, his rough-edged voice very low and a bit uncertain.

Jayne watched him as he stared down at Rocky and realized she had no idea why *this* man was here. "Why are you at the hospital at this time of night?"

He looked up at her, and she saw a bleakness in his eyes that made her want to withdraw the question. His eyes narrowed as he said, "I'm waiting for my partner to get settled in his room after surgery."

"Your partner?"

"I'm with the Santa Barbara Police Department."

A policeman? Weren't they all broken noses, hulking shapes, and inarticulate mutterings? Not tanned, blond, with incredible blue eyes, an outrageous Hawaiian shirt and a voice that made you think of rough velvet and security? "You wear a uniform?" she heard herself ask.

That brought the suggestion of a smile that twitched at the corners of his wide mouth. "No, I'm past that. I'm a detective. Most detectives wear suits and ties and look like any other citizen. We even get unmarked cars."

"I just showed my ignorance, didn't I?"

"No, most people get their information from television cop shows."

She fit right into that category. "What do you do?"

"I'm assigned to Homicide."

Her idea of television cops kicked in when he said Homicide, filling her head with visions of killers and wild shoot-outs. "What happened to your partner?"

"He was shot."

"How?"

"I'm not sure," he said. "I got there too late to see what happened."

"When did it happen?"

"Early this morning or yesterday morning since it's got to be after midnight."

And Brady had been here ever since, she thought. That explained the bristling of a beard and the weariness in his expression. "Is he going to be all right?" she asked softly.

"We hope so. Jack's pretty strong." He exhaled harshly. "The doctor seems to think he's got a good chance, but..." He shook his head. "I wonder just how much doctors really know."

Jayne had wondered the same thing herself many times in the past. "It's the patient who makes the difference," she heard herself saying, stating an absolute she had formulated over the past two years. "It's the patient's will to live. How badly he wants to fight and survive. Doctors can give up hope, but it doesn't mean a thing until the patient gives up. But if he does..." She shrugged as her voice trailed off, uncertain why she was discussing this with a stranger. She took a breath. "You deal with life and death all the time. I'm sure you understand."

"I do." He glanced at Rocky. "You're around it, too."

"Yes, I am. I chose to deal with the lives of these babies." In some way that choice had given her own life back to her, but she couldn't tell this man that. "You were on your way to see your partner when I waylaid you, weren't you?"

"I was going to check and see when I could go in. I must have pushed the fourth floor button on the elevator instead of the fifth. I guess I've been walking around in a daze since I got here."

"When was that?"

"Five this morning—no, yesterday morning. It's nearly one a.m. by now, I imagine." Brady looked at Mandy. "Where's *her* mother?"

"No one knows. She was abandoned in an alleyway and almost died."

His expression tightened, and she could see his jaw work. "How could someone—never mind. I know how they could. This world really stinks sometimes."

"It can." She let her head rest against the back of the chair. God knew she'd seen more than her share of the bad. She wouldn't be here now if she hadn't. Bad things leading to good? Sometimes. "There are good things in this world, too, Brady," she murmured, telling herself as well as the man across from her.

"Sure, but sometimes they're damn hard to find," he said.

"If you look—" she began, but was cut off when Rocky let out a piercing cry.

Brady stood so quickly he seemed to be propelled out of the chair. "What's wrong with him?" he asked anxiously over the shrill shrieking of the baby.

Jayne got to her feet and shifted Mandy into one arm as she crossed to Brady. "Let me have him."

"But you've got her, and..."

"Here," she said as she reached up and awkwardly caught Rocky in the crook of her arm. Twisting, she managed to substitute Mandy in Brady's hold, thankful that the little girl didn't join in with Rocky's piercing screams. She shifted him until the tiny bundle was snug against her shoulder; then she began to pace back and forth while she murmured over and over again, "It's okay, honey, it's all right. It's all right. I'm here."

She patted his trembling back and jiggled him up and down while she kept walking and whispering, "It's all right, it's all right." Then she began to sing "Hush Little Baby," mixing up the words completely, but never stopping until she sensed the trembling easing in him, heard the cries falter and felt the rigidity in his tiny frame begin to go away. Then he shuddered and took a gulping breath, and the silence seemed almost as loud as his cries had been.

Jayne came to a stop by the door, but she didn't quit patting the tiny boy or humming softly. Relief flooded through her as she felt Rocky relax against her shoulder. It totally unnerved her when a baby cried like that. She carefully crossed to the chair and sank down in the softness of the cushions. Now that the terror for Rocky was over, she felt a sense of accomplishment. She'd been there to hold him. That meant something. Just being there for him.

"Is he all right?" Brady asked in a hushed whisper, and Jayne realized she'd completely forgotten about the man.

She closed her eyes fleetingly and murmured, "For now. They thought he was going to die last week, but he made it. I think he'll make it all the way."

She glanced at Brady with Mandy in his arms. He was still standing by the chair, and she was taken aback by the pain she could see etched on his face. "Why did he cry like that?" he asked.

"I don't know. Maybe he's in pain," she said. "Maybe he's scared. I don't—"

The door swung open, and Elaine rushed into the room. "I heard the screaming. It was Rocky, wasn't it?"

Jayne nodded. "Yes. He had a bad spell." She motioned to Brady and Mandy. "Can you take Mandy back to the nursery? I'll spend some extra time with Rocky. Mandy didn't get much to eat, but she's been really good."

"I'll take care of feeding her some more," Elaine said as she crossed to Brady and took the baby. "Thank you, Mr. Appleton. You people are life savers." Jayne didn't bother correcting the nurse as she left with the baby and the door swung silently shut behind her.

As she looked back at Brady, he ran both large hands roughly over his face. Then he looked at her as his hands fell, and she thought how completely exhausted he appeared, and how much older he seemed than her first guess. Maybe he was closer to forty. "I really owe you for staying like this," she said.

"No, I think I needed a diversion." He exhaled harshly. "I didn't expect one like this, but it gave me something to think about instead of Jack."

Pain mingled with the exhaustion etched on his face, and she found herself wanting to ease it. But she couldn't think of anything to say except platitudes. "I hope he makes it."

"So do I." He hesitated and looked at Rocky, who had fallen into a deep, exhausted sleep in her arms.

"Some people are just destined to make it in the world. I've got a feeling Rocky is one of them, and maybe your partner is, too."

"Thanks," he murmured, and she knew he was going to leave.

Quickly, she asked, "Do you think you'd like to come back and help? We could use an extra volunteer, especially since Mr. Appleton won't be with us."

He looked at her, his eyes so clear and intent that she felt a blush beginning to rise in her face again. "No," Brady finally said. "I don't have the time and—" The shadow of a smile tugged at the corners of his mouth. "I don't have the touch. Sorry."

"But you could learn," she heard herself protesting.

"No, I don't think so. But it's been interesting. Good night, Jayne."

"Good luck," she whispered to him as he turned and headed for the door, then disappeared into the hall.

Jayne rested her head against the back of the chair, closed her eyes and hummed softly under her breath.

One thing she believed in was Fate. Things happened for a purpose. She'd be crazy by now if she believed otherwise. Elliot had been meant to be in her life. But she hated the shortness of their time together. That brought a tightness to her throat. Short? Three months. The blink of an eye. The beat of a heart.

She suddenly felt incredibly sad, an emotion she hadn't experienced with such intensity for a long time. Now the feeling was mingled with loneliness. But why now? Why did the old feelings of isolation and aloneness come back with such clarity tonight? Certainly not because she had made a blunder and cornered a blue-eyed cop into holding the babies with her. Not because she had felt as if his voice had flowed around her until it echoed inside her.

Rocky stirred, then settled with a deep sigh. Maybe she should try to find Brady on the fifth floor after Rocky was taken back to the nursery. It wouldn't hurt to ask him one more time if he could come in and help with the babies. The idea of talking to the man again made the loneliness lessen just a bit.

Brady walked slowly along the main corridor on the fifth floor, trying to put Jayne and the babies behind him and to prepare himself for what might lie ahead. He saw the nurses' station, and as he approached it, a pleasant looking woman in a white uniform looked up. Brown eyes behind thick lenses studied him expectantly.

"I'm Detective Brady Knight. My partner—"

"Oh, yes, we've been expecting you, Detective Knight. The doctor just left."

"What about Jack Wills?"

She sat back, her face sober. "He's still unconscious and on the respirator, but his vital signs are stable. He's holding his own."

Brady felt the tension inside him ease just a little bit. Ever since he had stepped out of the Forest Room and closed the door on Jayne and the baby, he had felt a knot growing into a suffocating tightness behind his breast-bone. Now it felt just a bit less intense. "Is Mrs. Wills still here?"

"Yes. She asked for a room for the night." The nurse adjusted her glasses higher on her nose with one finger. "She doesn't want to leave until she knows...until there's a change."

Brady understood completely. "Can I look in on Jack?"

She hesitated, then said, "Just for a minute. The fourth door on the left. Room 510."

Brady nodded, then turned, and as he walked slowly down the hall, the nurse called out to him, "Detective Knight?"

He looked back at her. "Yes?"

"Your partner...he's on the respirator and has two IVs and a monitor..."

Her voice trailed off, but Brady knew what she wanted to say—Jack looked like hell. "I understand," he said and headed for the room.

He stopped outside room 510, hesitated, then reached out and pushed the door open. One hospital room was like the next—green, white, filled with the odors of disinfec-tant, medication, and sickness. This room was no differ-ent, except that there were machines to the right of the bed making rhythmic beeping sounds.

Brady stepped inside, let the door swing silently shut behind him, then crossed to the bed near the windows. He looked down at Jack and gripped the cold metal safety rail with both hands. Jack was still and drawn, his eyes shut, his short lashes dark against his abnormally pale skin.

Even the faint breaths that entered Jack's body through the tube that ran into his nose didn't bring comfort or reassurance to Brady. He deliberately didn't look at the tubes going from the IV holders to Jack's arms, or at the screen of the monitor. He kept his eyes on Jack.

He felt white-hot anger at whatever stroke of bad luck had brought Jack to this state, and when he spoke softly, he hoped Jack could hear him. "You'll make it, Jack. You have to." He could almost hear Jayne's words. *It's the patient who makes the difference. It's the patient's will to live.* He just wished he could will Jack to fight. He wished he could make Jack want to live as much as he wanted him to.

Brady let go of the cold metal and reached for Jack's hand, knowing that holding it wouldn't keep his friend from slipping away, yet feeling that it might, in some way.

"Just who's going to want to be my partner after this?" he asked, his whispered question rough and unsteady. He had to take a deep breath and swallow hard to control the unnerving burning of tears behind his eyes.

Then he felt a faint but perceptible pressure from his partner's hand.

Chapter 3

Brady held on to Jack's hand, waiting, watching, willing the pressure to come again.

But nothing happened.

The machine continued to beep, and Jack was completely still. The respirator went on forcing air into his lungs, and his hand lay motionless in Brady's.

Brady knew he'd felt the pressure. He knew it. "I know, Jack. You're fighting. Fight like hell," he whispered, bending low over the bed. "Don't give up. You're the only one who can do it."

When there was no more response from Jack, Brady said, "Don't give up, Jack, just don't give up." Then he eased Jack's hand down onto the white linen of the bed and turned away.

He went back out into the hall and paused. He wasn't up to seeing Jack's wife, so he turned and headed for the nurses' station again. A different nurse was there, a young girl who didn't look old enough to be out of high school.

"I'm Detective Knight," he said when he got to the desk and she looked up at him. "My partner, Jack Wills, is in 510. Could you point me to the nearest waiting room so I can get some rest?"

She motioned to the right, toward double green doors. "Through there, two doors down on your right. I don't think there's anyone in there right now."

Good. He wanted some time alone, he thought as he headed down the corridor. He needed it. He wanted to stretch out, stop thinking and sleep.

When Brady stepped into the waiting room, he thought fleetingly that the beige and green space with a vinyl couch along one wall and six chairs on the other was nothing like the Forest Room one floor down. No clouds, no cottage, and no Jayne.

He ran both hands roughly over his face, across the bristling of his scruffy beard, then crossed to the couch and took off his holster. How could she ever have mistaken him for a CPA? He stretched out, his legs over one end, his head on the other arm, and he pushed his gun and holster between his side and the back of the couch. He laid his forearm over his eyes, released a long slow breath and tried to let go of everything for a few minutes.

Jayne walked slowly down the corridor and glanced at the clock over the elevator doors. One fifteen in the morning. She adjusted her black shoulder bag and swiped at her slightly mussed slacks and simple white shirt. It had been a long day, with eight hours at her job as a fashion buyer for The Taylor Stores, a business dinner with two out-of-town salesmen, then her shift here. She felt weariness in every part of her body and hoped that sleep wouldn't be a stranger when she got back to her house.

As she stopped at the elevator doors and pushed the button, she thought about the house, a huge bungalow in the hills, big enough for ten people. Even this tired, she knew she didn't want to go there, not just yet. She would do what she had thought about while she held Rocky—try to find Brady Knight and ask him one more time to help with the program. If she was lucky, he would still be with his partner.

Something in her wanted Brady to become part of the program. She had felt a sense of loneliness in him, maybe an echo of what she had once felt. If she talked to him again, maybe he would come back. If his partner was in the hospital recovering, Brady might be around for a while and be able to fill the hole in the schedule. One way or the other, it couldn't hurt to ask.

She stepped off on the fifth floor and walked down to the nurses' station. A nurse who had worked on the psychiatric floor when Jayne had been there looked up and smiled, her glasses slightly askew. "Jayne. How are you doing?"

"Tired, Sharon, tired. But I'm not complaining. I was wondering if you would know anything about a policeman who was wounded."

"Jack Wills?"

Jack. That sounded like the name Brady had said. "Yes, I think that's him."

"He's out of surgery and holding his own, but it's going to be touch and go for the next twenty-four hours."

"Actually, I was looking for his partner."

"Detective Knight?"

"Yes."

"Poor man. He's worn out. He hasn't left the hospital since they brought his partner in."

"Then he's still here?"

"He was fifteen minutes ago, before I went for my break. He went in to see Detective Wills, but I'm not sure if he's still in there or not."

"Is it all right if I go and check?"

"Sure." She motioned to her left. "Room 510."

Jayne headed down the hall, knocked softly on the door to 510, then pushed it back. She took two steps, one hand still holding the door open, then stopped.

Brady wasn't here, but a doctor was, a tall, thin man in a white jacket, bending over the occupant of the only bed in the room. Even though Jayne didn't say a thing, the man must have sensed her presence, because he glanced over his shoulder. Slowly he straightened and turned to her, letting the IV tube he'd been holding fall from his hand.

Hair so blond it could have been white was thin and cut short, almost in a military fashion, and she thought his angular face had an oddly empty look, until she made eye contact.

Faded blue eyes with lashes so pale they seemed nonexistent were filled with a rage that Jayne could feel even across the room. Instinctively she took a partial step back toward the corridor. She had seen doctors get annoyed when they were disturbed, but she didn't understand this man's anger. "I'm really sorry to disturb you. I was just coming in to see if..."

Her words trailed off as the man abruptly walked toward her, one hand pushed in the pocket of his jacket. She let go of the knob as she backed farther into the hallway, but the doctor grabbed the door before it could swing shut. Right then the sound of people talking echoed down the hall.

The man looked away from Jayne for the first time since he'd turned and seen her in the doorway. His gaze darted behind her, then back to her face. Without a word he brushed past her into the corridor, letting the door go. Jayne turned and watched him glance at the group of doctors coming down the hall, then turn on his heels and head off in the opposite direction.

When the door struck her softly in the back, she released a breath she hadn't been aware of holding and turned to push the door open. From the doorway, she looked in at the dark-haired man hooked up to a monitor and respirator. His skin was horribly pale, oxygen tubes ran into his nose, and IVs were attached to his left arm and the back of his right hand. The monitors beeped in a regular rhythm.

Jayne could tell how far the man was from regaining consciousness, and she wondered if Brady had simply given up and left the hospital for now. He probably had, and she knew he wouldn't ever come back up to the Forest Room, so she would never see him again to ask him to help with the babies.

Disappointed, she turned to leave, but the monitor sounds stopped her. She looked back at the bed, then at the monitor. The beeps seemed to be gradually getting closer and closer together. Then she saw the IV tube with the pale liquid from the overhead pouch running through it in a steady stream into the patient's arm.

It was wrong. She knew it. IVs dripped, they didn't flow. The beeping suddenly became irregular, and Jayne looked back into the hall, holding the door open with one hand. Three doctors were clustered two doors down, and she recognized one of them. "Dr. Webb?" she called.

A short blond-haired man turned at the sound of his name. "Jayne?"

"There's something wrong in here." The monitor's beeping seemed to echo all around her. "The patient . . ."

At the same time the nurse was up and calling. "Room 510, stat!"

The doctors and two nurses came on a dead run. As they got to the door, Jayne moved aside to let them pass, and the monitor sound changed to a piercing buzz that cut through the air.

Brady knew he was lost in a dream, yet he found a pleasure in it that he relished, a pleasure that throbbed through his weary body.

He was holding a woman, touching her, feeling her heat and silky smoothness under his hands. But he didn't know who she was. A faceless woman, lying close to him, letting him rest against her, then feel her and know her. Her voice was as soft as her skin, crooning on and on while slender, long legs wrapped around his and the silken curve of her slim hips fit neatly against the lines of his body. A narrow waist, a flared rib cage. And her breasts, small, but perfect, were heavy in his hands.

His lips trailed along her collarbone to the hollow of her throat. He could catch the scent of flowers, delicate, fleeting, sweet, and feel the rapid flutter of her pulse, an echo of his own. The vibration of her voice was evident under his lips. His hands spanned her diaphragm and caressed her stomach.

A dream, yet it was so real that he wanted to look up, to see her face, to know who was giving him such pleasure. But when he began to draw back, the image shifted and shimmered, fading as surely as the sound of her voice. She was beautiful—he could sense that—but he couldn't make out her features, eye color, or even hair color. The silky strands lay soft against his skin, yet he didn't know if they were dark or light, curly or straight.

His body felt as tight as a bow string, ready to explode from frustration, but when he would have cried out, he heard his own name. In the distance a voice called out to him, and suddenly he remembered Jack and the call during the night. He bolted upright, violently thrown into wakefulness.

The glare of the overhead light blinded him for an instant; then he blinked at the blurred image of a woman bending close to him. For a fleeting instant he thought he had pulled the woman from his dream with him into reality; then his eyes focused on the stark whiteness of a uniform and the face of the middle-aged nurse who had been at the desk.

"Detective Knight."

He swung his legs over the side of the couch and sat forward, sleep gone completely as he scrubbed his hands over his face. "What is it?"

"The other nurse said you'd come in here. I thought you would want to know."

His hands fell as he looked up at her. "Know what?"

"There's been a crisis. We think Detective Wills will pull through, but—"

Before she could finish, Brady grabbed his holstered gun and was on his feet heading for the hallway. He broke through the double swinging doors, snapped his holster on as he passed the nurses' station at a run, then slowed when he saw a cluster of people by Jack's door—white coats mingled with police uniforms.

He hesitated, then saw a uniform coming toward him. "What's going on?" he demanded, his voice slightly hoarse.

A rookie cop whose name Brady didn't think he'd ever heard stopped a few feet from him. "The Captain wants to see you, sir. He's down there," he said, pointing back toward Jack's room.

Brady moved around the man, almost pushing him aside to get to Captain Burkhart, who was standing by Jack's door. But Brady's steps faltered and slowed when he saw Jayne no more than a foot from Burkhart.

Jayne? Here? Confusion made Brady lightheaded for a minute; then he knew with complete certainty that she had been the woman in his dream. The unsettling realization was all tangled up with memories and needs that were raw and unbalanced. Needs that he hadn't even known were there until now.

As he moved closer he heard the Captain call his name, but he didn't take his eyes off Jayne. She was staring at the floor, a leather handbag clutched to her middle with both hands and the wedding ring glinting in the overhead lights. Stupid, he told himself. His relationships with women might not have been solid and lasting, but he had never once considered getting involved with a married woman.

It didn't help his equilibrium when he realized that if any woman could have made him consider it, Jayne would be that woman. He came closer to her, feeling her presence as potently as if he were touching her. He clenched his hands at his sides. Jack's shooting had really set him on edge emotionally.

Jack. The thought of his partner brought everything back into perspective. As he got within arm's reach of Jayne, he looked at Captain Burkhart by her side. A tall black man with a precise mustache and wearing a perfectly tailored, gray three-piece suit, the Captain rocked forward on the balls of his feet.

"Captain? What's happened? Why are you here? The nurse said there was a crisis, but—"

Burkhart held up his hand. "It's under control...for now."

Brady sensed, rather than saw, Jayne look at him, but he kept his gaze on the Captain. "What's under control?"

"We aren't sure, but it looks as if someone tried to tamper with Jack's medication." He jerked his head in the direction of Jayne. "Mrs. Spencer just happened to come in, and the guy took off."

Brady finally looked back at Jayne. Tendrils of ebony hair had escaped from the confines of the French twist to curl softly at her temples, and her huge amber eyes were vivid against the paleness of her face. "What?" he asked.

Her tongue darted out to touch her unsteady lips, and she nodded, a jerky motion of her head. "I came into the room and saw this man...." She took a quick, shuddering breath. "I thought he was a doctor."

Burkhart spoke up. "Someone tampered with Wills's IV drip. It could have killed him. If Mrs. Spencer hadn't come in when she did, who knows what he could have done to Wills."

Brady tore his gaze away from Jayne, pushing aside the question of her being there to ask Burkhart, "He'll make it, won't he?"

"The doctors think the medication wasn't on long enough to have a lasting effect. It might make him slower to regain consciousness, but nothing permanent." Burkhart motioned to two uniformed officers talking together farther down the hall. "I've arranged for a man to be with Wills around the clock." He frowned. "It looks as if whoever shot him might not be happy he's still alive."

"Did anyone else see the man?"

"We're still asking around, but it looks as if Mrs. Spencer is the only one."

Brady looked back to Jayne, who hadn't moved. "You saw him clearly?"

Her face paled even more. "Yes," she whispered.

"You'd recognize him if you saw him again?"

She nodded without speaking.

Brady stuffed his hands in the pockets of his jeans to keep from reaching for Jayne and holding her to him. "What on earth were you doing here?"

"I . . . I came down . . ." She bit her lip hard and just stared at him.

Burkhart spoke up. "You'll have to come down to look at mug shots in the morning, Mrs. Spencer."

Brady couldn't take his eyes off Jayne. "Can you do that?" he asked her softly.

She closed her eyes for a fleeting moment, then looked at him and nodded.

Burkhart spoke to Brady. "*You* go on home and get some rest. I'll personally see to it that you're kept up to date on everything."

Brady hesitated, still uneasy about leaving. "I need to see Jack."

"Sure, but he's not going to know you're there, and even when he's conscious, he can't talk until they take the tubes out."

Brady remembered the pressure on his hand before and wondered just what Jack did or didn't know. "Still, I want to see him for a minute."

Jayne spoke up in a small voice. "Can I go now? I need to get home."

Burkhart shrugged. "I don't see why not. I can have a squad car take you."

She brushed an unsteady hand over her hair, vainly trying to smooth the curling wisps back off her face, then gripped her purse tighter. "No, I have my own car here."

Brady knew she was going to turn and walk away, and before she could, he realized he wanted to leave with her. "Can you wait just a minute, Jayne, and I'll walk you down to your car?" He glanced at his watch, trying to make his offer seem rational and not made because there was an irrational part of him that didn't want her walking away from him just yet. "I'm leaving in a few minutes, and it's nearly two o'clock. And I'd like to ask you a few questions of my own on the way down."

She hesitated, then looped the strap of her purse over her shoulder. "I guess so."

He clenched his hand more tightly in his pocket, trying not to remember the way she had felt in his dream. The illusion had lingered on well past when it should have faded. "Good. Good."

"I'll be at the nurses' station," she said.

"Fine," he murmured and watched her walk off down the hall. Dreams and reality were mingling in the most unsettling way.

Taking a deep breath, he turned to Burkhart and started to move around the man. "I need to see Jack before I leave."

The captain stopped him with one hand on his shoulder. "No, he's not in there. He's three doors down on the right. I'm posting a uniform at this door as a decoy in case the guy manages to get back to try again. And I'm putting a man inside Jack's room so no one knows he's there." He dropped his hand. "Do you have any other ideas?"

Brady shook his head. "No. I'll talk to Mrs. Spencer some more on the way down to the parking lot, then we'll have to wait and see if she recognizes anyone tomorrow."

"Thank God she was here," Burkhart breathed, then motioned down the hall. "Come on. I'll take you to Jack."

After looking in on Jack and talking to the guard on duty, Brady went out into the hallway and looked down toward the nurses' station. A part of him was ridiculously relieved to see that Jayne hadn't left without him and was standing by the desk talking to the older nurse. Before he could scrutinize his reaction too closely, he went down the hallway toward her.

As he approached the nurses' station, Jayne turned to him. "Can we go now?"

"Sure."

"You'll get more rest at home than on that couch, Detective Knight," the nurse said.

"I'm sure I will," he said, though he doubted it. "And thanks for letting me know about Jack." He gave her his home phone number and asked her to contact him if anything else happened, then turned to Jayne. "Let's go."

The nurse reached across the desk and patted Jayne's hand in a familiar way Brady almost envied. "Go home. Take a hot bath and try to forget this whole thing."

"That sounds good to me," Jayne said, then glanced at Brady before heading for the elevators.

They rode down to the lobby in silence, standing on opposite sides of the elevator car. Despite Brady's intention of asking her questions, he just stared at the floor numbers as they lit up in sequence until the elevator reached ground level. When he stepped out into the deserted lobby with Jayne, he kept silent, walking by her side across the thick carpeting, then pushed the entrance door open for her. He followed her into the softness of the October night lit by the yellow glow of the security lights in the hospital parking lot. The city far below looked like a sea of lights.

Few cars were in the lot at this hour, most of them clustered near the emergency entrance. Jayne led the way to the left, along a short walkway lined by sweet smelling jasmine, then stepped onto the blacktop and headed for a very staid looking import sedan.

He had pictured Jayne in something upscale, sleek and expensive. She didn't match this car, but then again, he'd never thought he matched his Camaro, either. He'd bought it for its size and engine power. That thought, the first he'd given his car since going to find Jack, brought him up short. He'd left the Camaro near where he'd found Jack.

As Jayne searched in her purse for her keys, he stood beside her. "I just remembered something."

She looked up at him as she drew a brass key ring from her purse. "The questions you were going to ask me?"

"No. Where do you live?"

She frowned. "Excuse me?"

"North? South?"

"Near Downer's Bend, south and a few miles inland from the coastal highway."

An almost rural area in the hills, but definitely in the right direction. "Can I ask you a favor?" She looked confused, so he just kept talking without waiting for a response. "I left my car where Jack was shot. If you're going home, it's more or less on your way, just before the freeway in the area north of the old train station. Do you think I can hitch a ride with you?"

She hesitated, and he couldn't decide if she hated the idea of him being with her, or if she was just trying to get her thoughts straight. He opted for the latter when she put the key in the driver's door and said, "Get in."

He opened the passenger door as soon as Jayne reached across the seat and undid the lock. Then he got inside and immediately caught a hint of the perfume Jayne wore. He didn't try to stretch his legs out in the cramped confines of the front but settled as well as he could in the small seat and spoke to Jayne as she started the engine.

"I appreciate this. I hate to try to get a taxi in this town after ten, and I didn't want to ride down in a squad car."

She looked at him, the glow from the dash lights barely illuminating the hollows and curves of her face. "What happened down there, where your partner was shot?"

"I wish I knew. He called me, said he had a lead on some case and asked me to meet him at Waylan and Glenn. I got there, saw him in an alleyway, but before he could get to me, someone shot him in the back. Twice. I never saw who did it."

"Why didn't you see who shot him?"

"The alley was dark, and by the time I got Jack to safety and went back, it was empty." He rotated his head slowly, trying to ease the tension in his neck. As she drove toward the exit and turned west, Brady asked his own question. "Why were you in Jack's room?"

"Actually, I was looking for you."

Maybe the night wasn't quite as terrible as he had thought it was. "You were looking for me?"

"Yes. I thought if I could talk to you again, I might be able to encourage you to get into the program. After all, you'd be at the hospital and . . ." Her voice trailed off.

He ignored the implied question and felt a bit deflated. Stupid pride, he reasoned. He had hoped she had wanted to see him again, that he hadn't been the only one to feel this awareness. "So you went to find me in Jack's room?"

"That was the idea. But when I opened the door, this doctor was there. At least, I thought he was a doctor."

"Why?"

"He looked like one. No, he didn't, not really. I mean, he did, with a white coat and all, but . . ."

"But what?"

"When he looked at me, he..." She fumbled for the right words, and Brady gave her the time. She finally said, "His eyes weren't like any doctor's I've ever seen."

"In what way?"

"They were blue, pale, sort of washed out, but his expression...they were filled with raw anger. The sort of look that feels as if it could rip right through you."

"And there aren't any doctors like that?"

"No."

"How do you know that?"

"I've been around enough doctors." She stopped for a red light on the narrow street in a refurbished section of town and glanced at Brady. "This side of the railroad station or the other?"

"The other," he said; then, as she drove on, he asked, "So you didn't think he was a doctor when he looked at you?"

"I did, but he made me so uncomfortable. Then he came toward me, and I backed up, and then there were people in the hall. When he heard them, he brushed past me and went off in the opposite direction."

Brady sat lower in the seat. "Tell me exactly what he looked like."

She spoke rapidly, words spilling over each other, and when she finished Brady could almost visualize the man. Blond, pale, thin, and with cold blue eyes. When she stopped, he prodded, "And what did he smell like?"

That brought a slight chuckle from her, and he felt the incredible need to hear her laugh. But there wasn't one funny thing he could think of saying to get that response.

"Smell?" she asked.

He looked out at the night. "People have their own fragrances." Jayne Spencer certainly did. "What do you remember from when he passed you and went into the hall?"

"I . . . I think I held my breath, but I remember something . . . disagreeable. Cigars. Maybe pipe smoke. But it was too sweet and sort of stale. It made me feel a little sick."

"Anything else?"

"Maybe starch, but that would be from the laundered jacket he was wearing, I think."

"Did you see or hear anything when he got close?"

"I don't remember. I don't think so."

"Tattoos, a limp, a wheeze?"

He sensed her looking at him when she said, "I would hate to be a suspect and have you interrogating me."

"No rubber hoses, I promise."

That brought a bubble of laughter. "I didn't think there would be. I just meant that you think of things no normal person would."

He chanced a look at her. "I'm not normal?"

The responding laughter lasted just a bit longer this time. "Of course. I mean, I hardly know you, but my guess would be that you are. After all, you're on the police force."

"Normal isn't a requirement for being a cop." He looked up and saw they were nearing Glenn. "Turn right here, then left when you get to Waylan."

Jayne followed his directions, then turned the corner. Brady could see his Camaro still by the curb right behind Jack's sedan. No broken windows, no slashed tires. Miracles did happen once in a while. "Here. Pull in behind the black car."

"Yours?" she asked, driving up to the curb behind the Camaro.

"All mine and the bank's."

She braked to a stop and glanced at Brady. "I think it fits you."

The statement stopped Brady, since he thought just the opposite. "Really?"

"Yes, I do."

He looked at her in the dim light, then asked something that had been at the back of his mind. "Were you able to get in touch with your husband and tell him what happened?"

She was silent for so long that he wondered whether she hadn't heard him or if she was just ignoring him. Then he heard the soft intake of air, and her tone of voice was flat when she said, "No, I wasn't."

He needed to get out of the car and away from her. At least he was rational enough to realize that. "Then you'd better get home. Call Police Headquarters around nine and you can set up an appointment to look through mug shots."

"Should I ask for you when I call?"

He almost said yes, then stopped himself. "No, I might not be there. Just ask for Captain Burkhart's office. They'll be expecting your call." He hesitated before getting out of the car. "Thanks for everything."

"This was on my way."

"I meant for being at Jack's room. For interrupting whatever was going on. For helping."

"I believe in Fate."

"Sure," he murmured, wondering why Fate would bring her into his life, then make her married and crazy about kids. Fate. He didn't even want to think about it.

He opened the door, got out, then bent down to look inside. "Take care, Jayne Spencer."

"You too," she murmured, and when he had closed the door, he stood back while she pulled out into the street and left.

Brady went to his car and got in, relieved that even the radio was still there. He shook his head as he settled in the seat, then glanced up to see the taillights of Jayne's car slowly getting farther away. After turning the key, he let a beige coupe pass before he swung out into the street and headed off. When he got to the first stoplight, he could see Jayne stopped ahead of the coupe, and he made an instantaneous decision.

When the light changed to green and Jayne drove on with the coupe behind her, Brady did the same. The short distance between here and the freeway was pretty rough, and since she had only come here to bring him back to his car, he felt a certain sense of responsibility to see that she got safely onto the freeway.

But instead of going to the freeway, Jayne turned south onto the road that ran alongside the ocean. Brady hesitated, then kept driving after her. The sedan increased its speed, and the coupe stayed between it and the Camaro, so he felt comfortable following. Jayne wouldn't even know he was there.

Chapter 4

Jayne had decided not to take the freeway at the last minute. She wasn't in any special hurry to get back to her empty house, and a drive along the water seemed incredibly appealing. She wouldn't think about the past that had been pulled closer by Brady's question about her husband. She looked at the simple gold band on her ring finger and quickly looked ahead at the dark road.

She drove more slowly, less and less anxious to get home. Home? No, it was just a house now, no more. It hadn't felt like home for two years. For the past few months she'd been considering selling it. It was too big, too empty. With the five acres it sat on, it would bring a good price. Someone would snatch it up, someone who had a big family and wanted to fill all that space with children.

She closed her eyes for a fleeting moment and swallowed hard, then stared straight ahead as she drove south along the coast. The horror of what she had almost witnessed was playing havoc with her. She felt an involuntary shudder course through her, and she gripped the steering wheel more tightly. Think about the good things, the positive things, she told herself, an old trick that had helped her get through some rough times in the past couple of years.

But when she started to change the direction of her thoughts, Brady Knight came to her mind immediately. A policeman? She would never have guessed that, yet after she found out, she knew Brady could never have been a CPA. She chuckled softly.

She was certain there were incredibly sexy CPAs, but Brady Knight seemed so... The only word that came to mind was "physical." His deep tan, his sun-streaked hair, his lean muscles. She shifted on the leather seat, a peculiar discomfort making her feel restless.

She glanced at the dark water to her right, and even though it was October, she wished she had a convertible so she could put down the hood and feel the gentle air of Indian summer on her skin.

She glanced in the rearview mirror, saw a few headlights behind her and wondered if the drivers of those cars were out at this time of night because they couldn't sleep. She'd driven mile after mile on the bad nights, during the small hours of the morning, the hardest time for her since Elliot's death. She looked at the digital clock—2:30 a.m.

For an instant she considered just driving all night instead of going back to the house. No, she couldn't do that this time. She had to get some sleep and go to work in the morning. And there were other things she had to do. Her hands tightened even further on the steering wheel. She had to go to the police station to look at mug books.

That brought everything back to her with a thud. When she got to the freeway crossing and saw the road into the hills, she swung east. Once across the freeway, she started the climb into the hills. She passed towering trees on either side that formed a canopy overhead in spots, then went higher until the trees thinned and she could see the partial moon and the star-sprinkled sky over the plateau.

She took the first bad curve, slowing to make it easily, and saw the car behind her get closer. The glow of another set of lights behind that car came from farther back. Jayne knew this road so well—three sharp switchback curves, then the level stretch along the ridge. The view was breathtaking from there, with the city far below and the dark water beyond.

Jayne flipped on her radio, letting soft rock filter into the car while she kept her eyes on the road ahead. She slowed a bit as she approached the next curve; then her breath caught in her lungs when she saw the car behind her swing out and come alongside her. She couldn't believe anyone would pass on this curve, but she knew of accidents where people had done just that.

Instinctively she slowed further to let the car pass and get back in the right lane as quickly as possible. Then she realized the car wasn't passing. It lurched sideways at her, and metal impacted metal. Fighting the wheel to stay on the road, Jayne hit her horn, pressing it as hard as she could. Surely the driver didn't see her. Or he was drunk. All she had to do was get his attention.

For a second it seemed he was backing off; then, without warning, the car careened toward her again. She hit her brakes, bracing herself for another impact as the squeal of her brakes and the stench of burning rubber filled the night around her.

In a burst of memory, the past flooded over her, mingling with the present—squealing brakes, her fighting the wheel, certain she was caught in a dream that would be over soon. But this time she knew better. It wasn't a dream, and all she could do was pray and try to keep the car to the left so she wouldn't head for the drop-off by the shoulder of the road. She fought the wheel, trying so hard to keep it from whipping out of her hands that she thought her shoulders would dislocate.

But before the second impact became reality, she heard the roar of another engine, the sound of metal tearing metal, and then the car beside her was jerking forward, past her, speeding off into the night. At the same time Jayne knew that whoever was trying to save her was too late. She had completely lost control. Her car fishtailed wildly, then whipped around in a breathtaking spin.

She heard her own scream and closed her eyes to a world gone crazy. Brilliant images of people she loved and cared about flashed through her mind—her family, Rocky, the other babies. She would never see them again. She would never know what life held for her sisters and her parents. She would never know if Rocky survived, or if the other babies made it.

Regret for what might have been overwhelmed her fear. And in that last moment, when she braced herself for the end, the image of Brady Knight was there. With a shattering blaze of truth she realized she would never know another man. She would never be held or hold someone. She would never love again or be loved. And that last thought only deepened her regrets.

She waited for the pain, then the blackness, for the drop into nothingness. She waited to die, but it didn't happen. There was no ceasing of being, just a sudden and complete stopping of all motion and sound.

She could feel the car shudder, then still. The steering wheel felt solid in her hands. The headrest pressed against the nape of her neck. Was the act of dying just like living, only slipping into another space, another reality?

No. She remembered too clearly the accident with Elliot, the incredible pain, pain so intense she couldn't even begin to locate its source, then total blackness, until she woke to more pain and tremendous grief that cut into her soul.

No, she didn't think she was dead, and, even more incredible, she didn't feel hurt.

She flexed her fingers, then realized both her feet were pressed on the brake pedal. Cautiously she inhaled, trying to force air into her tight chest as she slowly opened her eyes.

At first all she saw was light and darkness; then, as her eyes focused, she could make out the lights of her car ahead, the darkness of the night beyond and all around. For a split second she wondered if she had imagined the car trying to hit her, the impact, the spinning. Maybe she had imagined the whole evening starting from when Brady Knight stepped off the elevator.

But before she could do more than fleetingly consider that idea, bright lights were coming right at her, almost blinding her.

Was she in the eye of a storm? Had she been caught in the stillness before the accident? Or was this the same accident with Elliot? Had she been trapped in a time warp, only to be thrown back to reality just before impact?

Face reality, her psychiatrist had said. Only then can you put the accident behind you and rebuild yourself and your life. But she had no idea what reality was now. All she knew for sure was the terror that was engulfing her, and the fact that she had to get out of the car, to run as far and as fast as she could before death realized she had a chance to cheat it.

Frantically she fumbled with the handle, twisting it until the door finally popped open. She scrambled out, but even before her feet hit the ground, she knew this was all wrong. Terror was waiting out here for her, too, but it had taken a different form. There was no road under her feet, just a thin ribbon of gravel and dirt and beyond, nothing but space. And, everywhere, the brilliance of the lights.

Reality tipped again, and she gripped the door handle, but it could have been bricks under her hand. The ledge at the hospital could have been under her feet. The light could have been July sunlight, and she could have been standing next to nothingness, intent on flying.

Except she knew she couldn't fly. She felt cold all over, and she couldn't move. She felt robbed of the ability to do anything but stare at the black gulf inches from her feet.

She closed her eyes, and images came from nowhere. The scene at the hospital, the parking lot, the people yelling and screaming. But she was clinging to a car door.

She didn't dare open her eyes. She felt dizzy, and she knew that if she looked again, she would step forward and get this over with—this horror, this world where nothing made sense.

She didn't know what was reality and what was a dream. She didn't know if she had ever lost Elliot, or gone through the healing from her injuries, or lived for two years alone, or if she had ever met a policeman who had made her start to think of possibilities instead of just survival.

"Jayne, don't move. Don't move."

The voice came from nowhere. It echoed strangely in the stillness and pulled her farther into the past. She knew it was the same voice she had heard on the hospital ledge, and it told her she wouldn't die. He would pull her inside, hold her, lift her, and there would be blackness.

But that didn't happen. Instead, the voice kept talking. "Careful, careful. Pull the door open and get back in your car. Just ease back in, then slide across the seat and get out the passenger door.''

The voice surrounded her, grounding her so completely that she couldn't do a thing. ''I . . . I can't. I can't.''

''All right. Just stay still, then, and I'll get you.''

The voice was all around her. The voice. The same voice. The same tone. Yet when she opened her eyes, the scene in front of her wasn't the hospital. It was night now, and there were hills, and city lights in the distance. Then she looked to her right.

The lights blurred everything, but gradually she could make out a dark form coming toward her out of the brightness. Brilliance exploded all around him as he came closer. Bit by bit, his body blocked the light. Tall, rangy, with his hand reaching in her direction.

Brady? Was this reality? Yet that voice from the past persisted, even though the person coming toward her looked like Brady. ''I'm almost there. Almost. Hold on,'' he was saying.

Then a hand touched her, grasped her by her arm, and she was being eased sideways along the rough fender of her car. For a split second she felt her feet slip; then she was pulled to the right and into the comfort of strong arms.

''Thank God,'' Brady whispered hoarsely. ''He could have killed you.''

Reality was there, solid and sure in the form of Brady Knight, a reality that tipped sideways at the mention of the man who had tried to run her off the road. She closed her eyes tightly. Was Brady the man who saved her life two years ago? His voice told her that he was. Had she known that all along, and it had just taken a while for the memory to click in?

Memories. That time two years ago had been more real to her this evening than it had been since she and Elliot had left for their trip. In microseconds she had relived everything, including the day she had subconsciously wanted to die. Yet someone wouldn't let her. Brady?

She found herself clinging to him, balling his shirt in her fist and pressing her forehead into his chest. Circles in life, circles on circles. Two years since she had tried to fly and nearly killed herself in the process. Two years since everything had been turned upside down and inside out. Since Fate had brought someone there to keep her from dying, someone for her to hold on to.

Brady was easing backward while he still held her, his voice a rumbling vibration against her face. "Here. Get in my car. He got away, but I need to call in the plate number."

With great willpower, she loosened her hold on him, and without looking into his face, she turned toward his car. She was vaguely aware of her own car facing the wrong way on the wrong side of the road, so close to the cliff edge that one more step on her part would have sent her over the side.

She let Brady ease her into his car, and warmth enveloped her. The leather seat felt incredibly solid supporting her. Weakly she sank back, closing her eyes, but her hands were clenched on her thighs.

Could Brady be the voice from her past? Now that she was in the silence of his car, she couldn't quite grab hold of the sound of him saying her name, begging her not to move. She remembered her last thoughts when she thought she was going to die, the sorrow over never knowing love again. Then Brady's voice.

She felt the car move at the same time Brady spoke softly to her. "Jayne?"

Right then, she knew the truth. Brady had saved her life twice. He'd spoken to her, encouraged her, anchored her to this world, then grabbed hold of her and refused to let go. She didn't know whether to cry or laugh, so she didn't do either. She simply sat there, letting the truth sink in.

"Jayne?" he said again, and she jerked slightly, his voice so close she knew she had only to turn to her left and he would be right there. Then his hand was on hers, his fingers strong and incredibly comforting on her clenched fist.

Comfort. That word stood out in her mind. Holding on to someone and being held.

"Are you all right?"

She nodded jerkily, feeling as if she could hold on to him forever, yet knowing she couldn't. "I ... I think so." She almost asked him about the past. She almost told him who she was. But she never uttered the words.

In a moment of startling clarity, she knew she never wanted Brady to know she had been that woman on the ledge. She'd put that behind her. She'd refused to think about it. No, she wasn't that person anymore, not any more than she was the woman who had roamed the hospital halls at night when she couldn't sleep, or the woman who had been in the psychiatric ward for two months while she healed emotionally.

She didn't turn her hand over to lace her fingers through his and hold on to him. She didn't open her eyes. "I just hate heights. I'm sorry I reacted like that."

"Sorry?" His hand tightened on hers. "For what? You could have been killed."

She couldn't stop a tremor from running through her, and no words would come at all.

"It's all right," Brady murmured and withdrew his hand.

The sense of isolation she had experienced in the Forest Room after Brady left came back with a vengeance when he broke the contact, so she brought both her hands to her middle, pressing hard on the tightness just below her breastbone.

"Headquarters, this is Alpha William thirty-two. I need two squad cars." He explained where he was, what had happened, gave them the license plate of the car, then finished with, "And I need a patch-through to Captain Burkhart at home."

There was static and crackle on the line; then a voice Jayne recognized as belonging to the Captain who had been at the hospital came over the radio. "All right. What is it, Knight?" he demanded curtly.

"I think the guy who shot Jack just tried to get rid of the one person who's seen him."

"What the hell?"

Quickly Brady explained, then asked, "What now?"

There was static; then Burkhart muttered, "I'll get right back to you."

Jayne could feel Brady moving, and she finally looked at him. She was thankful to see that the lights of her car had been turned out and the emergency flashers put on. The interior of the Camaro was in deep shadow broken sporadically by the yellow flashes. She knew she couldn't meet his gaze. He didn't know who she was. Or that Fate had brought him back into her life when she needed him the most. "What do we do now?" she asked.

"Wait. They're sending out help. And they'll check on the license plate of the car."

"Do you really think it was the same man? I mean, how could he know...how could he...?" Her words were stopped by a gulp.

In the next heartbeat, Brady had her by her shoulders and was pulling her to him. The gearshift between them cut into her hip, but Jayne let him gather her to his chest. It felt good to lean on him and she felt so weak she doubted she could even stand on her own right now.

She had no idea how long she sat like that, simply letting Brady hold her and anchor her. Then, out of the night, came the sound of sirens, and she drew back to see flashing lights. In a second, two squad cars pulled to a stop, and Brady eased her back onto the seat. "Sit tight," he said, then got out.

Jayne watched him hurry to the nearest squad car while the red and blue flashing lights played across his face. Even from this distance, she could tell that he looked exhausted. Lines cut deep beside his mouth and between his eyes. He spoke intently to a uniformed officer, raking his fingers through his hair, then disappeared behind her car.

In less than a minute he was coming back toward the Camaro and slipping inside. "Where do you live, Jayne?"

She had to try twice before words would come. "About two miles farther up the road."

"What do you think about having me for a house guest for the night?"

She didn't understand. "What?"

"Captain Burkhart wants me to stay with you for the night, then bring you to the station first thing in the morning."

The idea of not having to break her contact with Brady just yet was more appealing than it should have been, but she could hardly believe the accident had been any more than the mistake of a crazy driver, someone who didn't know the hills. The man at the hospital couldn't be that desperate. "You . . . you think that car, the person driving it, was the man at the hospital?"

"Either a crazy driver or the man who shot Jack and then tried to finish him off. If it's the first, he's long gone. If not, he's not finished with you yet."

"He couldn't know where I live," she breathed. "Could he?"

"He knew enough to follow your car, didn't he?"

When it was put that bluntly, she couldn't refute it. "Yes, he did."

"So I'll stick with you for a while."

"Thank you," she heard herself saying. "You can follow me, or should I follow you?"

"Neither. One of the men will take your car back to the station to check it over and make sure it's all right. We can take my car. The damage isn't too bad."

The past was receding more and more. "Damage?"

"A crumpled fender. Nothing much."

"I'm sorry about your car and I...I appreciate what you're doing. I know you've had a rough day."

"We both have." He hesitated, then asked, "Will your husband mind if I camp out at your house?"

The question came from nowhere, and for a split second she felt blank. There was no response left in her. Every emotion had been on the edge tonight and used up, and her mind seemed unable to zero in on his question. Then she automatically touched the gold band on her finger, the precious metal solid and real. "I'm not married."

"What?"

Until now she had always said she was a widow. She had never felt "not married," not really, and the words hadn't been there for her—until now. For a fleeting second she felt a stab of disloyalty to Elliot, mixed with a surge of incredible sadness that maybe he was finally beginning to slip into the realm of memory.

The idea scared her almost as much as her fear of dying had minutes ago. He couldn't be a memory, never that. He had been so real, so much a part of her life and the future she had envisioned. Yet life did go on. It always had. The sadness began to fade.

She made herself look directly at Brady in the strange shadows cast by the flashing lights from the squad cars. They played havoc with his face, showing shadows and planes, then robbing him of any definition.

"I'm a widow." There, she'd said the words right this time. She'd kept things in their normal order. "I live alone."

Brady stared at Jayne, hearing her words, yet uncertain whether he had only heard what he wanted to hear. He gripped the steering wheel tightly, absorbing an odd mingling of relief that she was single with a real sorrow for what she must have gone through losing her husband. The face of Jack's wife flashed in front of him, the pain, the anguish, the vulnerability. And Jayne had gone through that.

He hated the idea of anyone going through that, and he especially hated the idea that Jayne had. Yet, at odds with that, he felt relief. She wasn't married, not anymore. He knew he shouldn't feel this way, and he passed it off as a by-product of lack of sleep, but he had the momentary thread of an idea that she wasn't totally out of his reach.

"I'm sorry," he murmured, knowing the words should be said, yet feeling slightly hypocritical saying them.

"It happened a long time ago," she said in an oddly flat voice, yet he couldn't help noticing the way her fingers worried the simple ring on her finger.

Obviously not long enough, he thought, his relief not quite so clear now. She still wore the ring. There were still ties. And without any more proof than how loving she had been with the babies, he knew she had loved her husband deeply and completely. Jayne Spencer was a woman of commitment. That knowledge put a distance between them as even her being married hadn't been able to do. She wouldn't be a person who cared passingly.

"Won't your family be worried if you don't go home tonight?" she asked, her voice coming to him through the shadows. "I mean, you aren't at the hospital anymore, and you need to sleep. You probably need to get home."

"There isn't a family," he said when she took a breath. "I am divorced." But he didn't elaborate. His divorce didn't rank up there with having someone you loved die. He barely remembered it anymore. "And I'm sticking to you like glue until you get to look at the mug books tomorrow."

"I appreciate it," she murmured, but he could hear the slight tremor in her voice.

She'd been through the mill tonight, and still she kept going. Brady reached for the key to start the car, a good alternative to touching Jayne just to feel her reality under his hands. His mind felt fogged with weariness and irrational thoughts, along with a sense of loss that he had no basis for.

"Tell me where to go," he murmured as he pulled out into the road, waved to the patrolmen, then drove off up the hill.

In less than five minutes Jayne had guided him onto a narrow, tree-lined street. A scattering of lights penetrated the thick foliage of ancient oaks, which created a deep darkness on either side of the rural road. "See that fence?" she asked.

He looked ahead on the right and caught glimpses of a high, ivy-covered white rail fence. "Sure."

"My driveway is just ahead, where the stone pillars are."

Brady saw huge fieldstone pillars in the sweep of his headlights, turned between them and headed up a steep, cobbled drive that wound under huge eucalyptus and pepper trees. As he got near to what appeared to be the apex of the hill, his headlights caught a ten-foot high retaining wall overrun with bougainvillea vines, then, above it, the shadow of a rambling house.

He turned left and the drive finally leveled out as he headed for a garage that looked big enough to house four cars. It was attached by a breezeway to the house, a huge, two-story bungalow with a wraparound porch and shaded by a massive oak tree that stood in the middle of a sprawling front yard. For a flashing instant Brady thought the house sat almost smugly in its surroundings. It had been there a long time, and it looked as if it intended to be there for a long time to come.

As he pulled the Camaro up to the front of the garage and stopped, he realized Jayne's home looked big enough to house ten people. Then his mind added unerringly, *or ten children*. The thought stopped him dead. Jayne had been married. She could have a whole brood of children, for all he knew.

He remembered her ease with the babies, her natural ability to soothe Rocky, her obvious caring. She could be a mother ten times over. "Lots of room," he muttered, just to say something.

"Lots of room," she echoed softly, then got out, so he did, too.

He stepped out into a stillness that could only exist this far from the city. There wasn't silence, not with the crickets and the cries of night birds, but a peacefulness that didn't exist anywhere near his apartment.

The sky hung heavy above, with a sweep of stars brushed in the darkness and a crescent moon arching toward the west. When he looked in the direction of the drive and the gates below, he could see past the tops of the trees, and the view almost took his breath away. The city was miles away, yet he felt as if he could reach out and lift a single light into the palms of his hands and hold it there.

He shook himself sharply, and looked at Jayne as she hurried past him and onto the porch. He followed her to the right, away from the front of the house and toward a side door. She unlocked it, pushed it back, then disappeared inside.

Brady hesitated, then stepped inside Jayne's home. He took no more than two steps before stopping when she flipped on an overhead light in what he would have called a laundry room.

Gleaming hardwood flooring was partially covered by a round braided rug. A washer and dryer with shelves above them sat to the right, and closets were to the left. Dead ahead, beyond Jayne, who was stepping out of her shoes, were an arched doorway and darkness.

Jayne moved forward, flipped on a light and disappeared to the right. Brady went after her, then stopped inside the doorway and looked around.

What had he expected? Upscale modern? Affected country? Determined Victorian? Or a clutter of toys? None of them was the reality he faced.

Chapter 5

The room Brady stood in appeared to be a family room. It was dominated by a river-rock fireplace on the left wall that was framed from floor to ceiling by oak shelves filled with books. The furnishings were nice but ordinary—a tweed couch facing the fireplace, leather easy chairs and heavy wood tables. Even the walls, textured plaster done in off-white and decorated with oak framed pictures of hunt scenes in deep red and green, weren't out of the ordinary.

Yet the room seemed special. It looked inviting, comfortable, lived in. Almost. There wasn't one thing out of place. Furniture made to be used, and used well, looked as if it was hardly touched.

He glanced at Jayne as she walked through another doorway across the room and flipped on a light, and he could see a huge kitchen. He went after her.

The yellow accented room was as immaculate as the rest of the house. White tiled counters were clear of clutter; the floor, a ceramic inlay, was immaculate. Jayne stopped by double sinks under a bank of curtained windows along the back wall and turned to him. "Coffee?"

"No, just a shower and a place to lie down and sleep."

"There's a guest room. I'll make it up for you."

"The couch is fine. Just give me a blanket and pillow."

"You can't sleep on a couch."

"I can sleep anywhere. Just point me to it."

She went past him, back out into the laundry room, then met him in the family room with a stack of sheets, a blanket, and pillow. "If you're sure?"

"I'm sure." He crossed and took the linen from her, amazed at the shock that ran through him when he accidentally touched her hands in the exchange. He drew back, studied her upturned face for a moment, then murmured, "Thank you."

"Thank *you*," she said quickly. "I hadn't even thought about coming back here alone tonight."

"There's no family at all?"

She looked at him directly. "My family lives in L.A. Elliot and I…" She nibbled on her bottom lip. "It was just the two of us."

No children. That knowledge took a weight off him. He didn't know what to say, so he turned and looked around the room for a phone. "I need to call in. Can I use your phone?"

"It's in the kitchen, on the wall to the right of the sinks."

"Great." He forced a smile that he didn't feel and found himself trying to reassure Jayne. "Listen, this will be all right. The Captain and I are probably being overcautious about this, just making sure and covering all bases. After tomorrow morning, when you make an ID from the mug shots, this guy won't have any reason to go after you—if it was him in the car in the first place."

"Thank you," she said softly, then glanced at her watch. "Three a.m. The night's half over." She looked back at Brady, barely covering a soft yawn with one hand. "This has been quite an experience," she said as she began to take pins out of her hair and loosen the dark mass until it fell heavily over her shoulders and framed her face.

Brady stared at her, almost unable to think straight. As she shook her head, the ebony veil shifted and shimmered around her face, and he couldn't breathe. Beautiful. Absolutely beautiful. And so young to be widowed.

That thought brought him up short. Jayne Spencer should never have known sadness in her life. Hell, no one should. But everyone did. Jack's family certainly did. That brought him back to the present, to the reality that he was a cop, here only to make sure Jayne got to the station in the morning in one piece.

"Are you going to make your call?" she asked as she looked up at him from under a sweep of dark lashes.

His call. "Yes." He turned, tossed the linen onto the couch, then looked back at Jayne. "When I'm done, I'll need to take a quick look around the house and make sure everything's secure." He saw the widening of her eyes. "Just as a precaution. Just to make sure the windows are locked. That's all. And I need the basic layout of the house in my mind."

Jayne motioned around the room. "This is it. This and two more rooms. My bedroom, an extra bedroom and a bathroom."

Brady narrowed his eyes with a squint. "I don't understand. This house is huge."

"It is huge, but the rest isn't used. It's been shut off for a long time." Her sister Sara had done that. She'd come here while Jayne was in the hospital and taken care of everything. The bedrooms upstairs had never really been used in the three months Elliot and Jayne had lived here. Four had been extras, space for the future, for the family they'd planned, and the other had been the master bedroom, a huge room that faced the front, shaded by the oak and overlooking the city.

Sara had taken care of everything, including getting Jayne's things arranged in one of the two downstairs bedrooms, with a double bed not at all like the king-sized canopy bed upstairs under dust sheets.

Brady was watching her intently. "You never go into it?"

She shook her head, unusually at a loss for words.

"What is there besides this section you live in? What's in the closed off part?" Brady asked.

"Bedrooms upstairs. Five of them. Two baths. Down here there's a parlor, a formal dining room, a study of sorts, a foyer." She shrugged, hating the way she was cataloging a house she was feeling more distanced from all the time. That moment in the car when she had felt Elliot slipping from her came again. Once again she could feel herself beginning to let go of the past, including this house. She clasped her hands tightly together, as if she could delay the process by holding on to herself, at least until she had time to adjust, to rearrange her thinking. "It's been locked up for quite a while. I don't think you need to bother—"

"Just a precaution. But first I need to call in."

Without another word, he turned and headed into the kitchen. Jayne reached for the linen and absentmindedly began spreading it on the couch, her hands busy with the mundane task while her mind wrestled with the past.

She'd thought about selling the house, but could she walk away from it? Could she close the door on the past so completely? The idea tore at her, yet she had always known the time would come. She couldn't stay here. There was nothing here for her, not even a lot of memories. There hadn't been time enough for too many memories.

She hated the tears that suddenly burned her eyes. Letting go would probably kill her, if this maniac didn't do it first. Where had normalcy gone? Where had her common, everyday existence gone?

A few irrevocable moments had changed everything. The accident; the time when she had been stopped from killing herself; finding the babies and getting involved. She had always stopped there before, but now she silently added, meeting Brady Knight face-to-face, having him walk back into her life. The man who had saved her life twice.

She stopped smoothing the pillow, sensing, rather than hearing, Brady come back into the room. When she looked up he was in the doorway, one hand braced on the frame. His face looked tight; the tanned skin stretched across high cheekbones was touched with paleness.

"Your partner?" she asked as her hands stilled.

"Jack's holding his own. And there haven't been any more visitors." As he came into the room, stopping a few feet from the back of the sofa, she realized he was simply exhausted. He took a deep, harsh breath. "The news is that they got an ID on the car that tried to run you off the road."

"Who owns it?" she asked as she stood and absent-mindedly tucked her loose hair behind her ears.

"The owner is one Henry Reed, an orderly at the hospital. The car was stolen from the hospital parking lot, and

Reed didn't know it was gone until he was contacted at work a few minutes ago."

"Then the driver . . . ?"

"Was our man, or a kid out joyriding." He shrugged. "Either way, the car's a dead end, if or when we find it."

She motioned to the couch. "Your bed's ready."

He came closer, glanced at the sheets and pillow she'd laid out, then yawned. He shook his head sharply as if to clear it. "I'll check the windows and doors to make sure they're locked, then I'll take that shower."

She knew she didn't want Brady to go upstairs. There was no rhyme or reason to it, just the certainty that she didn't want him up there. "I can check the locks. You go ahead and take your shower. It's through there." She pointed across the room. "The middle door. There should be towels in the cupboard just inside the door and a razor in the cabinet . . . if you don't mind using one that's pink."

"I'm past minding anything right now. And I'll take you up on your offer. Just check and make sure everything is locked. And if you see one thing out of place, get right back here."

She nodded and crossed to the sliding doors that led into the formal living area. She slid them open, and they protested slightly with a low squeak. She felt as if she had just opened a door to her secrets.

She hated the unsteadiness in her hand when she reached for the light switch and pressed it. The two-tier, tulip chandelier in the dining room burst with light that was almost painful to the eyes. No one had been in here for almost two years except the cleaning service that came once a month. Now Jayne looked at the space before her, a painfully disused, silent space.

The oval oak table and chairs were hidden under dust covers, and the hardwood floor was exposed. The Oriental carpet had been rolled to one side and covered. She hurried through the room, into the foyer and over to the wide staircase that led up to the short balcony that overlooked the entry. After taking the carpeted steps two at a time, she was slightly breathless when she got to the top and flipped on the hall lights.

The hall went both right and left from the balcony. "The east wing and the west wing," she used to kid Elliot. But she felt no humor now, just a peculiar emptiness. An echoing hollow feeling that the house seemed to radiate, too.

She hurried to the right, checked the windows of the two empty rooms and the shared bath, then went back to the balcony, crossed it and headed in the other direction. She looked into the two smaller rooms at the back, which stood empty except for a few boxes that had never been unpacked.

She stepped back into the hall and turned to the only door on the other side. She hadn't been in this room for so long. The last time she had left it, the world had been right, everything had been right.

For an instant she considered telling Brady the windows were locked and not going inside; then she braced herself and pushed the door open. Total darkness confronted her until she took a deep breath, felt on the left side for the light switch and flipped it up. She closed her eyes against the onslaught of brightness that flooded the room, then braced herself and looked at what had been the master bedroom.

The carved four-poster bed was stripped; even the canopy had been taken down and put away. The dresser and armoire to one side of the bank of front windows covered with heavy antique satin drapes had nothing on them. The floor was bare, the carpet rolled the way the one downstairs had been. Even the pictures that had hung here were down on the floor, turned face in to the wall.

She waited for a surge of emotion, for the sadness or the pain, but, strangely, nothing came. She inhaled deliberately. There wasn't even a particular scent to the room. Nothing but mustiness and disuse touched with a trace of lemon wax.

Why had she thought she would walk in and sense Elliot here? Why had she feared this moment for so long? This was a room, the way all the others had been. As she quickly checked the windows, the feelings of disassociation from the past she had experienced in Brady's car, the sense of the past slipping farther and farther from her, became sharper and more focused. She felt the distancing, welcoming it on one hand, cursing it on the other. She swallowed hard as she backed out into the hallway, then closed the door and stood motionless, staring at it.

In the hospital, during those confused, blurred days, her mother had tried to help, saying things that had had no basis in reality for Jayne then. "The pain of loss won't ever go away, but it changes. You forget and readjust until you can remember and still go on living."

Jayne *had* gone on living, finally establishing a pattern for her life that filled the emptiness. She'd gotten involved with the babies, gone back to her job, but she'd known she wouldn't forget. Never. She had known it was irrational, but she'd felt that if she forgot anything she'd had with Elliot, it would be as if he had never existed. That couldn't happen.

Yet now she knew it was. She was forgetting, rearranging memories, and she didn't know how to deal with it. She felt her stomach knot and sickness sting the back of her throat.

Elliot. She closed her eyes, and tried to envision him, but all she could come up with was a blurred picture. She knew he had been her height, with dark hair and eyes to match, a man of gentleness and love. Yet the image she came up with was from an old picture she had of him, one she'd kept with her during that time in the hospital, not an image of the real man.

It was the events of the night, the spinout on the way up here. Something was out of kilter, and she couldn't fix it, not now.

She turned away from the door and hurried down the hallway to the balcony. In a rush to get away from her thoughts and the past, she headed downstairs and stopped just short of running headlong into Brady, who was standing at the bottom of the stairs looking up at her.

She stopped one step above him, putting herself almost at eye level with him, and her mouth went dry.

The man was almost naked, barefoot and wearing nothing more than his jeans. He smelled of a crazily provocative combination of freshness and soap and masculinity.

His hair, damp from the shower, was darker and brushed straight back from his face, making him seem all angles and planes dominated by the deep blueness of his eyes. His bare chest and flat abdomen were just as she had imagined, without one ounce of extra fat. Muscles rippled under the tanned skin, and a pattern of dark hair formed a definite T across his chest and down his stomach.

Jayne felt her mouth go dry and her heart lurch painfully in her chest. Her last thoughts when the car had spun out of control came back to her. The stinging regret that she would never be held by a man again, never be loved by a man. And Brady's image had been there in her mind.

Now the reality of him made it so hard for her to breathe that she literally had to make herself draw in air. She was aware of him in a way she hadn't been aware of any man for a long time. It was a basic response, a physical response, a man and woman thing.

The strength of it shook her, and it both shocked and embarrassed her at the same time. Brady had come here to make sure some crazy man didn't kill her. He was just doing his job, and she was looking at him like a teenager with a bad case of lust. She knew she was blushing, and she hated it. She couldn't look right at him, so she stared at a spot somewhere near his left ear. "Everything up there is fine."

"Are you sure? Nothing wrong?"

Only the fact I feel like some idiot sophomore, she thought, hoping the heat in her would subside. "Everything's locked up tight," she said quickly. "I'm really tired. I think we both need to get some sleep. I just..." Her voice trailed off. "I'm going to bed," she finished finally.

"I think that's a good idea. This has been a terrible strain on you."

She didn't want understanding from this man. In a way it was his appearance in her life that had set everything in motion, she realized. And his physical appearance now had actually weakened her legs so much that she reached out to grip the wooden banister.

In that moment she came close to hating the man in front of her. She hadn't felt like this for so long. It had always been Elliot for her, never anyone else. Now Brady Knight had shown up instead of Mr. Appleton, and all she could see was the expanse of his chest, his tanned skin, the pattern of chest hair, the undone top button of his jeans. She closed her eyes for a quick moment, then made herself look right at him. "Yes, it's been terrible. I was just thinking that if Mr. Appleton had shown up the way he was supposed to, none of this would have happened. You wouldn't have been in with the babies, and I wouldn't have—''

''You wouldn't have been drawn into this craziness, that's for sure. But you're the one who said you believed in Fate.''

Fate. Things that were meant to be. When she looked right at Brady, she was incredibly aware of his eyes, blue, so blue, and intent. ''And you don't.''

''I never said that. I just think a man makes his own fate, every moment, every hour, every day.''

''Even his own death?''

His expression tightened, and his mouth thinned. ''Chance. The toss of a coin. The wrong place at the wrong time.''

She felt her stomach knot. This was the wrong place and the wrong time to be discussing this, maybe the wrong life.

Unexpectedly he reached out to her, barely touching her cheek with the tips of his fingers. ''You're tired. I'm tired. Let's get some sleep.''

The contact, as insubstantial as it was, sent a shock through her, so she ducked her head, broke the contact and went down the final step and past Brady into the dining room. As she stepped through the open sliding doors into the family room, she could still feel his touch. She rubbed at the spot with her hand and spoke without turning as she crossed the room toward her bedroom door. ''We have to be at the police station at nine?''

''That's what the captain said,'' she heard from behind her. ''But we can go a bit later, if you want to. I know it's late and you won't get much sleep.''

''No, nine's fine. I need to get to work as soon as I can after that.''

"Nine it is, then."

"Good night," she murmured and went into her room, closing the door behind her.

She looked around the square space, with its double bed, chest of drawers, and stacks of well-read books on the floor.

Quickly she stripped off her clothes and crossed to the small bathroom. As soon as she stepped in she felt bombarded by a male presence. The air was still steamy and warm, touched with the scents of soap and freshness. A towel had been discarded on the wicker hamper, and Brady's shoes were by the shower stall.

She couldn't hide from what she was feeling anymore. She hadn't been with a man for what seemed like forever, and she found out that, having thought of it, she couldn't escape the idea. It made her tense and uncomfortable. She wanted to be held and to be made love to by a man who cared, who was gentle yet demanding.

Brady Knight had brought those feelings flickering back to life for her. It couldn't be him. It really wasn't him. She was just returning to life, in a way. And two years of being by herself seemed like an eternity right now.

She stepped into the shower stall, slid the door shut and turned on the water. Could it be that primal, the need to be with a man? No, it couldn't be, yet her body was screaming and had been since she had seen Brady at the foot of the stairs.

"You'll hit a point where you can get on with your life, where you meet someone—" She cut off the memory of her mother's words. She had tried to get on with her life, but she had never expected to want to be with a man again. And this wouldn't have happened if there hadn't been a mix-up, if Brady's partner hadn't been shot, if she hadn't thought a lanky man with incredible blue eyes was a CPA.

As the steamy spray bombarded her, she began to shake. She hugged her arms around herself as the water streamed over her body and closed her eyes.

Brady woke instantly, but he didn't move. He knew immediately where he was and what he was doing, but he didn't know what had awakened him from a deep, truly dreamless sleep. He felt the tangle of sheets around his legs and the arm of the couch pressed uncomfortably against the back of his neck. Then he felt the hard shape of his holstered gun caught between his hip and the back of the couch.

With his eyes closed, he visualized the layout of the room he was in and the rest of Jayne's house. When he heard a soft, muffled sliding noise, he zeroed in on it. It sounded as if it was coming from somewhere beyond the kitchen.

He inched his hand down to his side, found the holster and silently slipped his service revolver out, then grasped it as he opened his eyes just a slit. In the pale gray light of dawn filtering into the family room, he couldn't see a thing moving. Silently he slowly disentangled his legs from the sheets; then he stood, the soft braided rug under his feet, and looked toward the kitchen.

Nothing stirred. No more noises. He glanced at a clock on the wall by the bookcases. Six-fifteen. Less than three hours' sleep. He listened. The noise hadn't come from Jayne's bedroom or the bath, but from beyond the kitchen. He was sure of that. He looked at the closed door of her room, the one to the bath, the third to the extra room; then he slowly started for the kitchen.

Gripping his gun securely and curling his finger around the trigger, he pressed himself against the wall by the kitchen door, then eased forward until he could see into the room.

It was completely empty. He stepped inside and crossed the floor, the tiles cold and hard under his bare feet. Then he heard it again, a sliding sound that came from outside a door to the left of the sink. The door wasn't closed all the way, and it opened outward instead of inward, the way a lot of exterior doors did on older houses.

Brady hurried to the door, touched the knob and gripped his gun tighter. His adrenaline was surging. His heartbeat sped up. He took a deep breath, then kicked the door back and stood squarely in the doorway of a sun room, the gun braced in both hands.

"Police! Freeze!" he yelled as the sound of his own voice was overlaid by a piercing scream.

At first all he could make out was the blurred image of a person against the backdrop of windows and the outside world bathed in the colors of dawn. Then his vision sharpened, and he slowly lowered the gun.

Jayne was no more than four feet from him, facing him, both hands held out in his direction as if to ward off a blow—or a bullet. He felt sick at the shock in her eyes and the trembling in her hands as she drew them back to clutch at her middle.

"Oh, God, I'm sorry. I had no idea you were out here."

"I . . . I couldn't sleep," she said. "I came out here for a while to think." She was staring at the gun. "I didn't know I'd made any noise."

"And I didn't know there was a sun room out here. You didn't tell me." Brady heard the faint rebuke in his words, fed by his fear of what could have happened and the look of absolute shock and fear in her eyes.

He ran a hand over his face, then looked at her again. He couldn't reconcile the woman from last night—tailored and sleekly elegant—with this Jayne in front of him, a woman with a wild tangle of ebony hair framing a decidedly pale face and dressed in a short, white terry robe that showed the length of her shapely legs.

Something about her struck Brady to the core, something beyond the fact that she was even more stunning this way. He had a peculiar sense that he knew her, the same sense he had felt for an instant when she walked toward him in the hallway of the hospital. It was as if he had known her forever and she had just walked back into his life.

As he stepped closer to her the feeling flitted away before he could examine it or really understand it. On impulse, he reached out to her, as if contact could make him understand. And it hurt like hell when she flinched and drew back before he could touch her shoulder. His hand fell to his side, and he clenched it into a fist.

"I heard a noise, and..." His voice trailed off when her eyes went back to the gun. He could see each unsteady breath she took and the trembling in her body. He took a half-step toward her, thankful that she didn't back away from him when he reached out to her once more. He gently cupped her chin with one hand.

"I'm truly sorry, Jayne."

"I...was restless. I thought..." As her voice trailed off, her tongue darted out and touched her lips.

Her beauty at that moment stunned Brady. There wasn't a flaw in her face, or in the lines of the body under the short robe. She all but took his breath away, a more startling reaction than his shock moments earlier. His mind went in its own direction, the same direction his body took with this woman so close to him. And he wondered what it would be like to make love to her, to know her intimately and hold her far into the night. To feel her heat under his hands and hear her sighs of pleasure mingling with his.

Without taking time to sort things out, Brady lowered his head, and before Jayne could avoid him, his mouth touched her parted lips. Her taste was sweet, her lips soft, yet there was no response at all. The instant he realized what he was doing, he drew back and found himself looking into eyes huge with bewilderment. She hadn't moved; she hadn't invited more, but her face was deep crimson.

Brady felt so foolish that he knew if he could blush, he would have right then. What had possessed him to do that? He realized how stupid the question was as soon as it formed in his mind. The answer was simple and obvious. Jayne Spencer stirred him in a way no woman had for a long time.

Chapter 6

Brady's number one law," he said, searching for something to take the edge off, for humor in a tense situation. "Always let a cop know where you are." He tapped her on the chin and drew back, hating the loss of contact. "Especially if that cop is working on three hours sleep and is so disoriented he wouldn't know which end was up unless it was labeled."

There was no response at first; then Jayne spoke in a low voice. "I'll remember that. I...I need coffee. Do you want some?"

He was thankful that she didn't press the situation, looking for an explanation when he had none to give her that would make sense. "Yes, thank you."

Brady watched her move away from him and experienced a peculiar sense of loneliness as she disappeared through the door into the kitchen. Loneliness? The concept held little reality for him. He had always enjoyed his own company. Hours at the beach alone had been therapy for him so many times. Yet now he felt alone, and it was a real loneliness somewhere in the pit of his stomach.

He turned to the windows and stared blindly out. Yes, the beach. He fingered the gun still in his hand. As soon as he could, he was going to take a few days off and head for the Pacific—and solitude.

The change in his appearance gave him courage. It always did. So he felt no qualms about walking back into Santa Barbara Memorial six hours after he had tried to kill Jack Wills for the second time.

His outward appearance drew no curious glances as he passed the main desk and headed for the elevators. Gone were the hospital whites he'd stolen from the linen closet to get into Wills's room. They were in a dumpster a good five miles from where he'd abandoned the car he'd used to try and take out the dark-haired woman who'd seen him tampering with the IV. He'd walked over a mile before taking the chance of calling a cab; then he had only taken it to a point close to the hospital. The last mile, he'd walked again.

Once back at his rental car, he had tugged a baseball cap over his pale hair, then slipped into an orange wind-breaker that covered his beige shirt. Orange was a memorable color. And if someone asked for a description of a man who walked into the hospital around dawn, they would only remember the jacket. The dark contacts he slipped in were never comfortable for him, but they were necessary on occasion.

He rode up to the fifth floor, got out and took his time unzipping his jacket so he could get the lay of the land. He hated loose ends. Wills was a loose end, and the woman who had walked in on him had become another. In his career, loose ends could be fatal, so he would take care of them.

He'd almost had the woman until the other car had rammed him from the rear. He hadn't had time to find out who the driver had been. Now he had to find the woman, and to do that, he had to start at square one. Then he'd get Wills and get out of town.

He walked down the hallway, watching for cops. He spotted one sitting on a chair outside Wills's room. Another barrier he'd have to hurdle. Later. As long as Wills was unconscious, he had time.

He walked up to the nurses' station, then went into his act. "I want to talk to someone in charge," he said in a voice loud enough to make the woman behind the desk look up at him and frown.

"Sir, could you keep your voice down?"

He sensed the cop looking at him. The idiot had no idea who he was looking at, and it gave him a sense of power. "I heard that someone was almost killed here last night. My aunt's in this hospital, and if that's the kind of thing that can go on here, I'm getting her out."

"Sir, sir, please," the nurse sputtered. "I'm sure you're concerned, but let me explain."

"I heard that if that woman hadn't been here, God knows what would have happened to the poor man."

She looked vaguely taken aback by that. Obviously the cops were trying to keep everything under wraps. "I'm sure you've heard rumors, but—"

"There wasn't a woman who saved the man's life?"

"I suppose you could put it that way, but—"

"You're damn lucky she was here. I hope it's in the papers. She should get some recognition."

"Mrs. Spencer doesn't want that, and I'm sure you wouldn't—"

"Spencer?"

"Jayne Spencer, she—"

Jayne Spencer. He had a name and a general idea of where she lived. Enough. He held up one hand, knowing better than to push for more right now. "You know, I'm sure things aren't as bad as they say. You're obviously trying to do a good job."

The woman looked relieved and bobbed her head. "Yes, sir, we are."

"What was your name again?"

"Sharon, Sharon DeMarco."

He smiled at her. Sharon DeMarco would never know who she spoke to, and never know she helped kill Jayne Spencer.

Jayne stopped in the doorway of the sun room, a mug of coffee in each hand. Brady was standing in front of the windows, the morning light silhouetting him.

For a moment she couldn't move. The memory of his lips on hers robbed her of the ability to put one foot in front of the other. She had tried to block the image while she made the coffee, but the sight of him, barefooted and wearing only his jeans, brought it back with a jolt.

A barrier had broken in her in the past eight hours. It wasn't due to Brady but to the simple fact that something in her was coming back to life, something she thought had died two years ago. Brady had just happened to be there when it happened, and he happened to look almost painfully male.

She moved silently on the stone tiles and stopped within a few feet of the man, inordinately aware of the way his strong shoulders lifted with each breath he took. He was staring outside, and she looked past him at the slightly blurred shapes of the large oaks that framed the lawn in the back. The darkness of the higher hills loomed in the distance, and the sky above was washed in pale yellows and pinks.

Then she spotted the swing set to the right under a sprawling oak. She'd all but forgotten about it until now.

Brady sensed Jayne's presence at the same time he saw the swing set under the old tree. One of the swings stirred in the early morning breeze, the same breeze that ruffled the long grass, and it seemed to chill Brady without touching him. Children. It seemed as if Jayne's life was always touched by the specter of a child.

The question of just who Jayne had been married to nudged at him. What was the man like whom she had loved and made her life with, the man she had wanted to have children with?

"It's not really kept up now," he heard Jayne say from close behind him. "When I first saw the house there were flowers everywhere. It was breathtaking."

He turned. She was less than three feet from him, holding two mugs of steaming coffee. The gentle light of the new day touched her face, renewing his awareness of her. She turned and went to a small glass-topped table near a bank of side windows, but even the extra distance didn't lessen her impact on him. God, he could feel his whole body tensing, and he took a deep breath to try to ease it.

He found himself saying the one thing that he knew would help him get perspective. "And the swing set?"

She sat down, putting the mugs on the table top, then looked up at him. "What about it?"

"Did you buy it, or did it come with the house?"

"It came with the house. It's been there for years. The old owners told me they put it up for their children when they were young. That must have been years ago, because their children were all married and gone. That's why they sold the house. They said it was made for children."

"It's big enough," he murmured.

"Too big."

He narrowed his eyes on her. "I thought you must have bought it for its size."

"For its size, its location, its sense of belonging here. It seems as if it was almost grown in this spot." Her voice was low. "But it's not right for one person. It needs a family to give it life, to fill it up."

"That's what you planned?" he asked, almost not wanting an answer.

"We did. Elliot was from a large family, and so am I. We both wanted the same thing. Four or five children." She took a quick drink from her mug. "It didn't work out that way."

Brady looked at Jayne and knew deep in his heart that it would work out that way for her someday, with some man who wanted what she wanted, who wanted her. Brady almost felt jealous of that future man, the man who would be able to be everything Jayne wanted and everything she deserved. The things he couldn't be for anyone.

He heard her take a shaky breath; then she nudged one of the cups in Brady's direction. "I hope black is all right. I don't want to sound stupid like I did about your job at the hospital, but I thought since you're a policeman, you wouldn't want anything in it."

She spoke in a rush, and Brady felt the tugging of a smile at the corners of his mouth. She made him feel almost light-headed. Or maybe it was just lack of sleep and the mention of a house full of children—four or five.

"Black's fine," he murmured and walked over to sit in the other chair across the table from Jayne. "But I don't think it's a job requirement. Actually, sugar and cream tend to hide the flavor of the coffee I usually get at the station.''

He laid his gun on the table and reached for the mug, cradling the heat between his hands before he tested the steaming liquid. Then he sat back and looked out the windows. But instead of the outside world, he saw his image along with Jayne's reflected back at him. She looked like an illusion, a shimmering specter of darks and lights, the whiteness of her robe, the blackness of her tangled hair. A far cry from the woman he had thought was a doctor at the hospital.

He turned and put the mug down on the table top. ''Since we're up, why don't we get an early start going through the mug books?''

Jayne agreed immediately, thankful for the suggestion. She wanted to get this over with. ''Yes, I'll get dressed. I can go from there...'' She hesitated. ''My car is down at the police station, isn't it?''

''It should be in the police garage.''

''Fine, I'll go right from there to work.''

''Where is work?''

''On the north side. Taylor Industries. I'm a wholesale buyer for their department stores.''

''Do you do your work in an office?''

She found a bit of humor in that. ''Of course. And you do your work out of your car.''

His laughter was a welcome respite, a gentle sound that ran pleasantly over her nerves. ''Touché. I'm ignorant. I've never even seen a wholesale buyer on television.'' He looked at her and tapped his temple. ''No preconceived ideas.''

She fingered the mug on the table. ''I buy stock for the stores, but most of the sellers come to me.''

''Now I know.''

"Yes, you do." She felt an easiness between them, and she liked it. "I called the hospital when I got up. Rocky had a peaceful night. Maybe it was you holding him. The contact. He needed that."

Brady looked at her intently for a few seconds. "No problems?"

"He's still not able to suck. You know, he—"

"Did you ask about my partner?" he asked, cutting her off.

"He's still unconscious and on the respirator. But his vital signs are strong."

He exhaled harshly. "Good. Let's head down to look at the mug shots. Then you can get to work, and so can I. I need to put an end to this nightmare as soon as I can."

When they were getting ready to leave in the Camaro, Brady looked at Jayne. "We could have had a disaster because I didn't know about the sun room. Are there any other places in the house I should know about?"

Jayne shifted in her seat and looked at him; his Hawaiian shirt was definitely the worse for wear. At least she'd been able to put on fresh clothes: pleated brown slacks, a copper silk blouse with full sleeves, and leather pumps. "No, not in the house."

"But?" he asked, slanting her a sideways glance as he started the engine.

"There's an extra garage you can't see from the house, beyond the tree where the swings are." She looked straight ahead as he headed down the driveway and onto the street down to the city. "It was a carriage house of sorts, I guess. But it's full of junk now. I didn't mention it because I really forgot about it, and it's not part of the house, and I didn't—"

"Another law is don't omit something because you don't think it's important. Let me decide what's important and what isn't."

"Do you have these laws of yours etched in stone?" she asked.

He laughed softly at that, a pleasantly rough sound that echoed in the confines of the car. "A few of them. The really important ones."

"I guess we all have our laws."

"You too?"

"Sure."

"Tell me one."

She hadn't really thought about it, but one came to mind immediately, one that had gotten her through a lot in life. "Never give up. Keep going and do what you know is right."

"Isn't that another way of saying you're stubborn?"

"Probably." She took a breath and plunged into something she wanted to ask Brady. "I meant it when I asked you to come back and help with the babies. You'll be at the hospital a lot until your partner is better, and it could be a break for you. And the babies could really use the contact. You might find out you like doing it."

She kept talking quickly, barely stopping to take a breath. "I mean, the babies would love it, and I really think Rocky did better last night because you held him for a while. It does make a difference."

Brady downshifted at the corner. "You are stubborn, aren't you? You were right about that."

"Will you help?" she persisted.

"I don't have the time."

"But if you're at the hospital, you could—"

"I don't like children. I never have."

That blunt statement took her back. "But you held Rocky and you—"

"I had no choice, if you remember, but Rocky...he looks like an alien to me. All children do."

"That's probably because you haven't been around babies enough. If you were there day in and day out, you'd find yourself falling in love with them. They're so helpless, so needy."

"And so are the homeless on the street, but I can't take them home with me."

"But you want children of your own, don't you?"

"No. I never even thought about it."

"Not even when you were married?"

"Especially not then. I found out then how badly I do at relationships. I never even considered bringing a child into my marriage. I guess it boils down to the fact that my wife couldn't deal with my sort of life. I don't think a cop should ask anyone to deal with it, and certainly not children along with everything else."

"Surely cops get married and live happily ever after with families?"

He shrugged sharply. "Maybe. Then there are some who get shot, and their wives die a bit with them. I'm a good cop, but I figured out that I don't have what it takes to commit myself to one person, and I wouldn't wish me as a father on any child."

"So you chose to be in police work *and* be alone?"

"Not consciously, but it turned out that way." He shifted again. "I'm not complaining. I don't mind being alone. I could be happy spending my life at the beach by myself. I did, for quite a while. There are worse things in this world than being alone."

"Worse than loneliness?" She couldn't begin to think of one.

"I didn't say I was lonely. There's a difference between being lonely and being alone."

"Is there?"

"Isn't there?" he countered.

She didn't know. She was both alone and horribly lonely at times, even with her family as close as the phone. That was why the babies had become so important to her. Why her hours at work and at the hospital had grown longer and longer as she healed physically. That was why she lived in only a small fraction of the space in the house. And maybe why she was so inordinately aware of the man next to her in the car.

Jayne stared at Brady, and for some reason she felt sadness for the man.

"What about your parents? You let them into your life, don't you?"

He turned onto the main highway down to the city. "No. They live on the outside of it. They never say I'm a cop, they say I'm 'involved in the law.' My mother might admit to what I do under duress, but my father chooses to think of my job as a hobby, a passing fancy until I come to my senses."

"And when you 'come to your senses,' what then?"

"He thinks I'll go into his business and make good on my potential."

"What is his business?"

"The development company that negotiated for the land where the Taylor building stands. The A.K. Corporation leased to Taylor, then contracted for construction." He fingered the steering wheel. "A boring, routine job."

"Nothing as exciting as almost getting killed, I suppose," she muttered.

He glanced at her, and she could see his annoyance in his expression. "I'm not stupid. I wouldn't be doing this if I thought I was going to die. No cop would."

Jayne turned to the side window, away from Brady's barely veiled rebuke. But as they rounded a corner and she saw the skid marks her car had made the night before, she knew she'd gone from bad to worse. She hated the sight of the black rubber strips on the asphalt, of the grooves in the dirt shoulder where the car had skidded to a stop. Inches from the edge of the drop-off. She barely controlled a shudder and murmured as she closed her eyes, "But some do die, don't they?"

"Sure. And they leave families behind." He downshifted on the steep road. "Let's change the subject. Why don't you tell me just why you were up at the crack of dawn?"

She wouldn't tell Brady how restless she'd been, how she'd woken up for no reason just a few hours after falling into a fitful sleep, or how she'd known sleep wouldn't come back for her. How she had gone through the family room to the kitchen without once glancing at him on the couch, yet had been totally aware of every breath he took, each soft movement he made. Then the kiss, a mere brush of his lips on hers, a touch for comfort or apology, yet she had felt it as a jolt that could have been equaled only by a shock of raw electricity.

"I was awake. I was a bit on edge," she finally said, then laughed softly. "And that's an understatement, a real understatement. I don't know how you can deal with this day in and day out. It's crazy." She was talking quickly, and she had to make herself stop. "Life's crazy," she said simply.

"Amen to that," Brady murmured and sped up as they came to the bottom of the hilly road and headed for the freeway.

He signaled a right turn and never glanced at a blue car passing them to go up into the hills. He didn't see the driver slow down and look in his rearview mirror, recognizing the Camaro by its crumpled fender. Or see the man pull a navy baseball cap low over pale hair, then turn and follow them.

Jayne's eyes burned and blurred after more than an hour of looking through the thick, awkward volumes of mug shots. She sat back in the hard wooden chair in the small, glass-walled room and closed her eyes for a moment, then looked up at the door, surprised to see Brady staring at her intently.

The rumpled Hawaiian shirt had been changed for a blue T-shirt with a wave logo on it and fresh jeans. His white running shoes looked well used. He must have seen surprise on her face, because he shrugged. "I keep fresh clothes here, just in case. Did you find anything?"

She shook her head and closed the heavy book. "How about you?"

Brady had told her that he would go over the files of the open cases he and Jack had been working on while she looked through the books. "I can't find anything, but then, I didn't get through a quarter of the files, either."

She pressed her hand flat on the top cover of the thick book. "I wonder if I'd even know the man if I saw him again after looking at all these faces."

"You would, believe me," he murmured. "I talked to the police artist, and he just got here. If you can describe the man to him, he might be able to get a reasonable like-

ness, something that will give us an idea of what he looks
like."

She nodded. "I can try."

Brady turned and called out, "Novak!"

Jayne saw a small man dressed in a baggy gray suit get
up from a desk across the squad room and hurry toward
Brady. He carried a briefcase under one arm and a huge
sketch pad under the other. He slipped into the room,
crossed to where Jayne sat and took the chair to her right.
He looked at her with intent brown eyes. "I'm Tom
Novak," he said in a reedy voice. "Brady told me about
you, Mrs. Spencer."

"Tom, explain to Jayne what you want to do," Brady
said.

"We could do a composite," the man said as he laid out
his sketch pad and briefcase, then snapped the case open.
"But composites end up looking like someone from outer
space. Bits and pieces all stuck together. What we want is
something more natural." He took a thick pencil out of a
pack in the case, then flipped up the cover of the pad. "I'll
do a sketch while you tell me everything you remember
about the man. Don't leave out anything, no matter how
minor. If anything doesn't look right to you, anything at
all, stop me and we'll figure it out."

Jayne nodded and Tom looked at Jayne. "The shape of
his head . . . ?"

Within half an hour Tom had a sketch that shocked
Jayne with its likeness to the man in Jack's hospital room.
The face and hair were right; the whole look was right.
Even the eyes—cold and hard, yet not intense enough, not
really. She exhaled as she sat back. "That looks a lot like
him."

"But?" Tom prodded.

She glanced at Brady, who hadn't moved from the door. And she remembered his words in the car that no matter how unimportant she thought something was, she should let him decide. Then she looked at the sketch again. "The eyes. They were more intense."

Tom made a few small changes, deepening the lines at the corners of the pale eyes, then narrowing the lids. The look was almost perfect.

"Yes, that's it," Jayne breathed, feeling as exhausted as if she had run ten miles.

She realized she had been tensing while she watched Tom draw, and a faint headache was beginning to throb behind her eyes. Besides that, the face on the page made her feel distinctly uncomfortable.

Brady crossed to the table and looked down at the sketch, studying it. "We need copies, Tom. As soon as we can get them."

Tom stood and gathered his things together. "Ten minutes. I'll bring them in."

When the man left, Jayne looked up at Brady. "Will it help?"

"Sure. Now *I* know exactly what he looks like, too. It's not a photo ID, but it's as close as we can come for now."

"There wasn't anyone like that in your files, anyone you remember?"

"Not yet. But, as I said, I've just started."

She nibbled on her bottom lip. "This won't stop him trying to get **me**, though, will it?"

He hesitated. "Honestly, no. He'll still be after you. And that means only one thing."

"What's that?"

"I'm going to Taylor's with you."

The Taylor Building was glaringly new in a city that was full of red-tiled roofs, textured stucco, and adobe. The glass and steel structure stood six stories high, towering over the nearby buildings, and it had a deep blue sign on the top. Brady remembered hearing that the light had to go off at ten p.m. because the neighboring residential area complained about its blue brilliance flooding over them. Another of my father's contributions to the city, he thought as he drove into an underground parking structure. An attractive nuisance.

"Your father did this?" Jayne asked as he parked in a loading zone directly in front of three elevator doors.

"Every bit of it," he muttered as he got out and came around to walk with Jayne to the nearest elevator. He jabbed the button to go up and exhaled. "This took him over three years to complete. He slept and ate and breathed this project for all that time. And when he finished, he had a building that looked as if it belonged in downtown New York and not Santa Barbara."

She glanced at him from under the sweep of her lashes, and he could have sworn he saw a twinkle of humor in the amber eyes that almost matched the tone of her silky blouse. "Are you an architectural purist?"

He shrugged, a bit annoyed with himself for being so adamant. "If a city is unique because it looks like a Spanish mission town, which Santa Barbara was at the beginning, why try to make it look like every other city in the country? The hospital, I understand. They need it that tall and that utilitarian. But not this."

"You've got a point. But if you were in your father's business, couldn't you do something like that?"

The logic of her question didn't escape Brady, but as the elevator doors slid open and the two of them stepped in, he turned and watched Jayne push the fourth floor button. "If I wanted to sit behind a desk and make phone calls

all day, then go to business dinners every night with clients,
I'd be in that business."

"And you don't want to do that."

Not a question, but a statement. "I don't want to do
that," he echoed as the car slid silently upward. "I never
did, never will."

"I bet your parents think you're an aberration."

He couldn't help smiling, thinking that was probably
mild compared to what they really thought. "When I was
little I used to wonder if the hospital switched babies in the
nursery."

He could see Jayne's expression literally tighten at the
mention of babies and nurseries. "I told the nurse I'd call
back in a few hours." She glanced at her watch. "It's almost ten now. That was five hours ago."

"You said everyone was holding their own."

She leaned back against the wall, a frown line forming
between her eyes. "They are, but I'm worried about
Rocky. He's so tiny, so fragile and vulnerable." She stood
straight and adjusted her small leather purse on her
shoulder as the elevator stopped and the doors opened.
"Life gets tough sometimes, and he's hardly had time to
live at all. That's why holding him is so important, that
contact, that lifeline. It's really all he's got right now."

Brady watched her step out into the hall, and he felt a
rebuke in her rush of words even though there was none in
her tone. She didn't say that it was the least he could do to
hold a baby for a few minutes in the evening. She didn't
throw his words back at him, that he was too busy and
didn't even like children. But nonetheless, he felt incredibly selfish for a moment.

Then the bottom line came to him. What would happen
to Jayne if the little boy died? She obviously loved him. If
Brady had had any control over her at all, he would have

put a stop to her going to the hospital night after night and putting herself in line to be devastated.

He followed her out into the hall, an elegantly understated area done in pink, turquoise, and lavender underscored with beige. She led the way to the last door on the right and stopped as she turned to Brady.

"This is my office. I'll be fine now."

He looked up and down the quiet corridor. "Where's your security office?"

"On the first floor."

"Let me come in and call them."

She nodded and pushed open the door. Her office was as neat as her home, but even more sterile looking. Beige on beige didn't make a room exciting, Brady thought, even with the modern swirl of pink and yellow that passed for a painting on the far wall. Then he looked to his left at the view from the bank of glass windows that faced down the hills to the south. The one good thing about the building was the view. He turned to Jayne.

"I'll get someone from security up here to stay with you, then I'll stop at the hospital and go from there to the station to keep going over the files."

She crossed to the desk and dropped down in a swivel chair with its back to the view. She didn't argue with him, just made a call, then held out the phone to him. "Mike Leone is the head of security. He's on the line."

Brady crossed and took the phone from her, very aware of the heat of her touch still captured in the plastic receiver. "This is Detective Knight, SBPD," he said into the receiver. "I need a man of yours to stay with Mrs. Spencer today."

After the security man agreed to send up a guard within five minutes, Brady hung up and looked at Jayne, who was opening the morning paper that had been left on her desk.

She leafed through it, then looked up at Brady. "There's all sorts of coverage about DeForest Miles campaigning for the Senate, and that's months away. But there's just a single paragraph about Jack on page six. It says he was shot by an unknown assailant while working on a case."

"Good. We wanted to keep the rest of it quiet for now." Brady crossed to the windows and looked out at the brilliant summer day. "What a view."

Jayne spoke from behind him. "I guess so."

He turned back to her as she bent over the paper. She guessed so? It almost took his breath away, but she was so used to it, she probably didn't even see it anymore. "The guard's going to be here any time."

"I understand what you're doing, but I really don't think it's necessary." She refolded the paper until the front page was faceup on the desk, a photo of DeForest Miles in grainy black and white dominating the page. "I'm safe here."

"As safe as you were in your car?"

Bright color stained her cheeks. "I see what you mean. I'm not used to this sort of thing. You deal with it all the time, but it's foreign to me."

He looked at her intently. "And it should be. You shouldn't have any part in this. I'm sorry for that."

Chapter 7

A knock sounded on her office door, and Jayne called out, "Come on in."

A gray-haired man in a blue uniform came into the office, his hat in one hand. "Mrs. Spencer? You needed me?"

"Yes, Gus." She motioned to Brady. "Detective Knight needs to talk to you."

Brady quickly explained that he wanted Gus to stay with Jayne until he could come back to get her. He finished with, "Don't let her out of your sight. Stay outside her door or in here with her. She'll have lunch brought in, and I'll be back to get her when she's off work."

Gus nodded, not asking any of the questions Brady was sure the man had. "I'll stick with her, no matter what, Detective Knight."

Brady knew he should leave, yet he felt reluctant to go. He took a folded copy of the sketch they'd done at the station out of his jeans pocket and handed it to the man.

"If you see anyone like this even looking at the building, call me right away. No matter what."

"Yes, sir," Gus said. "No problem."

Then Brady turned to Jayne. She was a sleek, confident woman once more, obviously in her element. The fitted slacks and soft blouse looked simple and elegant. Her hair was pulled back from her face, confined in a low knot at the nape of her neck, yet instead of looking severe, it emphasized the line of her cheekbones and the tilt of her chin.

He remembered the urge he'd experienced at the hospital right after they had met, the need to touch her, to trace the line of her throat. Then he'd wanted to comfort himself. Now the same urge was there, but this time he wanted to comfort her. He wanted to make things right, to let her know he would do whatever it took to protect her. But he didn't touch her. He simply let his gaze meet hers, a totally unsatisfactory connection. "When do you get off?"

"Between five and six." She glanced at her desk and touched an appointment calendar with one finger. "I have a dinner appointment with a client at seven."

"Cancel it."

She looked back at him and didn't argue. "I guess I'll have to."

"I'll be back to pick you up," he murmured and turned away from her.

Brady walked into Jack's room, then stopped when he saw Marcia sitting by the bed, holding her husband's hand. She glanced up at Brady, and the tension in her face was underscored by the deep shadows under her eyes and the slightly dishevelled condition of her hair.

"Brady," she said in a hushed voice. "They said you went home finally."

"Hours ago." He came closer to the bed and looked down at Jack. He was still, but maybe not quite as pale. Or maybe Brady was just imagining it, wanting it to be so. "Any change?"

"No, but he's holding his own. The doctor says that's good. He's hopeful. That's what he said." She looked up at her husband. "But Jack's not waking up."

"He will."

Marcia looked back at Brady. "Are you blaming yourself for this?"

"Are you blaming me?" He had to ask.

"I thought you knew me better than that. I understand this job. I know the risks. And I know you'd do whatever it took to protect Jack."

The words made sense but didn't lessen his burden. "I should have known what he was up to. He didn't tell you anything when he came home that night, did he?"

"He didn't come home, Brady. He called, said he had to see someone, and that he'd be home in a few hours. That's all. That's the last time I talked to him."

"No idea who he had to see?"

"No, not at all. He didn't tell me much. He didn't want me to w—worry." Her lip began to tremble, but she took a deep breath, and her voice steadied. "He didn't understand that I worried every time he left the house."

Brady touched the woman's shoulder. No one should go through this, he thought for the hundredth time. From nowhere he remembered his thoughts about Jayne and the way she was attached to the babies. He wished he had the power to take her out of that situation, just the way he wished he had the power to make Jack whole again.

"He'll make it," he murmured, remembering the pressure on his hand when he had been with Jack last night. "And he knows you're here. I'm sure of it. Just keep talking to him." He stooped and kissed her lightly on her cold cheek. "If you need anything, or if you remember anything Jack told you that you think might help, call me. I'll be at the station going over the files."

She nodded, and Brady left, stepping out into the hallway, then stopping by the door to take a few breaths. He had never really felt like the protector of the world until right now, and the feeling was totally uncomfortable. He couldn't change what was going on behind the hospital door, not any more than he had the power to get Jayne away from babies that had the potential for ripping her heart out.

He strode past the decoy room with the officer outside and nodded, then kept going to the elevators past the nurses' station. The doors slid open as soon as he pushed the button, and as he got inside, he hesitated, then acted on impulse and pushed the button for the fourth floor instead of the ground floor.

When he stepped out of the car, Jayne wasn't there coming toward him in her white cover-up, and he didn't have her soft voice filling his ears as he headed for the Forest Room. He paused at the door, then pushed it back and looked inside.

Three people were there, two men in the chairs to the left, both in cover-ups and both holding babies. Then he glanced to his right and saw a woman in the other chair. She had dark hair and was bent over a baby in her arms. For a heartbeat he thought it was Jayne, that she had come down here despite the fact that he had left her at work an hour ago.

"Jayne?" he asked, his immediate annoyance overlaid by a sense of pleasure at seeing her. Then the woman looked up. Her blue eyes and long face were so different from Jayne's that it startled Brady.

"You looking for Mrs. Spencer?" a balding man to the left asked.

Brady stayed in the doorway. "No. I was just—"

"She's not here days. She'll be here tonight after ten," the other man said.

"After ten?" Brady asked.

"Maybe closer to eleven, but she'll be here. She doesn't miss a night. She's got a second home here, and she just gives and gives to the babies. She's a natural with them."

Brady knew the truth of that statement. He didn't have any trouble picturing her with a lot of children of her own. He could see that as clearly as he could see himself alone. The difference between the pictures left a sour taste in his mouth, yet he knew what he was and that there was no point denying it. He knew he wouldn't ever have come in here if it hadn't been for Jayne.

Or was this Fate at work? Was Jayne right about that, that some higher power had brought him here? No, he couldn't buy that. It was a quirk, a flip of the coin, the luck of the draw, and he was honest enough to admit he had stayed with Rocky because he had been attracted to Jayne, to a woman who spoke quickly, yet softly and soothingly. A beautiful woman.

A beautiful woman who wanted everything in life that he *didn't* want. A beautiful woman who could never be a passing fancy in any man's life. He was smart enough to know that once a man had her, he wouldn't want to let her go. And also smart enough to know he couldn't give her what she wanted.

"You want to leave a message?" the balding man asked.

"No, I—"

"Or do you want to sign up for a shift? We could sure use more people. Jayne's always looking for volunteers. I swear, she'd go out into the streets and drag people in here if she could.''

''Yes, she probably would,'' Brady muttered and made his escape.

''He's the one? Are you sure?'' Sara asked over the phone.

Jayne closed her eyes, sitting back in the swivel chair. ''I'm sure. I would never have known except…'' She didn't want to explain to her older sister about the attempt to run her off the road, or her standing on the edge of the cliff. ''…I heard his voice, and it all clicked.''

''And he just happened to be at the hospital last night?''

Jayne had called her sister on impulse, needed to share what was happening with someone, yet knowing she couldn't bring attempted murder into the conversation. If Sara knew what was going on, she would be here in a few hours, and Jayne didn't want any of her family involved. ''He was visiting someone,'' she hedged, ''and he got off on the wrong floor. I thought he was someone else, a man who had promised to take that shift with the babies. I dragged him in thinking he was this Appleton person. The man never showed up—Appleton, that is. He promised to come that night, and he didn't even call.''

''And he stayed to help?'' her sister asked.

''Who?''

''The man you said was the policeman who helped you before.''

''Oh, yes. His name's Brady Knight. He says he doesn't like children, that they're aliens to him, but he did fine with Rocky.'' She remembered the way he'd held the baby. ''He was awkward, but he tried. Now I'm trying to talk him into joining the program and helping out. I'm hoping he'll do it. But I'm not too—''

"Jayne?" her sister interrupted.

"Yes?"

"What's going on?"

"I told you."

"What else?"

She hated the way her sister could pick up on her moods so easily. "Why do you think there's something else?"

"You're talking a mile a minute, the way you do when you're excited—or when you're nervous. And you usually don't call to talk when you're at work." She paused. "What does this man look like?"

Jayne cringed at the tone of the question. She'd heard it before from Sara when they were younger. "Like a man, Sara, just a man."

"Is that all?"

She sat back in her chair and swiveled slowly from side to side. Calling Brady Knight "just a man" was like calling breathing a hobby, but she wasn't about to tell her sister that. "He's a policeman. He's nice, and he's a potential holder for the program."

There was silence, then, "And you aren't going to tell me any more, are you?"

Jayne regretted the call. She hated hedging with Sara, and putting her impressions of Brady into words made everything seem more complicated. "That's all there is to tell," she lied.

"I suppose I'll have to accept that, even though you sound different in some way."

She couldn't say, "You would, too, if someone was trying to kill you," so she settled for, "I'm tired, and work's slow today."

"Nothing else?"

She looked at the clock on her desk. Twelve-thirty. "I have to go and get some lunch. Say hello to everyone, and give your boys a kiss from me."

"Sure. You take care of yourself."

Jayne hung up, then sat back in her chair. So Sara thought she sounded different. Well, this day in her life *was* different from any day for a long time. And there was no way she could explain to Sara that she was literally seeing things she hadn't seen before, and not just the attempted murder of Jack Wills, but things she had passed by and not paid any attention to for two years.

Her office, a square space on the fourth floor, had always been a place to work, a refuge of sorts. As she settled back in her chair, she looked at the beige color scheme and realized how flat it was, how lifeless. The place needed some plants, or a painting with some recognizable subject in it. A bright, cheery painting would certainly help. Maybe one of animals, or a sunrise over a meadow.

She swiveled around to face the view. The city spreading down the hills had been a rolling sea of tile-roofed buildings against blue sky before. Now she saw the intensity of the red clay tiles, the brilliance of the white adobe and stucco, the deep greens that surrounded Mission Park in the distance, and the blue purity of the cloudless sky.

She nibbled on her bottom lip. She was feeling strange things, too, emotions she'd thought had gone forever. And she didn't have to think too long to know why. Brady Knight. The man had saved her life before, and that, she reasoned, was why his presence now had stripped away the grayness that had been surrounding her.

She had always cared about the babies, always fallen just a little bit in love with each one, and she was intensely interested in her job. But beyond that her day to day existence had been a vast grayness. Oh, she'd been able to grieve for Elliot and get on with life, but life had not been like this. Suddenly there was color everywhere, and it was almost painful.

She hugged herself tightly. What a time for this to happen, for the curtain to begin to lift. Why with Brady? A man who was isolated. A man who didn't want another person in his world. Yet a man who could send lightning through her with his touch.

She ran a hand over her face. *Adolescent.* That was what it was, she told herself. She'd reverted back to the emotions of her teenage years. Brady had just happened to be there when the change began, when the past began to truly become the past. As she thought about the past receding into memory, her uneasiness began to lessen.

But another sort of uneasiness waited just below, the uneasiness of knowing that Brady was the first man in years whom she had looked at and thought of as a man. And he was also the man who had saved her life once before.

A knock on the door drew her attention, and she called out, "Come in."

Gus, the security guard, looked into the office. "Mrs. Spencer, that cop called to find out how you are. I told him everything was calm, about the same. He said he wanted to check when you'd be off. I told him around five. I hope that was all right."

"That's fine, Gus," she said.

"You should send out for lunch. It's after twelve. Why don't I call down to Mrs. Murphy to get your usual lunch for you?"

She swiveled back and forth, clasping her hands on her lap. "I'd appreciate that, but I don't want a salad today. See if she can get me..." She had to think for a minute.

"How about something Mexican from that little restaurant across the street? Whatever's on special today."

"Sure thing," the man said, then slipped back outside.

As the door closed, Jayne glanced at the excuse for a painting on her wall, then reached for her phone. She punched one number for the receptionist's desk. "Stella? Jayne Spencer on four. Can you get me the number of an art gallery near here?"

"Mrs. Spencer," the guard said as he came back into her office just after five o'clock. "Detective Knight left a message that he'll meet you in the parking garage. I'll walk down with you as soon as you're ready."

Right then her phone rang and when Jayne answered it, it was for Gus. She held the receiver out to him. "It's Mr. Leone."

Gus hurried to take the receiver from her. "Yes, sir?" he said, then hesitated. "Yes, sir. I will. Right away."

He handed the receiver back to Jayne. "I need to go up to the top floor and check on a problem with one of the fire escape doors. It's been tampered with." He frowned. "Thing is, Detective Knight wants you in the garage in five minutes."

"You don't have to go with me."

"Yes, I do," he cut in. "Detective Knight gave me strict orders this morning about that."

"All right. How about this? Why don't you see me to the elevator and watch the doors close. It'll go right down to the garage."

"I don't know—"

She grabbed her purse and smoothed at her hair. "I'll be fine, and you can see about the door."

The old man glanced at his watch. "He said five-fifteen on the dot. Told me to make sure you were there then."

Jayne came around the desk and headed for the door. "And I will be."

Gus walked her to the elevator, pushed the Down button, and when the doors opened, he reached inside and pressed the button for the parking garage. He stepped back as Jayne got on, then touched his peaked cap. "You sure you'll be all right?"

"Fine. Thanks for everything."

"You take care. See you Monday."

She smiled at him as the door shut, then she leaned against the coolness of the elevator wall as the car slid silently down to the underground parking area. When the car stopped, Jayne gripped her purse, waited for the doors to open, then stepped out.

With its low ceiling and heavy pillars that supported the weight of the building above it, the garage had always seemed tomblike to Jayne, but tonight it looked even stranger than usual. The lights seemed awfully dim, and the place was almost empty, since it was Friday and most people left before five for the weekend.

She looked around, but there wasn't a black Camaro in sight. Slowly she walked to the far corner to see if Brady had parked in the visitor area.

As she approached the corner, she caught a flash of her own reflection in the glass door over the emergency fire-hose housing to her right. As she turned to look, she caught another flash of movement in the glass, the movement of someone or something a few cars away.

She stopped abruptly to turn and see what was going on, and at that moment she heard three sounds that came almost simultaneously—a faint pop, a rush of air, and the explosion of the glass door less than two feet from her head.

Shards of glass were propelled everywhere, raining down onto the concrete floor. She didn't understand what had happened, but she instinctively knew she had to get out of there. If she could get back to the still-open elevator, she would be safe, but as she spun around to head for it, she saw a man straighten from behind a nearby car, and he was between her and the elevator.

For an instant, in the dim light, she thought Brady was there, that she'd missed seeing the Camaro, that she was overreacting. Then the man moved, taking a step toward her, and she saw the slender build, an orange jacket, and the gun in his hand.

Fear and panic drove Jayne in the opposite direction with one thought—to get around the corner. It was the same as those moments of eternity during the accident, when everything had slipped into slow motion. She felt her feet slip on the shattered glass; then her hand was grasping at the rough block wall as she raced to put that wall between herself and the killer.

She lurched around the corner, and her momentum sent her into the nearest car. Then she had control and the world sped up to the frantic pace that fear dictated. Her hip struck metal, sending pain down into her leg. She caught herself by pressing both hands onto the cold fender, then spun to her right, ready to take off running to the far end of the garage.

Screams that she knew were her own echoed and re-echoed in the cavernous parking area. But before she could do more than turn, she knew her cries were being drowned out by the squeal of tires and the low throbbing of a powerful engine. She looked, and felt her heart leap when she saw the Camaro at the bottom of the entrance ramp, speeding toward the elevator area like a black bullet.

Without thinking, she took two steps toward it, leaving the protection of the corner wall. Exposed, she froze when she saw the elevator doors sliding shut and the killer staring at her, the gun lifting toward her. But the doors closed before he could shoot.

Jayne stared at the metal barriers, knowing there was something different about the man besides his change of clothes, something not right, but she hadn't yet figured it out when she heard the Camaro right beside her.

As she turned, she heard Brady calling out to her. "Jayne!" And she saw him jumping out of the car and running toward her. Then he was there, his hands on her, pulling her to him in a crushing hug. "Oh, God, did he hurt you?" he gasped.

"No," she managed and pulled back enough to point to the elevator. "But it's him, Brady. He's . . . he's in there."

Brady twisted to look at the elevator, gripping her shoulders almost painfully. The floor indicator lit up at "1," and Brady looked at Jayne. "Stay here," he said, then let her go, taking off at a dead run for the stairs. When he got to the door and pulled it back, he called over his shoulder, "Get in my car and lock the doors. Call for backup." He looked at her for a split second. "The keys are in it. If anything happens, get the hell out of here!"

Jayne watched until the door to the stairwell swung shut; then fear overwhelmed her, and she ran for the Camaro. She scrambled in on the passenger side, hit the door locks and took several deep, shaky breaths to try to steady herself. Brady's scent was in the car, and it gave her a certain degree of comfort. When she reached for the police radio, her hand was surprisingly steady.

She might have gotten all her knowledge about police work from television before Brady fell into her life, but she did know enough to press the thumb button at the side of the transmitter before she tried to speak. "Detective Knight needs a backup," she managed in a tight voice and was relieved when she let go of the button and a voice said, "Give me your location."

By the time Brady got to the landing for the first floor, his heart was pounding painfully in his chest, partly because he had taken the stairs at a dead run, but mostly because of the raw fear that had surged through him when he had turned the corner into the parking structure and spotted Jayne running from the man with the gun.

There had been few times in his life when he had experienced such all-encompassing fear—and never when another person had been involved. Always for himself, when he had been in tough situations—facing a drug-crazed kid with a loaded gun, or going in without his gun to talk face-to-face with someone holding hostages. Feeling such fear for another person, for someone beyond himself, made him even more scared.

He already had his gun free of his holster, and with his other hand, he pushed the door back. He looked out into the empty corridor, then broke into a sprint, heading for the elevator. The indicator was locked on "1," and the doors were shut. He reached out, pushed the button and stood back to squarely face the opening doors with his gun braced in both hands.

As the doors slid back, Brady moved a fraction closer and saw that the car was empty. He gulped air, looked down the hall, then took off at a run for the front of the building. As he ran into a formal reception area dominated by a semicircular desk and the color blue, the woman behind the desk looked up at him.

"Oh, God," she gasped when she saw the gun.

"Police," he said quickly, fumbling in his pocket for his badge case, then flipping it open. "Did anyone come this way?"

"I don't—"

"A man in an orange jacket wearing a baseball cap?"

The woman shook her head. "No. What's wrong?"

He crossed to the glass entry doors and looked out into the street. He didn't see anyone or anything out of the ordinary. No one running, no car taking off in a hurry. He scanned the scene, the people leaving work, the cars parked along the curb, the street congested with rush hour traffic. Everyday people, everyday cars, a day like any other, yet he couldn't quite catch his breath or make his fear go completely away.

He looked back at the receptionist. "Call security for me and get Mike Leone on the line."

She pushed some buttons, then handed the receiver to Brady, who said, "This is Detective Knight. I talked to you this morning. I've got an emergency, and I need this building sealed right now. I'll explain later, but for now, just don't let anyone leave. Get a man up to the front, and have someone cover the back exits and the fire doors. No one leaves until I say so."

"Most of the people have left, and it's past quitting time," the other man said. "The rest of the people—"

"—will have to wait until I say they can leave," Brady muttered. "Get someone up here right now."

He didn't wait for a response before he handed the receiver back to the receptionist. "Can you lock the front doors?"

She nodded as she put the receiver back in place. "I could, but—"

"Then do it, and do it now. I'll take responsibility for it."

Before the woman could do more than nod, Brady ran back to the elevator, then went past it, down the corridor that ran back into a maze of offices. He couldn't look in every one. He would have to wait until backup got here to find out where the guy went. Then he had a thought that made his heart lurch. The killer could have doubled back down to the garage.

He turned, ran for the elevator and got in. Being careful not to touch the heat sensitive floor buttons in case there were fingerprints, he pressed the one for the garage level with the tip of his gun barrel. As the car slid silently downward, he took several deep breaths to try to ease his tension.

His heartbeat was nowhere near normal, and the sour taste of being out of control sat at the back of his throat. First Jack being shot right in front of him, with him unable to do anything, and now Jayne. The thought made his stomach clench. Jayne.

By the time the elevator stopped and he saw Jayne safe in the Camaro, he didn't know what he felt. Then he grasped at the nearest emotion and came up with anger. He'd told her to stay in her office until he came for her. He headed for the Camaro. He'd made very sure she understood before he'd left her this morning. And then she'd come down to the garage alone anyway.

His anger grew as he got closer to the car. Anger was a cleansing emotion, an uncomplicated emotion that he could understand and deal with.

He pushed his gun back into his holster, and in three more strides he was almost to the Camaro. He didn't look directly at Jayne, yet the image of her when he'd first turned into the parking area was burned into his brain. Her pale face, her frantic scrambling to get around the corner.

He felt anger sear through him, engulfing the last of his fear as he got to the car, pulled the door back and slid inside. For an instant the anger faltered when he was assailed by her provocative scent, which seemed to be saturating the very air he had to breathe. For a second it hit him hard, making his heart begin to race again; then he grabbed for his anger and held on to it for dear life.

"I didn't find him," he said as he turned in the seat, gripping the steering wheel with one hand to brace himself as he met her gaze full force. Words came immediately.

"Why the hell didn't you do what I told you to? Why didn't you stay in your office until I came for you? Damn it, you could have been killed!"

Her pale cheeks were suddenly infused with brilliant color. "You're the one who called and said to meet you down here!" she gasped. "I wasn't just going for a stroll."

"I never called. You should have—"

"What? What should I have done?" she demanded, turning to face him fully. "You called. You said to come down here, that you'd meet me. Gus told me so."

Facts hit Brady like a bolt of lightning—the man knew him, knew his name, knew that he was guarding Jayne, probably even knew that he'd been late getting out of the station because his car wouldn't start at first. The loose coil wire had been enough to stop the circuit. The man's thoroughness stunned him. Jayne could have died, he admitted, and raw fear came in a flood. He fought it with anger once more.

"And you didn't check? You didn't make sure? It's only your life we're talking about. You're going to get yourself killed. I'm just trying to do my job, to keep you safe because of what you've gotten yourself into here."

He could see her stiffen and her hands clench on her purse until the knuckles were bloodless. "Me?" she gasped. "What I've gotten myself into? Have you forgotten that it was you who got off on the wrong floor and sat there like an idiot without telling me you weren't Mr. Appleton? And you're the reason I went up to your partner's room and saw that man. I didn't ask for this to happen. I wish I . . . I . . . was . . ."

As Jayne's words sputtered to a stop, Brady felt both his anger and his fear beginning to fade. All he could see was a woman who was so angry at *him* that she couldn't even finish what she was saying. A woman he would never have guessed had this kind of fire in her.

That stopped him. Fire? He'd sensed fire in her, but the fire of passion. The fire of need and kindness. This anger was totally unexpected, and he found himself beginning to smile. His moods when he was with Jayne seemed ridiculously volatile. He'd been chasing a killer, and all he wanted to do was hold Jayne against him and feel her reality.

Jayne couldn't remember when she had been so furious with one person in all her life. Never, she thought. Surely she would remember this sort of explosion. The brilliance of feeling she'd been beginning to experience in the past twenty-four hours was even stronger now. At a time when she could have died, she felt more alive than she had for a long time.

Now Brady was actually smiling at her, deepening the brackets etched at the corners of his mouth and narrowing his blue eyes. "I thought you blamed all of that on Fate, not me," he drawled.

"But you . . . you . . ." She stumbled to a stop when she realized that she wouldn't even be here now if Fate hadn't brought Brady to the hospital two years ago.

That thought and the way he was looking at her, gentle humor mixed with rebuke, made all the anger she had been experiencing dissolve as if it had never been. Suddenly she could smile; then she heard unsteady laughter actually bubbling out of her. And that laughter was echoed by Brady's soft chuckle.

When he reached out to her, she went to him, letting him surround her with his arms, and she buried her face in the heat of his shoulder. His soft laughter rumbled around her, and the absurdity of what was happening struck her full force, almost as forcibly as the presence of the man who held her.

She felt bombarded by sensations. His hard muscles contrasted with the gentleness of his hold, the heat of his body mingled with hers, and the coolness of the console pressed against her hip. When she drew back, unnerved at the comfort she experienced just being held by him, her face was only inches from his.

Chapter 8

Brady looked at Jayne and felt such a surge of protectiveness that it rocked him. The next instant that protectiveness mingled wildly with a desire that came from nowhere to fill his being. The need to kiss Jayne was a living, vital thing within him. Without taking the time to think about what he was doing, he tasted her lips, realizing that the sensations of softness and heat that he had experienced early this morning had not been illusions.

But this time the merest touch ignited a passion that exploded deep in his being. And when Jayne gasped softly and her lips parted, he didn't hesitate. He tasted her deeply, completely, letting her flavor fill him and the feeling of her body against him filter deep into his being.

For an instant Brady simply let himself experience the moment. He let Jayne's unique essence seep into him, the smoothness of her teeth, the uncertain touch of her tongue against his, and he felt something he couldn't begin to comprehend. It overwhelmed him, how completely she was beginning to fit into his life, how completely she could fill a need he had never known existed until he met her.

Then he realized that he couldn't let it happen. He couldn't let himself need another person this way. He didn't have any space for another person in his life. He never had. He never could. There was no way he could give her what she wanted, what she deserved. As he began to move back, to break the contact before it could be anything more than impulsive mutual support, sirens cut through the air.

Jayne jumped, her eyes wide, her lips parted and slightly swollen from his touch. The same shock he felt at what had just happened was echoed in her face, and it unnerved him. He wanted to touch her face, to feel the silky warmth of her skin under his fingertips, yet he didn't trust his hands to be steady enough or trust himself to stop at that. Out of a need for self-protection, he looked away from her, moving back in the seat to turn and look over his shoulder at the squad cars screaming down the ramp into the parking area.

As the cars came to a screeching halt beside the Camaro, Brady got out without saying anything to Jayne, trying to put everything in perspective. He was doing his job, protecting Jayne, literally saving her life so she could live it with a man she would meet someday. That man would be her future and give her everything she needed. And that man wasn't anything like him.

Perspective—hard, cold perspective. He needed clear, precise thinking, and he tried to concentrate on what needed to be done right now. What he really needed was a few hours at the beach—alone. But that was a luxury he couldn't afford just yet.

He swung the car door shut and strode toward the nearest squad car. He spoke quickly to the patrolmen, giving orders for searching the building, then made a decision. He was getting out of here with Jayne, getting out now. He would let the others take care of the search, but he would get Jayne safely out. She was the target.

Jayne sat in the squad room back at the police station, watching through the glass walls of the side office as Brady talked to Captain Burkhart.

The dark-skinned man had arrived five minutes ago in formal dress: a finely cut tuxedo, a snow-white shirt, and a perfectly done bow tie at his throat. He'd nodded to Brady, who had been at a desk with Jayne near the entrance, then motioned to the office.

They had been in there five minutes, with Burkhart standing behind the desk and Brady in front, leaning across it, his hands braced on the top to steady himself. Jayne could feel the intensity of the exchange, but she had no idea what it was all about, because the glass walls of the office killed most of the sounds, and the noises of the busy squad room killed the rest.

No one had been found in the building when they searched it. There had been no usable fingerprints in the elevator. In fact, the only useful thing that had come out of tonight was that Brady had seen the man, too.

Jayne sat on the hard vinyl chair by Brady's desk and suddenly felt cold. She couldn't forget that face, yet she knew there had been something different about it. She'd been trying to think of what it was since then, but she hadn't been able to remember. She closed her eyes, but instead of seeing the man's face in front of her, she found herself suddenly reliving the kiss with Brady.

She'd blocked it out during the trip over and during their wait for Burkhart, but now it came back to her in a rush.

The brilliance of the world was growing with each moment that passed. She wondered if it had ever been as clear for her, or as painful, as it had been since Brady kissed her. She couldn't remember a time when every emotion she felt had been so sharp, so alive, so vibrant. Fear, caring, excitement, passion, pain.

She closed her eyes more tightly. She'd heard how life and death situations brought people together who had nothing in common. For the duration of the emergency they clung to each other and were closer than seemed humanly possible. But once the emergency was over, they lost contact. Their lives were different, with nothing but shared survival in common.

She touched her lips with the tips of her fingers. Talk about different lives, she thought. Brady Knight was from a different world.

"Jayne?"

She opened her eyes and looked up at Brady. He seemed huge as he loomed above her, a shoulder holster she'd never seen him wear before looking incongruous with his blue T-shirt. Her hand fell to her lap and curled into a fist. "Why is Captain Burkhart so angry?" she asked.

Brady shrugged as he raked his fingers through his sandy hair. "He was on his way to a fund-raiser for our future senator, DeForest Miles. He paid five hundred dollars a plate, and he wants to get there as soon as possible."

Right then Captain Burkhart strode out of the office and across the room, stopping at Brady's desk. "We're doing all we can, Mrs. Spencer," he said to Jayne as he tugged at the cuffs of his tuxedo jacket. "Hopefully this can be settled soon. Detective Knight will explain our plan to you." He glanced at Brady. "I'll be in contact with you," he said, then crossed to the doors and left.

Jayne looked up at Brady. "What now?"

"Burkhart wants you safely out of the way, and the best place for both of us is at my place."

"That's the plan?"

"That's your part of the plan."

"Hiding with you?"

"Staying out of sight until this is settled."

"For how long?"

He picked up a folder from his desk. "As long as it takes."

Jayne got to her feet, noticing the way Brady took a step back to avoid any contact. "But I've got work, and—"

"Not for the weekend. Maybe this will all be like a bad dream by Monday," he muttered and moved away from her. But he stopped almost immediately and turned back to her. "Give me your house key."

"Why?" she asked as she dug in her shoulder bag for it.

"I arranged for a policewoman to go by and pick up some clothes and things for you. Is there anything in particular you want?"

"Just jeans and a few tops." She had her key and held it out to him. "Everything's in the downstairs bedroom, and my toiletries are in the bath. There's a small suitcase in the bedroom closet, an overnight bag. She could use that."

He took the key, his fingers never touching her at all. "Stay here," he said.

Before he could walk away, she spoke up. "I was thinking, why don't I just go back to my house myself and get my things?"

Brady looked down at her, his blue eyes hard and intent. "Understand this one thing. This creep knows where you work. He knows *you*. You're not just some anonymous face to him anymore. He undoubtedly knows where you live, too. You're listed in the phone book, aren't you?"

"Yes, but how would he know my name?"

Brady shook his head. "Who knows? The important thing is, I'm *not* listed in the book. No one's going to give out my address, and I'll make damn sure no one's following us when we go to my place."

Then he crossed the squad room to talk to a tall red-haired man. After handing him the key, he came back. Without a word, he gestured for Jayne to follow him as he pushed back the doors and led the way into the hallway. She hurried after him, catching up to him as he opened the side door to the parking lot.

At seven o'clock, dusk was just beginning to fall. The Indian summer air was balmy, and the bell at the town hall chimed in the distance. A line of black and white police cars along the far wall looked like soldiers to Jayne, still, silent, but ready to go when they were needed.

She hurried after Brady as he moved down the steps toward the Camaro. Her car was there, too, parked behind chain link fencing in a storage area. She averted her eyes from the body-length scrape and the rippling indentations where the other car had struck her.

Jayne swallowed hard and got into the Camaro. As Brady drove out of the lot, she saw a squad car right behind them. It followed them onto the street, where it stayed two car lengths behind them.

Brady drove in silence past the landmark city hall, an imposing Spanish structure, then waved as the squad car turned left onto a side street. Staying on the one-way street until they were out of the business district, Brady steered silently through the evening traffic, then swung west.

Jayne held tightly to the purse in her lap. "Can I ask you something?"

He nodded without speaking as he checked his rearview mirror.

"If you didn't call and tell Gus to get me to the garage, that man did, didn't he?"

He nodded again. "Seems that way."

"Okay, I accept the fact that this man could find out about me, about where I live and all that, but how did he know when you were coming back for me?"

"I guess he could have found out when you got off by asking someone who spoke when they shouldn't have. Maybe by making an educated guess. If I were him, I'd find someone at Taylor with the need to talk."

She remembered Gus telling her that Brady had called around lunch time. "Did you call to check on me today?"

He slanted her a look, but his eyes were shadowed. "I thought about it, but I didn't."

"Gus told him."

"He what?"

"Someone called around noon, saying they were from the police, wanting to know how I was doing and to re-confirm the time I expected to get off."

"Bingo," Brady said softly.

"But if he knew you would be coming back, why would he try it then? He could have been caught. He almost was."

"He knew when I wouldn't be there," he said.

"He what?"

"He thought he'd made sure I wouldn't be there. When I tried to start the Camaro to go and get you, it wouldn't start. I looked under the hood, fiddled with the coil wire and got it to run. My guess is he loosened the wire just enough to break the circuit. He knew it would slow me down and give him time. I just lucked out that it was the first thing I tried. Otherwise I wouldn't have been there for ten or fifteen minutes more. I would have had to go and get a garage man and have him look at it.''

"But it didn't work. I mean, he was on the elevator and the doors were barely closed when you were out of your car. He must be crazy or something. That's it. He's mad. Why else would he be doing this?'' She was rambling, but she couldn't seem to stop. "If you had come just a few minutes earlier, he would have been scared off. He would have wasted all that time and trouble.''

"Or he would have shot me first, then you.''

He said it so matter-of-factly that it almost made her heart stop. "He would have. He's crazy.''

"No, he's a pro. I've been thinking about everything, and I'm convinced we're dealing with a pro.''

"What sort of pro?''

He hesitated, then said, "A pro who messed up something so badly he has to finish off Jack and get you before either one of you can finger him. And he almost succeeded, at least with you. A neat, simple plan. Lure you down there and shoot you. He wasn't going to mess with cars again. He doesn't care if it looks like an accident or not.''

"Why? What did he do that he's so afraid of being discovered? I mean, is he an international terrorist or something?''

"In Santa Barbara?'' Brady countered. "I don't think so.''

"He's walking around trying to kill people, Brady,'' she said, staring at him, wanting him to say something, anything, that would make sense out of what was happening.

But he said only, "And it's up to me to make sure nothing like the garage incident happens again.''

She sank back in the seat and pressed a hand to her eyes. "I can't believe I didn't know there was something wrong down there. I didn't know, not even when the lights were so low, or when your car wasn't there. You must have a sixth sense or something. If something like that was going to happen, I should have felt it, like the hairs at the back of your neck prickling, or having a premonition of some sort. There was nothing at all. Nothing and—''

Brady glanced in the rearview mirror again and cut off her words. ''Do you always talk this much when you're nervous?''

She bit her lip, the heat of embarrassment flooding her face. ''Yes, I guess so. It's a bad habit of mine. I'm sorry.''

Unexpectedly he touched her hand. ''Don't be. Everyone has trouble coping with something.'' His hand tightened fleetingly before he pulled it away and settled it back on the steering wheel. ''For your information, I don't have premonitions. I don't have visions, and I've never had the hairs at the back of my neck prickle. I just do my job the best way I can without any psychic advantage.''

''How do you cope with your life?''

''Do you really want to know?''

She looked at him, the angles of his face softened by the blurred shadows in the car. ''Yes, I really do,'' she said softly.

''All right. I'll show you my secret weapon.'' He turned right onto the coast road and headed north.

Jayne looked out at the Pacific, the limitless expanse of rolling waves bathed in the last traces of twilight. She couldn't remember the last time she'd driven down here. They passed cars lining both sides of the road, then got past the tourist and commercial area and started climbing into the north section.

As they went higher, paralleling the water's edge, Brady pointed out to the ocean. ''That's my secret weapon, my medicine.''

"The ocean?"

"Everything about it."

"You live here?"

That brought a rough chuckle. "Don't I wish. No. A policeman's pay doesn't allow that sort of luxury."

She remembered him talking about being happy by himself at the ocean. "But you spend a lot of time here?"

"When I can get away." He sounded almost wistful for a moment. "I've got a theory that some people are healed by the ocean. Not medically, but emotionally." He drove on, putting the main beaches behind them and turning onto a narrow winding road that ran along the top of the cliffs. "It's the rhythms or the tides or something like that. Some people respond to it. I do. I always have."

She understood the tan that touched his skin and the deep squint lines beside his blue eyes. "Do you swim, or just sit and watch?"

"Swim, surf, just sit and watch. Everything."

He pushed a button, and her window slid down; then his did the same. Jayne inhaled, the softness of the warm evening touched by the tang of salt air. She could feel, actually feel, the tension easing in her. "Do your parents live near the ocean?"

"No, they live at the old homestead in the Dumbarton area, about ten minutes from here."

Jayne knew the area, filled with what she would certainly call mansions and set well up in the hills.

"I had to hitchhike down to the beach when I was younger. Then I got my driver's license, and I'd strap my surfboard to the top of an old Volkswagon I had and head down to the beach. During the summer, I'd stay for days."

"Stay where?"

He slowed and turned left, onto a road barely wide enough for the Camaro. Scrub brush and a few low growing trees scraped against the sides of the black car. They followed the zigzagging path until they came to a wide area blocked with a chain across the road.

"I'd stay near here," Brady said, turning off the engine and the headlights.

Jayne looked through the window to a ribbon of dark beach a hundred feet away. "Where is *here*?"

"Tidewater Cove. It's been part of the county's reclamation system as long as I can remember. There were guards coming by every so often, but only during the daylight hours. All night long, no one showed up. I had it all to myself." He sank back in the seat, the wistfulness fully evident now. "Surfing at night is awesome."

She looked out at the dark waters and the first of the stars flashing to life in the heavens above. A gentle breeze drifted in through the windows to tease her hair, which had fallen free during her escape. "When did you stop coming here for moonlight surfing?"

He chuckled again, the sound soft and pleasant. "Never."

She looked at him in the dimness. "What?"

"I still come down every once in a while. I park here, head down to the beach and go for it. Or I just sit for hours thinking. Another of my laws I suppose—sea air clears the mind and soothes the spirit."

"It's legal for you to be here?" she asked.

That brought more laughter from him. "Haven't you ever heard the old adage about 'stolen fruit being the sweetest?' "

"But you're a policeman, and you're—"

"Supposed to uphold the law? I know, and I do—most of the time." He moved abruptly, stepping out into the gathering shadows of night; then he leaned down to look back in at Jayne. "Come on. Let me show you something special—the mysterious healing properties of the ocean.'' He hesitated. ''I don't know about you, but I need that right now.''

''We can't just . . .''

''Sure we can.'' He straightened and closed his door, then walked around the car to open her door. When she didn't move, he said, ''I can't leave you here, and I want to go down to the water for a little while.''

She looked up at him; the night shadows couldn't hide the tension in his face and stance. ''All right,'' she conceded. ''Just for a while.''

''Good. Let's get out of our shoes.'' He held on to the door with one hand and tugged off his shoes and then his socks with the other. As he tossed them into the Camaro, he looked at Jayne, who was still sitting there. ''Your turn.'' Then he went around to the back of the car and snapped open the trunk.

Jayne slipped off her pumps, then her knee-high nylons, and put them on the floor by her seat. When she looked up, Brady was beside her, a blanket over one arm. ''I'm being a bit more civilized tonight,'' he said, indicating the blanket.

She didn't ask ''more civilized than what?'' but just got out, feeling the ground cool and firm under her bare feet. She swung her door shut and followed Brady, stepping over the low chain, then heading down the road.

They came to the beach, where coarse sand formed a thin ribbon of no more than twenty feet before it disappeared into the dark waters of the Pacific. Jayne felt the sand beneath her feet as she followed Brady to the right. The only sounds were the surging of the ocean slapping the shore and an occasional night bird crying before it dipped low, looking for food.

Finally Brady stopped near an outcropping of rocks. "We're here," he said as he unfolded the blanket in front of a rock that jutted sharply up out of the sand. He smoothed the wool, then motioned to Jayne to sit. "The best seat in the house."

She moved past him to sink down on the blanket, where she crossed her legs Indian-style as Brady dropped down beside her. For a long, peaceful interlude they sat side by side, simply staring out at the ever-changing ocean and the star-studded sky.

The silence between them felt right, with no need for polite chitchat. Jayne watched as the moon rose over the water, an almost full moon casting its silvery light on the world below. She could feel something changing in her, a sense of peace that she hadn't experienced for a long time. She wondered if Brady was right about the healing properties of the ocean.

She dug into the warm sands with her toes. "You were right," she finally said in a hushed voice.

"Why are you whispering, and what was I right about?"

She felt the breeze ruffle her hair and skim over her face. "I guess I don't want to talk too loudly and spoil the mood. And you're right about the ocean being soothing. It's the rhythm, I think, simple and consistent. It doesn't change. Maybe it's something to do with humans developing in water for nine months, then having to leave it at birth."

"And maybe it's because it's so simple and quiet," Brady murmured. "And because there's nothing like sleeping by the ocean under a starry sky when it's summer and you're sixteen."

She looked up at the sky, the stars brilliant and sparkly in the blackness. "Do you know what I was doing the summer I was sixteen?"

"What?"

"Working at Galbraith's Hardware sorting out nuts and bolts."

She felt him shift, his knee brush hers, his arm bump against her arm. "You never slept on the beach?"

"No, of course not, not any more than I've been shot at before, or run off the road." She shivered from a combination of the suddenly cooler air and the invasion of reality into the conversation.

When Brady moved closer and casually put his arm around her shoulders, tension came to the surface in a rush. His body heat instantly warmed her, and she was inordinately aware of each breath he took, the way he shifted to get a bit closer. She closed her eyes for a moment, then looked out at the ocean again, fighting the urge to rest her head on his shoulder.

"Someday, when you're well out of this mess, you should think about broadening your experiences," he murmured.

She laughed, a nervous sound even to her own ears. "I think the past few days would qualify as broadening my experiences."

"That wasn't quite what I had in mind," he said softly by her left ear. "I meant good things...like sleeping on the beach."

"This . . . right now . . . it isn't all bad, you know."

"You're right. It's not all bad. And I needed it." He exhaled heavily. "I've needed this for weeks and haven't had the time to come down here, much less camp out."

She closed her eyes as he began to slowly stroke her arm. "I never even knew this beach was here. I've lived here for over two years and I've never seen it. If you hadn't brought me here, I would never have found it."

"You would have if you were supposed to. Isn't that what someone who believes in Fate would say?"

She slanted a sideways look at Brady. He was staring out at the horizon, the silvery light of the moon etching the planes of his face with lights and darks. She couldn't tell if he was being sarcastic or if he really meant what he said, so she opted for the latter.

"You're right. Everything happens for a purpose, for a reason. This isn't all chance, the luck of the draw."

His eyes narrowed on some spot in the distance. "I almost envy you being able to believe that."

She looked at the line of his jaw, the way his hair ruffled in the ocean breeze. She could even see the beating of the pulse just under his ear. Nothing was chance in this life, she was certain of that, not even Brady's role in hers. "What's my option? Should I believe that someone tossed up a bunch of cards that represented my life, and only the ones that landed inside the circle counted?"

He turned to her, his eyes shadowed and unreadable. "That's one way of looking at life. And it's easy to believe this is all luck, all chance. That way you're free to take what turns up, then keep going if you want to."

"Keep going where?" she found herself asking. "To another accidental set of circumstances, to another person who happens to be in the right place at the right time, then the next person, and the next? Is that why you got divorced?"

She felt his hand on her arm stop its gentle motion. "No, that's very easy to explain. Simply put, marriage wasn't what I needed or what I was good at. It didn't work out. So why not move on to something else, to another phase?"

"That's not chance, Brady, that's being alone. That's being completely alone. And that's terrifying." She exhaled shakily and stated a stark truth. "Right now, I'm thankful you're here. That I'm not alone."

He studied her intently, and even before he bent his head to hers, she knew he was going to kiss her. She knew it, and she found herself waiting for it with the same sense of expectation she felt when she looked forward to opening presents on Christmas morning.

As his cool lips touched hers, she accepted that Fate had brought Brady to her more than once, that Fate certainly hadn't left anything to chance in her life. When she opened her mouth to his, when she felt him hesitate, then take what she offered, she felt secure that nothing in this world was due to blind chance.

She lifted her arms, encircling his neck and turning until she felt his body against hers. And then Brady was easing her down onto the blanket. The sounds of the ocean rushed around them, the breeze whispered, and Jayne knew she hadn't really felt alone since the moment Brady had stepped off the elevator at the wrong floor.

She opened her mouth, willing him inside her, wanting him inside her. She tasted him, felt his tongue swirling over her teeth, penetrating her. And she held tightly to him, the world receding into a hazy reality somewhere beyond her reach.

When she felt the heat of his touch on her stomach, she realized he'd undone her blouse without her realizing it, freeing it from her slacks. His hand was gently caressing her bare skin, and it made her gasp. Then she arched toward the contact as his hand trailed higher until his hot palm was cupping her breast through the thin nylon of her bra.

Feelings exploded in Jayne, rocketing through her, honing the brilliance she'd been experiencing by degrees all day. She gasped, straining to meet Brady's touch, holding more tightly to him, needing to feel him under her hands the way he could feel her. She tugged at his T-shirt, pulling it up, freeing it from the waistband of his jeans. Then she was touching the plane of his stomach, the rippling muscles, the sleek strength. She heard him groan and felt him shudder under her spread palms.

She was fascinated by the way she could feel his heart thudding rapidly, the intake of each breath. Then Brady pushed aside the fine material of her bra, freeing her breast, and his touch on her nipple made it peak and throb. She curled her fingers across his skin, scraping over the soft hair on his chest, unable to take in the pure sense of pleasure that coursed through her.

She arched, moaning softly, her arms encircling Brady's back, holding him tightly, anchoring herself to keep from crying out. She tangled her legs with his, felt the strength of his arousal pressed against her hips. His mouth trailed from her lips to her throat, touching the exposed spot just above her swelling breasts, robbing her of the ability to breathe or think or do more than just try to absorb what was happening to her.

"Jayne," he groaned against her flushed skin, then drew back just enough to look down at her. "God, you're beautiful," he groaned.

She could feel her breasts swelling just from his look, his glance.

With a low moan, he lowered his head, tasting the soft cleavage between her breasts; then his touch became more insistent, more demanding, his fingers closing over her nipple, tugging at it, kneading it, until Jayne was sure there was a sensual cord that ran from her throbbing breasts to a spot deep in her belly. She felt a heaviness that had been so long denied that she hardly recognized it for what it was until Brady moved his hand lower to her rapidly rising and falling stomach.

Then she knew what was happening. She throbbed and pulsed, and she was alive in a dazzling way she could barely comprehend. The night was all around, the scent of the ocean, the scent of Brady. Despite everything that was happening, Jayne felt centered here, with this man, centered and incredibly happy.

His lips moved over the fullness of her breast until they took the place his hand had just forsaken. She arched toward his lips as he tugged at her nipple, tasting it, drawing at it, his tongue circling it slowly, until it was a hard bud of intense feeling. The pleasure bordered on pain, strong, unrelenting, overwhelming.

She knew she should stop this while she still could, but there wasn't enough strength in her to be rational right now. She hungered for what she knew she would find with Brady, to be with him, to lose herself in him, to forget about everything but the stunning sensuality of this moment.

His hand fumbled with the button on her slacks as his mouth trailed up her throat to the hollow where her pulse beat frantically. Her mind was a jumble of images: the beach; the rhythm of the waves; the pounding of her heart in her own ears; Brady's ragged breathing brushing heat over the dampness of her skin. Then, frustrated by a button that wouldn't budge, he tucked his fingers under her waistband, finding the heat of her belly. Heat against heat. A touch that sent fire through her veins.

"What the hell do you two think you're doing?"

A voice intruded from nowhere, a rough, loud voice that brought the world to a grinding halt. Jayne jerked back and for a split second a brilliant light all but blinded her, then Brady put himself between her and the intruder.

Chapter 9

Jayne felt Brady freeze; then, in one smooth motion, he was turning, jerking his gun out of its holster, and the terror was back. Until Brady stopped, his gun out, aimed above them into the brilliant light.

Then he sank back, his body a shield between the light and Jayne. "Oh, it's you, Ted," he sighed, lowering his gun. "What the hell are you doing down here at this time of night?"

Jayne could sense Brady relaxing. He obviously knew who the intruder was, but even so, *she* couldn't relax. Awkwardly she pushed herself back until she was sitting against the cold rock, the front of her blouse clutched together in her hand. Then the light was gone and the darkness was back.

"I'm doing my job," the man above them said. "Keeping incorrigibles from using this beach for their own purposes. What are you doing here, Brady?"

"Watching the submarine races, Ted," Brady murmured as he pushed his gun back in the holster, then sat forward and encircled his bent legs with his arms. He never looked back at Jayne.

"I thought they'd been suspended when you got to be a big-time cop," Ted said.

Jayne closed her eyes, not about to think of what the man must have seen, no more than she would think about what would have happened if he hadn't come along. Her body was reminder enough of that. She felt overwhelmed by the heaviness inside her, the painful frustration. She literally ached for something that had been denied her. And she didn't know whether she hated this Ted person, or whether she was grateful he had shown up when he did.

"Some things never change," Brady was saying. "I thought the guard shifts stopped at sundown."

"They usually do, but I was restless and thought I'd take a walk." He looked at Jayne. "How did this guy talk you into coming down here with him, little lady?"

She swallowed hard and opened her eyes, her impressions simple—a medium built man in some sort of uniform silhouetted against the sky. She touched her tongue to her lips. "He...he promised me submarine races."

The man broke into laughter. "It works every time, doesn't it, Brady?"

"Usually," he said.

"You two enjoy yourself. I need to get back. Good seeing you, Brady. Take care," he said and waved as he walked off down the beach.

His light snapped on again, and as soon as it disappeared around a bend in the distance, Brady turned and looked at Jayne. "Ted's been working here for twenty years. He covered for me a lot of times with my folks." He shrugged. "Would you say Fate brought him along tonight?"

Even though the question was asked in a neutral tone, it seemed cutting to Jayne, painful after the enormity of what had almost happened, so she found herself reacting defensively. "Chance or Fate, he showed up just in time, didn't he?"

Brady stood abruptly, and when Jayne got to her feet, too, he bent and picked up the blanket. "Damn right," he muttered.

She bit her lip, horrified at what could have happened if Ted hadn't come along. Casual sex was something she had never believed in. She'd been a virgin before Elliot, a virgin by choice, and she'd almost thrown away her values simply because a man had walked into her life and made her aware that she was still a woman. A man who saw everything as temporary and the result of luck. She did up her blouse with very uncooperative fingers.

She hugged herself, suddenly cold despite the lingering warmth in the air. When Brady started back down the beach, she took off after him.

She had to take a couple of skipping steps to catch up with him. "Brady," she said. "I need to get to the hospital for the eleven o'clock shift. We've got plenty of time, but I—"

He never broke stride as he cut her off with one word. "No."

"But it's my turn. I have to be there."

"No, you don't," he said. "You're going to my place for the rest of the night, and we aren't stepping outside the apartment until daylight."

"I'm going to the hospital, Brady," she said, hurrying ahead of him. "The babies need me. Rocky needs me."

He stopped her by catching her arm. When she turned, he was looking down at her, the moonlight shading his face with silver. "And you need to stay alive to help them," he countered as he let her go.

She dug at the sand with her toe. "But Rocky isn't doing very well, and I just want to go and hold him for a while. He needs loving." She shook her head, then took off walking toward the road. "I'm not a prisoner. I'm going to the hospital, at least for a few minutes. I have to."

Brady was by her side, but he didn't speak until they climbed the road and came to the chain. "All right. All right. But we go *now*, and you only stay a few minutes. We can't take any chances."

She recognized a compromise when she heard one, and she wasn't about to push for more, then get denied everything. She'd been shortchanged enough for one night. She simply said, "Thank you," before she stepped over the chain.

The hospital seemed so normal and familiar that it was hard for Jayne to believe that anything had ever happened there. Maybe she was the only one who had changed. Brady was silent; he hadn't touched her after he'd stopped her on the beach. They'd put on their shoes in silence, driven here in silence, and ridden up on the elevator in silence. He was acting as if nothing had happened. Good enough, she thought, intent on forgetting the way he had touched her and the way she had responded.

When she got out on the fourth floor, Brady was right beside her as she headed for the nurses' station. Elaine was there and smiled when she saw Jayne.

"Hello there. We've all been worried about you."

"I'm fine. I'm not going to be able to make my shift later, but I want to spend some time with Rocky. Can you arrange it?"

"I'm sure I can. We didn't think you'd get here at all tonight."

"I wouldn't miss seeing Rocky or the others."

The woman looked at Brady. "Glad to see you're back, too, even after that mix-up. I'll get cover-ups for the two of you."

Brady spoke up quickly. "I'm not helping, just waiting. Just get a cover-up for Jayne."

Elaine left for a minute, then came back with a white cotton cover-up, handed it to Jayne and said, "I'll see about Rocky."

"I called earlier, and they said he's about the same."

The nurse's face sobered. "That's about it. He's still not able to suck, but he needs to be held. I'll bring him in to you in . . ." She looked at her watch. "In ten minutes."

"Fine." Jayne tore the plastic off the cover-up and handed the crinkly wrapping to the nurse. "I'll be in the Forest Room."

She turned and headed down the hall, sensing Brady by her side as she shook out the cover-up, but she didn't look at him. No more displays of emotion, no matter how raw she felt, or how stark the emotions were. Like now. Her fear for Rocky was mounting with each step she took. Babies hadn't made it before, and she'd grieved, yet she knew that if Rocky didn't make it, she wouldn't be able to deal with it. She felt things too deeply now, too clearly, the way she had right after Elliot's death.

And then, after the grieving had finally been done, she had slipped into that gray state of existence. Until Brady. Now she felt everything, every little detail. But after what had happened on the beach, she wasn't sure she wanted to anymore. What had been fascinating all day was almost unbearable now.

She stopped at the door of the Forest Room and turned to Brady. She could hardly look at him directly, and she knew she needed to get away from him for a few minutes. "Why don't you go and see Jack?" she suggested as she pushed her arms into the cover-up.

"I intend to, but not until a guard gets up here to stay with you until I get back."

When she awkwardly tried to tie the back of the gown, Brady abruptly moved behind her and fastened the ties at her back, then the one at her neck. For an instant his fingertips brushed her nape, and she barely covered a spontaneous recoil.

Then he was in front of her, his eyes narrowed and his jaw tense. "Go inside and stay put," he said abruptly. "Your guard will be here in a few minutes."

But before Jayne could go inside, Elaine called out to her. "Jayne?"

She looked up to see the nurse hurrying down the corridor toward her. She wasn't carrying a baby.

"What's wrong with Rocky?"

"Oh, I haven't gone for him yet. I forgot something. There's a man waiting for you inside." Elaine stopped in front of her, slightly breathless from hurrying. "He's been waiting for you to come. I told him you might not be here, but he said he'd stay for a while and see if you showed up."

Before Jayne could ask anything, Brady cut in abruptly. "Who?"

"He didn't say, just that he wanted to see Jayne and explain something."

"What does he look like?" Brady asked.

Elaine frowned. "Medium height, pale. He said—"

"Both of you get back," Brady said as he tugged his gun out of his holster. The guy was here. Right here. Right in the hospital. He looked at Jayne. "There's a cop outside Jack's old room and another in with Jack. If I yell, get one of them, and get him fast."

As soon as she nodded and he knew she understood, he stood back, held his gun braced in both hands, then aimed a sharp kick at the door to the Forest Room. It flew open, hitting the wall with a crack. In the next second Brady yelled, "Police! Don't move!"

The only person in the room, a man by the windows, spun around, his hands out.

Brady tightened his finger on the trigger, ready to use the gun if he had to. Then he saw dark brown eyes behind horn-rimmed glasses, a pale face robbed of any lingering color and unsteady hands lifting into the air.

"Hey, wh—what are you d—doing?" the stranger gasped.

Brady stared at him, then eased his finger off the trigger and lowered his gun to his side. "Who are you?" he demanded.

The man blinked rapidly. "Me? Who?"

"You," Brady repeated. "Who are you?"

"A—Appleton, Charles Appleton. I was w—waiting for...for a lady. I was..." He gulped in air. "I swear, I...I was just waiting for...for..."

Brady pushed his gun into his holster and had the passing thought that Charles Appleton did indeed look like the stereotypical CPA. Pale, glasses, slight build and a brown bow tie worn with a white shirt and black slacks. "Put your hands down, Mr. Appleton. Please. This is all a mistake." Brady called back over his shoulder, "Jayne, come on in."

He heard footsteps behind him; then Jayne was at his side, looking past him to the man by the windows. "He's not the one," she said. "He's not anything like him."

"I know," Brady said. "Meet Charles Appleton."

"Who?"

Brady looked at Jayne. "Your Mr. Appleton, the CPA."

Appleton coughed, then spoke in a reedy voice. "I must insist on knowing what's going on here. I just came to see a Mrs. Spencer, to explain, and instead I'm accosted like this."

"I'm Mrs. Spencer," Jayne said as she took a step toward him. "And I'm really sorry about this."

"Well, I'm sure I don't know what this is all about, but I came to explain to you about last night. I got my dates mixed up. I thought I should explain. I thought it was the right thing to do."

Jayne shot Brady a quick look, and he saw the laughter in her eyes veiled by her long lashes before she turned and crossed the room to Appleton. She held out one hand to the man. "I'm so glad to see you, Mr. Appleton. I can't tell you how much I appreciate you showing up. Better late than never..." she was saying as Brady slipped out the door and into the hall.

He stopped and leaned against the wall. He'd overreacted. He should have asked more questions before going inside. He should never have confronted Appleton that way. He'd pulled his gun for no reason, and in a hospital, too.

He'd made up his mind on the drive from the beach that he would ask Burkhart to find someone else to watch Jayne, and this only underscored his need to be off this bodyguard detail. His perspective was distorted. He was on the defensive all the time where Jayne was involved, instead of on the offensive. He worried about protecting her more than he worried about finding the man who was after her.

Wrong, all wrong, as wrong as it had been to give in to his needs on the beach. Any contact with Jayne was too much contact, not matter how fleeting or unintentional. And their contact on the beach had been monumental. He could have taken her there. He had wanted to so badly that his body still ached when he thought about what had happened. He rubbed his hands together, not at all surprised that he could feel a tightness growing in his body when he remembered the feel of her under his hands, the way her breasts swelled and her nipples tightened. Or the sound of the soft whimpering she made, the way she wound her arms around him.

Now, just glimpsing the nape of her neck, just because he had happened to touch the softness of her skin there, his body responded. For the first time in his life he seemed to have no control over his reactions to a woman.

For a moment he tried to remember the others, even the last woman he had been with, but all he could conjure up were blurred images. The image of Jayne Spencer seemed to have taken over his entire life, not just his dreams. The only face he could envision was Jayne's. The only touch he could remember was hers, and the only thing he wanted right now was to go back inside, get her away from Appleton and take her where they could be alone and he could finish what Ted had stopped on the beach.

Brady reached out with one hand and pushed the door open a crack to look into the Forest Room. Jayne was standing by the windows with Appleton, deep in conversation, her dark hair falling forward to veil her face. Slowly he let the door swing shut.

He was honest enough to admit that what Jayne stirred in him wasn't entirely physical. He could feel her presence filtering into his soul in a way he couldn't begin to define. He knew that he needed to distance himself from her, yet he couldn't let her out of his sight.

He would do what he'd decided to earlier—talk to Burkhart as soon as he could and ask for someone to take over for him as her bodyguard.

"Detective Knight?"

He turned and looked down the corridor at a uniformed officer coming toward him, the rookie he'd met the night before. The kid got closer, and Brady wondered if he had ever looked that young and anxious. Probably, but years ago. "Were you looking for me?"

"Not really. I was just walking around a bit before I took over the next shift in Detective Wills's room, and I saw you here."

"When do you start your shift?"

The man looked at his watch. "In fifteen minutes. At ten o'clock."

"Could you do me a favor?"

He stood a bit straighter. "Yes, sir. What do you need?"

"I need you to stay right by this door and check anyone and everyone who goes in or out of this room. Mrs. Spencer is in there with a man named Appleton." He saw Elaine coming down the hall with a tiny blue bundle. "Don't let anyone else in or out except that nurse with the baby. I'll be back in fifteen minutes, at the most."

"Yes, sir," the kid said. "No problem."

"By the way, what's your name?"

"Neibauer, sir, Peter Neibauer."

"All right, Neibauer, I'll see you in a bit," Brady said, then motioned to Elaine as she got closer. "Go right in," he said, then walked away toward the elevators without looking at the baby. As he pushed the button for the next floor up, he forced himself to concentrate on seeing Jack.

When he stepped off at the fifth floor, he looked ahead to the nurses' station, then beyond to a uniformed officer standing outside the decoy room where Jack had been at first. He walked down the hall, nodded to the cop by the door, then kept going.

He stopped by Jack's room, looked both ways to make sure the corridor was clear, then quickly slipped inside. After glancing at the uniformed officer sitting by the door, he looked at Jack in the single bed and Jack's wife standing by the windows. Marcia turned when she heard Brady, and he could tell she'd been crying. But now she looked controlled—pale and tight, but in control.

He nodded to her, but he didn't say a thing as he walked over to the bed and looked down at Jack. Brady studied the man, the closed eyes, the tubes, the machines still keeping to their own safe rhythms.

Was there more color in Jack's skin and a less blank look to his face? Brady looked closer; it might just be wishful thinking, but he could have sworn Jack looked almost peaceful.

He looked back at Marcia. "Anything new?"

She shook her head but didn't come closer to the bed. "He's doing all right, the doctor said, but he's..." She bit her lip. "He's still in a coma and needs the respirator. The doctor says we just need to wait, to let time take its course." She clenched her hands in front of her. "Time, everything takes time."

"I think he looks better," Brady said, as much to comfort himself as to comfort Jack's wife.

"Do you really think so?"

He looked back down at Jack. "Yes, I do. He's fighting. I can tell, and that's important. Being a fighter, being a survivor." He felt his focus becoming clearer as he stood by Jack's bed. His mind was settling on what to do, how to do it.

"Brady?"

He looked at Marcia. "Yes?"

"Have you got any idea who did this, or why?"

He wished he could tell her that he did, that it was just a matter of time, but he couldn't lie. "Not yet. I've been going through the files, and we've got a good sketch of the assailant. We'll get him. It'll just take—"

"—time. I know." She turned back to the windows.

"That's right. The stack of files is monumental."

"Files. Jack pored over files all the time. A couple of days ago, he brought home a stack and stayed up to all hours going through them."

Brady stared at her. "What files?"

"He didn't tell me. He just said reopening a case was such a mess that Burkhart wouldn't thank him."

"What?"

"You know how the captain is. He's so tidy, so intent on every loose end being tied up, then left alone."

A closed case? "When did he tell you this?"

"The night before..." He heard her take a deep breath. "Two nights ago."

"And what did he do with the files?"

"He took them back to the station with him." She turned to Brady. "Why?"

"Did he mention a name, a place, anything about a specific case?"

"No, just that he had to be right before he did anything." She nibbled on her lip. "And..."

"What?"

"I don't remember, exactly, but something about a professional person. I don't know what it meant."

A pro. A hired gun? A businessman? Brady looked down at Jack. How he wished his partner would open his eyes. Then the tubes would come out and he would name names. How he wished he'd paid more attention to Jack's obsession with their past cases. A closed case? A professional. That changed things, including which files he had to go through first.

He went over to Marcia and spontaneously hugged her for a moment. When he stepped back, he felt unnerved by the unsteadiness he'd sensed in her. He wanted this suffering to stop, to be put to an end. "I'll check back with you as soon as I know anything, and in the meantime, take care of yourself," he murmured, then left the room.

He walked down to the nurses' station, made sure they still had his home phone number so they could call him if Jack's condition changed, then went to a pay phone on the far side of the elevators. He called the station and asked to have a complete computer readout on all the cases he and Jack had worked on that were closed and a list of any felons for hire, and said he would be by in a bit to pick them up and the suitcase for Jayne. After he left a message to be relayed to Burkhart, he hung up and went to the elevators.

When he got back down to the Forest Room he walked up to Neibauer, who was standing right by the door. "How is everything?"

"Quiet. No one in or out except the nurse. Do you need anything else before I go upstairs, sir?"

"No, not now, but thanks for your help."

"Anytime," the rookie said, then touched the peak of his cap and headed down the hall.

Brady touched the door, pushed it open and stepped quietly inside. He stopped after a few feet when he saw Jayne holding Rocky, swaying slowly back and forth while she talked in a steady stream of soft words to Appleton, who sat across from her in one of the easy chairs.

She glanced up when Brady came into the room, but the tone of her voice didn't change. "Anything new?"

"Not much," he said, but he didn't move any closer. He needed his distance from Jayne, even if it was only a matter of a few feet. He leaned back against the closed door. "How's Rocky?"

He saw the way her face tightened before she looked down at the baby in her arms. "He's about the same, I guess. You know, there's always a turning point with everything, and I don't think he's gotten there yet. Maybe that's good. I hope it is." She stroked the baby's cheek with one finger. "He seems more settled, less restless, or maybe I'm just looking for something that isn't there." She sighed softly. "At least he's not fussy and crying."

No one needed this uncertainty in their lives. He wasn't bearing up well not knowing about Jack, and he could see how much it took out of Jayne not knowing about the baby. "He is quiet," he agreed for lack of anything else to say.

Jayne looked back at Brady. "Do you want to hold him for a while? I can get Elaine to bring you a cover-up."

The idea of holding that tiny human being wasn't something he wanted to consider. He didn't want even that responsibility, so he crossed his arms over his chest. "No, he's doing fine with you."

Jayne didn't press him. In fact, it surprised him just a bit when she gave up so easily. She bent back over the baby and began to speak in a soft voice to Mr. Appleton. "I was telling you about the mix-up last night, Mr. Appleton. Well, Detective Knight is the man I brought in here. I thought he was you. And he held Rocky for a while. They got along just fine. You know, this program is so important, that's why I'm pleased that you came after all. I was hoping you would, but when you didn't come that first night, I didn't expect you to ever show up."

"I certainly am sorry," Appleton said, his face creased with concern as he watched Rocky begin to squirm. "I'd like to be part of the program, I really would, but, you know, I think I should give this more thought." He stood abruptly. "You're doing a wonderful thing here, you really are, but I'm not sure I'm suited for it."

Jayne looked up at him. "Anyone's suited for it, Mr. Appleton. It's just a matter of caring enough to come, to hold the babies, maybe feed them. It's the contact that's important."

Appleton shook his head and held his hands out as if to ward off the possibility that she might thrust the baby at him. "You're right, I'm sure. But I'll have to think it over and get back to you. Good night, Mrs. Spencer." He went to the door, and as Brady moved out of the way, he murmured, "Good night, detective," and left.

Brady looked at Jayne, at the heart-wrenching disappointment on her face, and muttered, "I'll be right back."

He went out the door that had barely closed and saw Appleton already halfway to the elevators. He hurried after the man and caught up with him five feet from the elevator doors.

"Appleton?"

The man stopped and turned. "What is it, detective?"

"If you're leaving because of what happened earlier, I want to apologize and explain."

The man pushed his glasses up on his nose. "That's not necessary. Mrs. Spencer explained. I understand. I'm just not cut out for this sort of thing. I thought I was, but now I know I'm not."

"Why?"

He shrugged his narrow shoulders. "I thought . . ." His voice trailed off.

"You thought the babies would be all pink and pretty and cooing for you, didn't you, like some damn magazine ad?"

Appleton colored a bit but finally nodded. "I guess that's about it."

"And you don't want to be around a baby that looks like some alien creature. Is that it, too?"

The color in the other man's face deepened. "No, I never said that."

Brady glared at him. "You just thought it."

"Listen, I can do what I want, Detective Knight. I volunteered for this, it isn't servitude."

Brady had to control the urge to shake the man until his teeth rattled. But he kept his tone even and didn't touch him. "They need you on this program."

"I'm sorry," was all Appleton said.

So was Brady. He hated the disappointment he'd seen in Jayne's face, disappointment that bordered on pain. "You won't reconsider?"

"I admire the concept, I really do, but I don't think I want to be involved after all. You and Mrs. Spencer and the others will make this program work without me. I can see how important it is to both of you."

Brady wanted to protest, but he didn't. It didn't make any difference what this man thought. "It's important to the babies," Brady muttered.

"I'm sorry," Appleton said and turned to the elevators.

"Swell," Brady ground out, then turned to stride back to the Forest Room.

He braced himself, then went inside.

Jayne hadn't moved since he'd left. She was still rocking the baby, and when she spoke, her voice was as soft as velvet. "He isn't coming back, is he?" she asked.

So she'd known what he was doing all along, Brady thought, and that made him feel a bit foolish. "No, he isn't."

Jayne sighed. "I guess he expected a baby like the ones they show on TV, not one like Rocky. Maybe I should have shown him Mandy, or one of the others that are almost ready to leave the hospital."

Brady could hear an echo of his own words to Appleton. "Rocky isn't exactly 'baby beautiful,' is he?" he murmured.

"Not many babies are," she said. "And the irony is that these babies need love and attention the most. Pretty babies get holding and cuddling without anyone having to worry, but babies like these don't get anything, unless someone is their advocate."

Brady felt uneasy at the emotion in Jayne's voice. And uneasy, too, that he could fully understand why Appleton had been put off when he saw Rocky. Yet that didn't stop his anger at the pale man. "And you're their advocate?"

She looked at him, her eyes overly bright. "Someone has to be, Brady. Someone has to care."

Rocky stirred and whimpered softly. Without thinking, Brady went closer and looked down at the baby in Jayne's arms. Did the wrinkled face look less pinched now, the color less strange? And when Rocky slowly opened his eyes, was his gaze a bit sharper? No, not a pretty baby at all, but there was something about him that didn't seem quite so alien to Brady this time.

He crouched down by the chair arm. "Does he look better tonight?"

Jayne looked down at Rocky. "You know, I almost thought so myself, but I was worried it was wishful thinking. If you want something badly enough, you can pretty well imagine what you want to see. I was thinking that's what I was doing, but if you see it too...?"

Maybe he was looking for more than there was with both Rocky and Jack, but he could swear the baby didn't look quite so frail. Yet he couldn't set Jayne up for disappointment. "Maybe I'm wrong."

He surprised himself by reaching out to touch the small fist pressed against the baby's cheek. The hand felt tiny and about as substantial as a feather, yet it was silky soft and surprisingly warm. Rocky seemed to be looking at Brady; then, with a sigh, he closed his eyes.

Brady blinked, shocked at his desire to see this baby make it. Then he looked at Jayne, so close to him, her whole attention on the baby. From nowhere he found himself saying a simple prayer that the baby really was getting stronger, that Jack really was going to come around and be well, and that there really would be a quick end to this nightmare.

Chapter 10

When Jayne began to softly sing to the baby, Brady crossed to the chair Appleton had just left and sank down into the cushions. He felt foolish, yet he wished that Fate, or whatever it was that Jayne believed in, would take over and make everything right. At least that Jayne would be spared any more pain.

He watched her, marveling at the way she gave herself to others, the way she got so involved that she became a part of another person's life. Not just a baby whose beauty certainly wouldn't come for a long time, if ever, but a cop who had long ago decided not to let anyone get close to him again.

He looked down at his hands clenched on his thighs and made himself speak. "We'll have to leave soon."

"Five more minutes? He's just gone to sleep."

Brady looked up when the door opened and Elaine stuck her head into the room. "Detective Knight, there's a phone call for you at the nurses' station."

He stood. "I'll be right there," he said to the nurse, then glanced at Jayne. "Five more minutes. I'll be back as soon as I take this call."

He wished Jayne hadn't smiled at him. Even that simple gesture played havoc with him. "Thank you, Brady," she said softly.

"Sure," he muttered and went out into the hall and down to the nurses' station. Elaine handed him the receiver, then moved away so he could have privacy.

"Detective Knight," Brady said into the receiver.

He was surprised to hear Captain Burkhart's voice come over the wire. "We've got a big problem."

"What is it?"

"The policewoman we sent over to the Spencer woman's house."

"What about her?"

"She was getting the clothes when she thought she heard someone in the house. By the time she got into the kitchen, the back door was ajar. The sun room was empty, but she heard a motor, and when she ran out to see what was going on someone shot at her."

Brady closed his eyes. "Did she get hit?"

"No, I figure it was a diversion, just enough to let the intruder get away without being followed."

He hated the idea of Jayne's home being invaded like that. But wasn't that the very reason she wasn't going back, that she was in protective custody? "What now?"

"God knows. The guy obviously realized he hadn't found Mrs. Spencer and took off. That sort of knocks out the madman theory. He's picking and choosing. He's not killing just for fun, but with a purpose, whatever the hell that purpose is."

A pro. "What now?"

"Keep with the plan. Don't let her out of your sight, and stay low. I'll be in touch."

"Captain, did you get my message earlier?"

"Yeah. I'll see if I can dig up someone to take over for you."

"Good. I'm not a baby-sitter, I'm a cop. I hate being confined like this."

Burkhart spoke quickly. "Got to go. I'm still down here at the banquet, and the speeches are just winding up. I'll be in touch soon."

Brady handed the phone back to Elaine and had no difficulty deciding not to tell Jayne about what had happened at the house. She'd been through enough without knowing the creep had invaded her own home.

As Brady drove away from the police station, Jayne glanced at the dash clock—11:05. It was getting on toward midnight. She held the stack of computer paper Brady handed her after he'd put her overnight bag in the back seat. "What're these papers for?" she finally asked.

He drove through the night streets, constantly checking his rearview mirror and didn't answer until they were through the stoplight by the court building. "Computer readouts of all the cases Jack and I worked on that were closed. Also a list of any professional felons."

"Professional? Like career criminal?"

"Sort of. There's a class distinction in the crime business. There're your crooks, your cons, your thieves, your murderers. But they do what they do out of passion, or need, or because they're psychotic. Then there're the ones who do it for pay. They don't care one way or the other, as long as the price is right."

"Like a mercenary?"

"Close."

"You said something about closed files."

"Jack said something to his wife, Marcia, about a closed case maybe causing trouble if he had to open it up again. That narrows it a bit. And maybe a pro's involved."

She fumbled in her purse and found a small penlight, snapped it on and looked at the top of the first page. "Aaron, Roderick James," she read off.

"I remember him. He stole a car and ran down three people with it before he was stopped. He was convicted on two counts of murder two, driving under the influence, and possession of cocaine with intent to sell. Look at the bottom of the entry and see where he is now."

She glanced down. "Soledad. Eligible for parole in seven years."

"That lets him out. What's the next one?"

She read the entries to Brady, a bit impressed that he remembered most of them clearly. As they turned onto a steep street, she read off the next name. "Fletcher, Raymond Beau."

"Murder one. He shot a clerk at a convenience store. Six shots fired, five hit the man in the head. The prosecutor proved premeditation, and he pleaded innocent by reason of temporary insanity. It didn't stick. He got the works. He's still inside with parole at least twenty years down the road."

She snapped off the light and sank back in the seat. Seeing the records and hearing Brady talk gave her a glimpse into what he worked with every day. No wonder he was so cynical and unwilling to get involved with others. He had to deal on the most basic level with the worst people the city had to offer.

She looked outside at an area with older apartment buildings on either side of the street. "Do you remember every case you ever worked on?"

"Most of them."

Even though it was dark, Jayne could tell they had circled the block and were driving past the same apartments for the second time. "Where are we?"

"Outside my apartment building." He motioned to a brown stucco, two-story structure to the right.

"Why are we driving around the block?"

"Just making sure no one's following us." He looked in his rearview mirror again, then swung to his right and down a drive into underground parking. "It's clear."

He parked near the back, then got out, and by the time he had her overnight case in his hand and had come around to her side, Jayne was out and standing by the car with the computer printout in her arms, along with her purse.

"Wait for me before you get out," he said in a low voice. "Don't expose yourself like that."

She darted a nervous glance around the parking area, then back to Brady. "Could he be—"

"I hope not," he murmured, then took the computer printout from her and tucked it under his arm, shifting the overnight case to the same hand. With his free hand, he motioned to some nearby stairs. "Up there." Then he touched Jayne for the first time since they'd left the beach. It was a soft touch on her elbow, meant merely to get her moving, but the contact was riveting.

Yes, the world was clearer to Jayne now. She felt his fingers through the thin material of her blouse and was certain she could feel the heat of his touch, the way she had on her breast. She went with Brady but broke the contact at the stairs, more out of self-protection than because they were climbing to street level. She felt bombarded by life. Life and death.

They stepped out into a central courtyard ringed by apartments, and Brady paused, glanced around, then motioned Jayne to the right. She stayed close to his side as they crossed to the metal stairs that went up to the second level. At the top, he stopped by the first door and pulled his keys out of his pocket, then inserted one in the lock.

"I'm not sure how the apartment is," he said when the key clicked. "I mean, the cleaning service comes in once a week, but they keep changing days on me, and it could be pretty bad." He looked at her with a sideways glance. "It can be messy. I mean, I don't notice it too much myself, but my friends and family have been known to comment."

The door swung back, and Brady reached inside. When a light came on, Jayne found herself reluctant to step past Brady into his home. Being with him in the car had been hard enough. She didn't know how she would react to being in a place that was completely his.

As she stepped inside, she knew the place really was *completely* his. She couldn't have described why, but as soon as she saw it, she felt his presence there, his undeniable stamp.

The living room was square, with a couch and a few chairs, all in brown tweed, arranged in a half circle facing away from the curtained windows and toward a television sitting on a low bookshelf on the far wall. A kitchen, really little more than a nook, was at the back on the right, and at the rear on the other side was a closed door with a blue surfboard propped against the wall by it. The board was nicked, the color a bit faded, but she could still read *Brady* splashed across the top in red.

As she moved farther into the room, she thought she wouldn't have called the apartment messy but maybe cluttered. Newspapers were stacked on the floor by the couch, and clothes were tossed over the back of one of the chairs. Books leaned against both sides of the television, and the kitchen had dishes stacked to one side of the sink.

"It's not too bad," Brady muttered as he closed the door and walked past her. "I don't really look at this place. I sleep here. That's about it."

Jayne glanced at him as he put her case on the floor by the couch, then tossed the printout onto the coffee table. He bent and pushed the button on an answering machine on a table beside the couch.

There was a beep; then a woman's voice came over the machine. "Brady, this is Mother. We heard about your poor partner. Since you didn't call, I can only assume that you weren't involved. I wish you were here with us, instead of there. Your father sends his love. Take care."

There was a beep, then a second message, again from his mother. "It's me again, Brady. Your father says if you'd like, he'll send the plane for you. It's not a long flight. You could be here tomorrow when the sun comes up. Think about it and call us at the number I gave you before we left."

The machine beeped; then a third message began. "Knight? Captain Burkhart here. Nothing new on the shooting at the Spencer woman's house. I'm still working on your request. I'll get back to you."

Jayne stared at the machine in shock as it beeped twice, then fell silent. A shooting at her house? She turned her eyes to Brady, who was standing very still, just watching her. She had to try twice to get the words out. "What shooting, Brady?"

He motioned to the couch. "Sit down and I'll explain."

She took a step toward him. "What shooting?"

"First sit down."

She dropped her purse on the table beside the stack of papers, then sank weakly into the soft cushions. But she never took her eyes off Brady, who was still standing by the telephone. "All right. Explain."

He moved across the room while he spoke, and Jayne twisted to watch him take off his holster and toss it on a table by the front door. "I wasn't going to tell you about this, but the policewoman who got your things thought someone was in your house." He took his badge out of his pocket and dropped it by the holster. "She went to investigate and someone took a shot at her." He turned, meeting her gaze. "Don't worry. She's all right, and your house is fine."

Jayne closed her eyes and exhaled in a rush. "He *did* go there. You were right. He knew. He found out where I lived." She opened her eyes and stared blankly down at her hands clenched in her lap. "He's not going to stop, is he?"

"No," Brady said simply as he came closer. "He won't. That's why we have to stop him."

She looked up at him standing over her. "Why didn't you tell me this when you found out?"

"You were worried about Rocky, and after everything..." His voice trailed off, and a frown tugged his eyebrows together. "Enough is enough, Jayne. It makes no difference, and no one was hurt. Maybe I should have told you."

"This is so crazy," she said, huddling into the corner of the couch. "This man who never met me, never even knew me before yesterday, is after me, shooting me, getting into my house, trying to kill me any way he can. God, it's like a nightmare where everything's out of control, where there's no rhyme or reason to anything."

"Yeah, I know the feeling," he murmured, then said, "Enough of this. There's nothing we can do right now except go over files and lists." He looked down at her with narrowed eyes. "The big question right now is, are you hungry?"

She stared up at him, at first thinking that was a stupid question, considering what was going on; then she realized that, despite everything, she was starved. The Mexican food she'd had for lunch could have been eaten days, rather than hours, ago. "I . . . I guess so."

He seemed to relax. "How about pizza?"

She hadn't had pizza since... She couldn't remember the last time. "Sure, that sounds good."

He moved to the side table and picked up the phone, dialed a number, then looked back at Jayne. "Any allergies or aversions to anything?"

"Just to anchovies."

"An allergy?"

"Aversion," she said with a grimace.

He nodded, then spoke into the receiver, ordering a pizza with "the works." As he hung up, he looked at Jayne. "They'll be here in thirty minutes."

He crossed the room and flipped on the television. A news anchor with a huge map behind him took shape. He turned the sound to a level loud enough to hear but low enough not to be intrusive, then came back and sank down on the other end of the couch. "You can take a shower or clean up, if you want," he said to Jayne. "I want to catch the local news."

The news anchor, a red-haired man with a full mustache, was talking about acid rain, then moved on to the local scene. Pictures flashed on the screen of a formal dinner with people in elaborate gowns and full tuxedos in a huge, domed ballroom. Then a single man dominated the screen, a tall, lean man with silvery hair framing a deeply tanned face.

Jayne recognized sixty-year-old DeForest Miles, a striking man who seemed to command attention. He was the image of a politician.

"Tonight DeForest Miles, candidate for the U.S. Senate, hosted a five-hundred-dollar-a-plate dinner for his supporters," the voice-over was saying. "Among the guests were celebrities, financial giants, and city officials."

Jayne felt Brady move and glanced at him as he shifted lower until his head rested against the back cushions of the couch. He pulled one foot up to rest it on the opposite knee. Exhaustion etched lines in his face and softened every angle of his body. He ran a hand over his face, then glanced at the television screen from under heavy lids.

"In other news," the anchorman was saying, "police are still searching for the single gunman who left a policeman near death in an alley near Waylan and Glenn. Detective Jack Wills, who sustained two wounds that caught his lung, is in a coma and listed as critical at Santa Barbara Memorial."

Brady reached to his right and picked up a remote control from the table with the phone on it. He pressed a button, and the sound went off. "Duly vague," he muttered, still staring at the mute television as he spoke to Jayne. "The bath's through the bedroom." He motioned to the closed door by the surfboard. "You've got time for a shower, at least, before the pizza gets here."

Maybe Brady felt the way she did, that she needed a few minutes by herself, without his presence there to confuse her and remind her of the intensity of the recent past. "Thanks," she murmured as she stood. She crossed to pick up her overnight bag, then walked to the door.

She stepped into his bedroom, which was as big as the living room, but almost filled by a huge bed that was definitely long enough to accommodate Brady's height and size. The bed was a tumble of sheets, and clothes were scattered on a dresser to the left. For an instant she found herself looking for something feminine, some hint that there was someone in Brady's life, but everything she saw was male. Finally she turned from the sight and stepped into the bathroom.

The small, blue-tiled room was cold and sterile, with shaving products on the back of the sink, and the medicine cabinet standing open. A razor, a can of shaving cream, and a single toothbrush lay on the back of the sink.

She nudged the medicine cabinet door shut and stared at herself in the mirror. Jayne Spencer, rational person, career woman, stared back at her. Was it her imagination, or did she look different? Was there more character in her face, more life in her eyes? She stared hard at her reflection. Maybe she was imagining it the way she thought she saw improvement in Rocky. Rational thought and actions weren't her strong suit tonight.

She thought of the beach, of Brady, of the way he had touched her, kissed her. Maybe she was looking for more than she could ever have. Quickly she stripped off her clothes, took her white terry-cloth robe out of her overnight bag, then reached into the shower and turned on the water. She adjusted it until it was pleasantly warm, then stepped under the stream and let it flow over her.

He stood in the phone booth by the hospital's visitor parking lot and felt nerves crawl up his neck, a sensation that made him vaguely sick. Nothing like this had happened before. There had never been loose ends that could do him in.

He stared at the hospital, a tower of lights in the blackness of the night and drew on his cigar. The cop and the woman had disappeared. They had dropped off the face of the earth, but he knew they'd be back, and when they came, the woman would be his downfall. The cop he'd shot wasn't the threat the woman was, not yet. The cop had never really seen him, never really gotten a good, clean look at him.

He'd heard the sound after he'd made the hit. He'd been careful to stay in the shadows while he took care of business, luring his target to the meeting behind the surplus store by promising drugs at a price that would have drawn anyone. He'd never stepped into the light as he took out his target, then disposed of the body, moving with an ease he'd perfected over the years. Until that sound. Then his life had stopped.

He took a deep breath. It almost scared him that the cop had obviously been on his tail and he had never suspected it at all. He hadn't even known the guy was a cop until the other one came, yelling that he was the police. For an instant he'd been inches away from the tall one in the alleyway, but the man had never known. He'd blended with the darkness, something he had always been able to do.

Then, later, the woman had interfered. The hit could have been clean and over with. They would have blamed an attendant or a sloppy nurse for the faulty IV. The cop would have died and taken his knowledge with him. Then the woman had walked in.

He dropped the cigar to the ground and crushed it under his heel, then he pinched the bridge of his nose between his thumb and forefinger. "Think, think," he muttered to himself. "Focus."

He straightened as he realized what he could do. He would call his client. The man had contacts. He could find out where the cop and the woman had disappeared to. He gripped the receiver, pushed a quarter in the slot, then punched the number. His client should be more than happy to help. After all, it was his skin, too, if this ever came out.

And answering machine clicked in after two rings and the message was brief. "Leave a message after the tone."

He hesitated, then said, "Mr. King will call back in one hour. Be there."

Brady sat very still and stared at the mute news anchor on the television after Jayne left the room. He could hear her move through the bedroom; then the bathroom door closed. A few moments later the water went on.

He relaxed just a bit, exhaling softly, then glancing around the room. It felt like a lifetime since he'd really looked at the apartment. It didn't look much like anyone's home. It looked like what it was, a stopping over spot, a place to clean up, to sleep, a place to store his things. His choice.

"It looks like you live in a motel," his mother had said the few times she'd been here. "You don't have to live like this. You know you can stay at the house, or you can have the privacy of the pool house anytime you want it."

The "pool house" was a two bedroom cottage near the tennis courts at his parents' home. And he'd used it from time to time but not lately. He didn't belong there, no more than Jayne fit into this place of his.

That brought him up short. Not only didn't she fit here, there was no reason why he should even be considering the idea of whether she did or not. He let his head rest against the back of the couch and closed his eyes. No, Jayne fitting in here wasn't even a consideration.

He must have drifted off, because the next thing he was aware of was the sound of a door closing. He sat bolt upright, instantly awake, before realizing it must have been the bathroom door. Jayne would be coming back to the living room soon. He glanced at the wall clock. Less than fifteen minutes since she'd gone in to take the shower.

He could almost follow her in his mind, sense her coming through the bedroom to the door, opening it. And then she was there, coming toward him.

At that moment he knew he would never be prepared for Jayne's appearance in his life. She wore a white robe, short enough to show an expanse of bare legs, and her hair was slightly damp, with curls clinging to her forehead and temples. Her bare feet pressed into the beige carpet, and he realized she looked paler, younger, definitely vulnerable.

She was going through hell, and all because of his stupid mistake with an elevator button. A surge of compassion flooded through him, and he had the incredible urge to just hold her, to tell her everything would be all right, the way one would do with a child after a horrible nightmare.

While he had been staring at her, she had crossed the room to stop within a few feet of him, and she'd been talking to him.

"I'm sorry, what did you say?" he asked, sitting up.

She came closer and sank down onto the other end of the couch. "The policewoman didn't pack slippers or pajamas." She touched the hem of the robe. "Just this."

He sat forward and raked both hands through his hair. "She probably wanted out of there as quickly as she could manage it. I'm sure I can find something for you to sleep in."

He glanced at her as color rose in her cheeks. "I didn't mean that. I just..." She bit her lip. "This is really awkward for me," she blurted out.

"Why? I slept on your couch last night." He was feeling more than awkward himself, but he wasn't about to explain that to her. He couldn't tell her that when she was this close, all he could think about was the way things had gotten out of hand at the beach. How he had needed her so much at that moment that he'd ached from it, or that even now he could hardly look at her without remembering the sight of her naked breasts bathed by the moonlight.

Instead, he got up and went into the kitchen. He rummaged around until he found two clean plates in the dishwater. When the tightness in him began to ease, he went back into the room and put the dishes on the coffee table. "We'll make the best of this. After all," he said, forcing himself to straighten and look right at her, "we don't have a choice, do we?"

Her color deepened. "You do."

"How?"

"Your mother. When she called, she said you could stay with them, if you wanted to."

He'd forgotten all about that. The offers came all the time, offers meant to bring him "back into the fold," offers he never took, and, he suspected, offers neither parent expected him to take. "That wasn't serious."

"When you call her back . . . ?"

"I won't. She doesn't really expect me to. She and my father are in Cabo San Lucas, in Mexico. They've got a home there on the cliffs. She knows I wouldn't go down there now. But she had to ask. It's part of her makeup. Try to get Brady away from his job, get him back in his old circles. Maybe he'll come to his senses."

He could see that she was surprised by his blunt statement. "Jayne, I have the feeling you had a pretty normal childhood. I didn't. My father worked every waking hour, and my mother had her *commitments*, everything from the local historical society to fighting the slaughter of baby seals. That doesn't mean they're bad people, because they're not. They're great. They're in love and they have a terrific time together, but parenting wasn't in their vocabulary. They weren't good at it. They loved me, but I doubt they liked having a child around. At least, not until I got to an age where I was considered the 'heir apparent' to the company."

She simply stared at him without saying a thing, so he turned and went back into the kitchen to open the small refrigerator. He looked inside at his idea of supplies—ketchup, steak sauce, two six-packs of beer, milk of indeterminate age, a bottle of red wine, and a huge half-full jar of peanut butter. "How about something to drink with the pizza? I've got red wine of questionable vintage or milk." He took out the milk, smelled it, then tossed the half-full container in the sink. "Scratch the milk. I've got beer, too."

"Wine sounds fine to me."

He kept silent while he opened the wine and found glasses in the kitchen. He didn't know what had possessed him to tell Jayne about his parents. The thought had been his and his alone for so long, staying inside him without being actually said since the time he'd been nine and figured the whole thing out. Now the thoughts were solid, real, because he had brought them to life and spoken them to a woman he barely knew.

Chapter 11

Brady filled the two glasses with wine, then took them and the bottle into the living room, where he put them on the table by the plates. Right then the doorbell rang. As he crossed to the door, he instinctively took his gun out of the holster and called out. "Who is it?"

"Paul's Pizza."

He opened the door a few inches, looked out at the boy with the pizza box, then tucked his gun into his waistband and took out his wallet. After he paid and took the pizza, he locked the door, then laid the box on the table after Jayne put the computer printout on the floor at her feet.

He returned his gun to the entry table, then crossed back to the couch and sat down, leaving plenty of space between himself and Jayne. Then he leaned forward to look at the pizza. "It looks good," he said to Jayne. "Help yourself."

She didn't hesitate before picking up a plate, then pulling a piece loose from the pizza. Sitting back, she tucked her feet under her and rested the plate on her thigh. Brady reached for a slice himself and, folding it over, bit into it. Then he picked up his glass and sipped his wine.

They ate in silence, but he had to smile when Jayne reached for her third piece. "You *were* hungry, weren't you?"

She looked up at him, and color rose in her cheeks. "Oh, I'm sorry. I—"

"Don't be sorry. I was just thinking this is the first time I've had pizza with a woman who did more than just pick at the toppings."

She ran her tongue over her lips, then sank back on the couch. "I didn't realize how great pizza can taste."

"This is only fair, not good, much less great. If you want great, there's a place on Larchmont and Vine that makes the world's best pizza, but they don't deliver."

She took a sip of wine. "I don't worry much about food. I'm either at some business dinner or I heat up one of those frozen dinners, the kind that looks beautiful on the package but tastes like cardboard when you eat it. How do you do it? I mean, you're on your own." She glanced at the kitchen. "Do you cook?"

"The secret to good cooking is to let someone else do it for you," he said. "There're a lot of good take-out places around here, and I know every one of them."

"I'm so far up in the hills that I would have to pay a delivery man mileage just to bring food to me." She smiled, a spontaneous expression that put lights in her eyes and forced Brady to swallow hard to get his next bite of pizza down without choking.

He finally washed it down with the last of the wine in his glass, then sat back and looked at Jayne. He couldn't believe she was alone very often. "Do your dates ask for mileage when they come to get you?"

The smile disappeared as quickly as it had come. "No," she muttered and put her plate down on the coffee table. When she picked up her wine, Brady felt taken aback to see that her hand was unsteady. "I don't date very much." She took a gulp of wine and looked at him over the glass. "But I'd guess you do, with your submarine races and all."

"A leftover part of my misspent youth," he murmured, pouring more wine into his glass. "More pizza?"

Jayne shook her head. "No, I'm full."

He sat back. "So am I."

"And you're exhausted."

He didn't bother denying it. He could have slept for days. "It's been a long time since I've had a good night's sleep."

"Just show me where to put this," she said as she stood and closed the box on the remaining pizza. "Then show me where the linen is so I can make up the couch."

Brady stood, but before he could do anything she was on her way to the kitchen. "I'll take the couch," he said while she looked into the fridge.

"No you won't. You had my couch last night. Tonight I get yours. You don't shop much, do you?" she asked as she straightened up after putting the pizza away.

Brady watched her, the way she brushed at her loose hair, then tucked it behind her ear. Then the way she looked at him from under the sweep of her lashes. "No, but as long as they carry peanut butter at the convenience store, I won't starve."

She swung the door shut and turned to Brady. "When I was in college I lived on peanut butter and jelly sandwiches. I always thought that was food for kids until I realized it was the easiest thing to make when I was in a hurry. You can read, even type with one hand, if you're eating a sandwich. But the sandwich needs to be filled with something that won't fall out. Peanut butter sticks to everything."

"I never thought of it like that."

She came back into the room and picked up both plates, then took them out to the kitchen, keeping up a running conversation all the time. "You know, I've read that kids don't actually eat much candy if you leave them to their own devices. They prefer peanut butter or potato chips." She slid the plates into the sink and turned to him with a grin. "I actually made a peanut butter and potato chip sandwich once. I figured that included several of the major food groups. It wasn't great, but it served the purpose at the time."

"To make you sick?"

"No. Didn't you ever put bananas in a sandwich with peanut butter, or lettuce?"

He grimaced at the idea. "No. I didn't even know living people ate things like that."

"Kids. They love it. I still do."

"I don't know much about kids." He picked up the wineglasses, carried them to the kitchen and handed them to Jayne. As she set them by the other dishes on the side of the sink, he realized again how disconcerting it was to be within inches of her. "I've always kept my distance from children."

"How about other adults?"

He moved back a bit, his actions echoing his next words. "I keep my distance, unless there's a mutual agreement to get closer."

Her face flooded with color again, and he found himself fascinated by the ease with which she blushed. "Then what happens?" she asked.

"When it's over, I go my way and she goes hers. I do my job and live my life the way I want to."

"Alone?"

"By myself."

"Can you really live like that?"

"I have so far, and I've survived. And for me to be a good cop, I have to keep it that way."

"Maybe when you're trying to survive you need someone the most," she whispered.

The ringing of the phone startled Brady, and he turned from Jayne to answer it. He lifted the receiver. "Hello?"

"Detective Knight?"

"Who is this?"

"Elaine Burrows, the nurse at Santa Barbara Memorial."

His stomach clenched. "What is it?"

"You left your number here, and since you've been with Jayne, I was hoping you'd know how to get in touch with her. There's no answer at her house, and I didn't want to wait to call her at work Monday morning."

"She's here with me."

"Oh, good," she said. "Can I speak with her?"

"Why don't you give me a message?"

"I'd rather speak to her. It's important, or I wouldn't have called you."

Brady hesitated, then turned to hold the receiver out to Jayne. "It's Elaine, from the hospital."

He could see the way Jayne paled. "What's wrong?"

He wished he knew. He wished he could protect her from what he thought the woman was going to tell her. But he couldn't. "She needs to talk to you."

Jayne came over and took the receiver. He could see her take a shaky breath before managing to ask, "Elaine, what's wrong?"

She listened in silence, then slowly sank back down on the couch. "What did they say?"

She nibbled on her bottom lip, then stared at her hand as she clenched and unclenched it. "When?" A pause. "All right, call me no matter what time it is. I'll be here."

When she put the receiver back in the cradle and didn't say anything, Brady couldn't stand it any longer. He went to her, standing in front of her. "Jayne, what is it?"

"Rocky," she breathed, then looked up at him, her eyes bright with unshed tears. "He's weaker. They had to put him on oxygen." She bit her lip hard. "He's not going to make it, Brady, he can't. I was wrong about him looking better. I wanted it so badly, so badly, but . . ."

Brady knew incredible pain at that moment, almost as if he could feel her grief on top of his own sorrow that the tiny boy was slipping away. It drove the breath from him, and he sank down on the cushions next to Jayne.

He looked at her, horrified that the fate of the boy was becoming so important to him, almost as important as this woman beside him was becoming. That was it. That was the hardest thing of all for him to absorb. He ached for Jayne and knew that if there were some way to take all the pain from her and put it on him, he would.

When she took another unsteady breath, he acted on instinct, the only thing he could possibly do. He had to hold her and not let her be alone in her pain.

He reached out, gently pulling her into his arms, and the way she swayed against him, the way she buried her face in his chest, made his heart lurch. He would have done anything to make things right for her. Anything. Then he realized that he wasn't holding her just for her sake, but for his own. He needed the connection, the support, the feel of her against him, her heart beating against his chest.

When she stirred and looked up at him, her amber eyes shadowed by her lush lashes, he knew that, even more, he needed to be with her, to know her and to never let her go.

He didn't give himself a chance to do more than let the idea settle in his mind before he dipped his head to taste her lips. They had spent so little time together, yet he felt as if he had experienced an entire lifetime with her, and the only thing left to experience was feeling her against him, surrounding him.

Her lips were unsteady, softly parted, inviting, and no matter how he tried to tell himself he was doing this for comfort, it didn't ring true. He wanted her, pure and simple. And he knew he had wanted her since that first glimpse he had had of her in the hallway of the hospital.

When she sighed, a shuddering release of air, and her arms circled his neck, reason gave way to feelings, and those feelings were melded with a white hot passion the likes of which he was certain he had never felt with another woman.

Jayne felt as if she had been fragmented by the news about Rocky, and now, in some unexplainable way, Brady was putting her back together again, healing her, sealing her soul and saving her life. The idea took her breath away, just as his kiss was doing at the same moment.

She felt his tongue invade her mouth, and she welcomed the caress, letting the sensations swirl around her, catching at her, tugging her into a gentle vortex. Then his hands were on her, pushing back her robe, and she fell back onto the couch cushions with him over her. His skin touched her skin, and there was no reasoning left.

Passion exploded in the air. Maybe it was a continuation of what had been stopped at the beach, but the feelings were wild and uncontrollable. His hands freed her of the robe, exposing her without any protection, and she knew no embarrassment. She arched to his touch, her breasts swelling, her nipples aching for more, tight and hard under his fingers.

Then his hands moved lower, and his mouth took their place. While his tongue played havoc with her nipples, his hands stroked her, teased her, drifting lower over her belly to the sensitive area between her thighs.

Her legs parted willingly, and she arched toward him, needing to have him know her, demanding that he touch her, and he did. His fingers slid into her damp heat, and the intimacy of his touch made her gasp with pleasure.

Frantic to know him, she undid his belt, fumbling with his zipper until it slid down; then she pushed her hands under the denim and the soft cotton of his shorts. He shuddered, and his hand on her stilled at the same moment that she felt his arousal. She was suddenly aware of the pleasure she could give him, and she felt a joy that seemed unbounded.

Then his touch began again, insistent, earnest, breathtaking. There was no turning back, no thought of stopping what she now knew had been inevitable ever since she had first met Brady. As inevitable as her falling in love with him. The idea drifted into her mind but did little more than flit past before his touch stopped all thoughts.

He had such strong, sure hands. Yet his touch was as gentle as it was demanding as his fingers continued to invade her. Her anticipation came close to pain, but it was a pain that she knew could turn into the purest of pleasures. She knew that without a doubt, and as her hands awkwardly pushed aside the denim of his jeans, she knew that Brady could truly heal her.

"Are you sure?" Brady whispered roughly against her hair.

Jayne had never been so sure of anything in her life. She answered Brady by finding his mouth with hers and kissing him so fiercely that she could feel her teeth against his teeth, her breasts crushing against his chest.

With a low groan, Brady stood away from her. In a moment his jeans were gone, then the white briefs were stripped from his deeply tanned skin. She only had a fleeting glimpse of his need for her, then his hands had hers and he was pulling her to her feet.

In one swift movement he had her high in his arms and was carrying her to the bedroom. Without turning on the lights, he crossed to the bed, lowered her onto the cool sheets and then was lost in the shadows. She lay very still, certain that if she moved, she would explode from need.

She heard him go into the bathroom. Then he was back, and as he came to her through the shadows, his voice was as soft and as sensual as any sound she'd ever heard. "I've been away too long," he whispered roughly against her lips as he brought her body to him.

Yes, too long, too long. The words formed a chant in Jayne's mind as Brady touched her and stroked her and drove her mad with wanting. Then she was answering touch for touch, kiss for kiss, caress for caress, and her soft whimpering sighs grew to deeply felt groans.

She raked her nails across his chest, then splayed her hand on his flat stomach, feeling the springy hair and the heat. Then she slipped her touch lower, until Brady groaned, "Yes, touch me." So she did.

She felt the protection he'd taken, and it touched her in a way she couldn't express. As she encircled him, she heard him gasp; then his tongue delved deeply into her mouth, invading her in the most intimate way.

And then, just as he was ravaging her with his mouth, he took her with his body. When she opened her legs, he found her with one quick thrust. Her back arched, her cry one of pleasure; then, as he began to move, she matched his pace, never slowing.

Suddenly it happened. Jayne felt such pleasure that she cried out Brady's name at the same time that he called out hers. The fullness of him within her healed her. It brought her the serenity she needed. She could feel all the pain and grief floating away and a happiness that left her stunned taking their place.

"Yes, yes, yes," she sobbed as the feelings began to mellow and drift off, leaving her awash in pure contentment.

"Yes," Brady echoed, and as he left her, he rolled to his side, pulling her with him.

She snuggled next to him and spread her hand on his chest, feeling the steady, strong beat of his heart under her palm. Had she ever felt so complete? She didn't know. Strangely, she couldn't remember much before Brady. She tasted the heat of the sleek skin on his shoulder and relished the heavy weight of his leg over hers. It felt right. It felt perfect.

As he grazed her forehead with a fleeting kiss, she closed her eyes. Perfect? It felt as if she had been waiting for this forever, and though she had expected to feel that she was betraying Elliot's memory, the feeling didn't come.

This was different. This man was different, the place was different, the time and the life. And it was a life she wanted more than anything.

Brady shifted, pulling her more tightly to his side; then his breathing became regular and deep. When she heard a soft snore, she knew he was asleep, so she snuggled closer, sighed deeply and let herself drift off into the soft gentleness of exhaustion.

"What the hell do you mean?" King demanded on the phone. "You get an address, a location for me, or your name's going to be on every newscast in the state within the hour.''

His client took a deep breath. "I told you, I tried. No one's talking.''

"You can't tell me that with your connections you can't get a cop's address and phone number. Go to the top. Go to the boss.''

"If you hadn't screwed up the job—''

"Me? How the hell did I know a cop would be snooping around, that a cop suspected the lies you told before? I didn't even know there was anyone following Gallagher until after I'd finished him off.''

"Now you know. And you're still messing up.''

"I'm improvising," he muttered. "I hate improvising.''

"You'd better improvise both of us out of this.''

"I'll end it. Then I'll be gone, but the money—''

"You've got the money. The mess is your own responsibility, and it's on your own bill.''

He couldn't argue with that. He should have sensed that someone was there when he took out Gallagher. He should have, and the fear came back with a rush. He hated it. "Just get me what I need.''

"Give me a number where I can contact you.''

He quoted the motel's number, then added, "Room 22. The name's Arnold. It's one a.m. now. I'll give you until nine a.m. That's it.'' He needed some sleep. "Don't let it go past that. I'm not a patient man.'' He hung up, then stepped out of the phone booth near the hospital and into the autumn night. Patience had never been his best asset. He wanted the cop dead. He wanted the lady dead. And the way it looked now, the other cop, that Brady Knight, had to go, too.

* * *

Brady woke instantly.

He sensed the early light of day on his closed eyelids, and he felt the gentle heat of Jayne at his side. That made his heart lurch. He'd never woken up with a woman by him in the apartment. That hadn't been in his plans. Nothing that permanent.

Now, he lay very still, afraid to wake her, yet feeling his body begin to tense just because her body was against him. This woman was a potent stimulus—her presence, her scent, her heat. This had been a mistake, a terrible mistake, yet he couldn't bring himself to regret it. There was no happily-ever-after in the cards for him. He knew that and felt a degree of sadness, yet he knew he would never forget what he'd found with Jayne for one night.

She was the first woman who'd stayed here for the entire night, and she was going to be the last. He couldn't think clearly with her lying next to him. He couldn't begin to reason why this was all wrong. All he knew was that, as she sighed softly in her sleep, his desire for her, his need, hadn't diminished just because he'd made love to her once.

When she moved against him, when her hand spread slowly across his chest, he felt his breath catch in his throat. Desire was there, potent, fiery, and undeniable.

When he looked down at her, her lashes fluttered, and then her deep amber sleep-filled eyes were on him, and he knew he was lost. His lips found hers, his hands knew her, and his need for her was a painful, intense, living thing that only one thing would quench.

The kisses, the soft sleepy murmurings, the touches, the explorations, built his desire, sending Brady reeling into white hot passion. When Jayne shifted, his hands spanned her waist; then she was over him, astride him, and he felt her heat as it surrounded him, welcoming him.

He groaned, his head back; then the two of them began to move at the same time. His hand found her breast, cupping its weight, feeling it swell under his touch. And Jayne bent to kiss him, her hair lying soft against his skin, the feathery contact sending fire through his veins. She leaned closer, her breasts skimming his chest, her nipples hard and erect, tickling and teasing his own.

As their rhythm grew faster and faster, Brady ceased thinking. He simply felt, and in that moment he knew a oneness that transcended the uncertainty and transient nature of their union. Then the fire exploded in and around him, and as Jayne threw back her head and called out his name, he met her cries with his own.

The two of them were lost in each other, beyond the reach of reason and sanity. Brady watched as reality was swept away, feeling a satisfaction he had never experienced before in his life.

Then Jayne sagged against him, her face buried in his neck, her hair veiling him. "Yes, yes," she whispered unsteadily. "Thank you."

For an instant he felt an incredible envy of her dead husband. Envy because Elliot had known this with Jayne every day, every hour. Because she still wore his ring.

Gently he rolled to his side, her legs still around his hips, and he didn't leave her. He kissed her face, her eyelids, her nose, her cheek, the sweep of her jaw, tasting the slight saltiness, reveling in her soft whimpers. He wasn't willing to let go of this, not yet, not for a while longer.

Her hand traced unsteady patterns on his shoulder, her lips tasting his chest. And even though his satisfaction was immense, he could feel the beginnings of need in him again. He wondered if he would ever have enough of Jayne, even if they had a lifetime together.

The thought brought him to a painful stop.

A lifetime? There wasn't a chance of that. Not the way it had been with Elliot.

He finally left her to sink back against the pillows and close his eyes tightly. No, there would be no lifetime. He wasn't what she needed. He wasn't what she would want, not after the first rush of physical awareness died. He tried to make himself put some distance between them, yet she was molded to his side, trustingly, intimately.

He couldn't take any more. Knowing there would never be another time like this, he swung away from her, pretending to check the bedside clock. But the numerals were blurred, and he wondered why he couldn't focus on them, why his eyes burned and his heart was beginning to pound against his ribs.

"Brady?" she said, the softness of her voice coming through the gray light of dawn, skimming over his nerves.

He let the idea of taking what he could from her do little more than materialize before he rejected it. No, Jayne Spencer wasn't a woman who could give everything, then calmly walk away. She was a woman who believed in commitment, in family, in forever.

He shifted onto his back, his arm over his eyes.

"Brady?" she said, so close he could feel the heat of her breath on his skin.

"Mmmm?"

He almost flinched when he felt her hand on his arm. Her fingers were cool, yet her touch had the power to scald him. What had he gotten himself into? More importantly, what was he going to do about it?

"I never..." He could hear her take an unsteady breath. "I wanted you to know, I don't...I never..."

"You haven't been with anyone since your husband, have you?"

"No," she breathed. "And Elliot was the only one then."

He didn't look, but he knew she would be blushing. Damn it, that made it all the worse. "I know. And I understand. This just happened. It didn't mean anything to you. Don't feel bad. You were lonely, frightened, and you needed someone."

"No," she said, the single word hanging between them.

He forced himself to lower his arm and turn to look at her. Wrong move, he told himself as soon as he saw her flushed face, the tangle of dark hair, the bright color in her cheeks, and the way she lay there. The sheet was tangled around her hips, but her breasts were exposed, their dusky tips beautiful against the perfection of her complexion.

He raised himself on one elbow. The need to touch her was overwhelming, so he did the safest thing. He skimmed her hair back from her face. "Yes. This doesn't have to be more. I understand. Impulses aren't all wrong, just overwhelming at times."

"Impulses?" she asked, her eyes wide and bright.

"You aren't in any condition to get involved, and I never have been." His hand stilled at her temple. He was doing this all wrong, but he groped for the words to make things right, to put them in perspective, so he could deal with it and be done with it. "This just happened."

She moved from his touch abruptly, scooting back and sitting up until her back was pressed against the headboard. He hated the way she clutched the rumpled sheet to her breasts, in some way shutting him out. Yet that was what he wanted. That was what this was all about, distance, making their lives separate once more.

"It didn't just happen," she whispered. "No, you...you were there for me. You helped me, and you cared about . . . about me and Rocky."

That was too much for him. Care? The feelings he had right now were well beyond simple caring, but he couldn't admit that to her. That was something he would have to deal with later—alone. He stayed very still, his eyes never leaving her face, and he created more distance with words. "Don't make this what you think it should be. I'm doing my job. I'm protecting you—that's all."

Chapter 12

Jayne could feel sickness rising at the back of her throat, a diametrically different emotion than the one she'd experienced moments ago. She'd given herself to Brady, shared herself in the most intimate way she could, and she knew she had done it only out of love.

She could barely think about that now, but she had to face it. In the short time she'd known him, she'd started to love him, to want him and to need him. And she couldn't take him pushing her away like this. Denying he was involved in any way with her life. She remembered the way he had touched Rocky. "You say you don't care about anything, but you went after Mr. Appleton tonight," she said. "Why?"

"You're reading more into it than there was. I thought the guy acted like a jerk. That's all. Period."

"So, you don't want to get involved? You don't want to become important to anyone, or let them become important to you?" She clutched the sheet so tightly over her breasts that her hands tingled. "You think you're going to slip through this life without having to emotionally support anyone, or be responsible for anyone's happiness? That you do your job, nothing more?"

He moved abruptly, turning from her to sit up and throw his legs over the side of the bed. "That sounds too cold," he muttered. "I simply don't ask anything of anyone, and I don't want anyone asking anything of me."

She barely controlled the urge to strike out at him, to pound her fists against his back until he felt the pain she was experiencing. She damned the day he'd come back into her life and made her feel things again. She didn't want to feel this pain, this anger, this sense of desertion. He couldn't do this to her, yet he was. He had brought her to life, literally, then turned his back. "You think you're so smart," she gasped.

He stood and turned to her, his naked body almost painful for her to look at. She knew him, she could almost feel him under her hands, yet he stood there as detached as any stranger could be. "No, I'm just realistic. I'm more like my parents than I ever thought. But, unlike them, I know my limitations, what I'm capable of and what I'm not."

She swallowed hard; then words spilled out that she had never thought she would say to him. "You never asked me how my husband died or what happened to me when he did."

Brady reached for his jeans and put them on, then turned to Jayne as he zipped them up. "What's that to me?"

"Aren't you at all interested?"

"It's none of my business."

"Yes it is. Elliot died in an automobile accident two years ago on May fifth. I was hurt. My head struck the windshield.'' With trembling hands she pushed back her hair to show the scars near her temple on the right side. ''They had to do a lot of work on me, and it took a long time for me to heal. A lot of pain. And during that time, a funny thing happened to me. I decided that I had to get away.''

Brady stood by the bed, completely still.

''And you know what I did, Brady?'' she demanded, her voice shaking so badly she could barely get the words out. ''I crawled out on the ledge of Santa Barbara Memorial, and decided I could fly. I was going to fly away and leave all the pain behind me. I couldn't take it anymore. There was no reason for me to stay around.''

She could see his shock, then realization as he remembered. But she kept talking. ''And I would have tried to fly, I would have plunged to my death, but there was this voice.'' She didn't realize she was crying until she tasted the saltiness of tears on her lips, but she kept going. ''A voice spoke to me, making contact with me. Then someone took a chance of dying himself to get hold of me and drag me inside.''

Brady knelt on the bed facing her. ''It was me, wasn't it?''

''Yes.''

''How did you know?''

''The voice. I finally knew when the car tried to force me off the road.'' She swiped at her eyes. ''You were there. You saved my life.''

He shook his head sharply. ''I was doing—''

''Your job? Baloney! You saved my life. That's getting involved. That's getting in on a gut level and caring beyond anything that most people ever experience in this life.''

''You don't understand.''

"Yes I do. You're the one who doesn't. You don't even know what you're capable of. You've got your ideas, and you push yourself to fit them."

Brady stood again, moving back, distancing himself. "God, I never thought it was you. I should have known."

"How could you? I was a mess. My face was bandaged. And it was two years ago. At the most it was an hour of your life, but it gave me the rest of mine. Fate brought you there and made it possible for me to start over, then start Loving Touch and help babies like Rocky. So even if you don't mean to, you changed all our lives, Brady. You've changed mine."

He shook his head, but before he could say anything the phone by the bed rang. He stood still, letting it ring; then the answering machine snapped on in the living room. Jayne heard Brady's voice on the prerecorded message, then a beep and the voice she recognized as Captain Burkhart's.

"Knight, just want to let you know I can't get anyone else to take over for you with the Spencer woman. You're in there as her bodyguard for the duration. Anything in the files you took home? Contact me as soon as you can."

There was a pause, a beep, then silence.

Jayne looked at Brady. He'd been trying to get away from her, even before last night. The idea made her feel incredibly foolish. At least he had no idea what their time together had meant to her, and she wasn't going to tell him. "You tried to get someone else to protect me?"

He shrugged sharply. "I'm not a baby-sitter. I'm a cop. I want to be out there finding the creep who's messing up everyone's lives."

"Even..." She couldn't put it into words, the way she had felt when he took time to get protection from the bathroom. Now she knew he'd been terrified of getting her pregnant and making a commitment whether he wanted to or not.

He turned from her and crossed to the bathroom door. With his hand on the knob, he looked back. "Don't believe in fairy tales. They only end up hurting you."

"I believe there's a reason for everything," she whispered. "There's a reason why you came into my life in the first place, and there's a reason why you're here with me now."

He shook his head. "Luck. Dumb, stupid luck," he muttered, then went into the bathroom and closed the door.

Jayne felt as if whatever it was that had made her feel alive and aware had been snatched from her. She could feel herself sinking into a place of nothingness. No feelings, no pleasure, no pain. And she found herself fighting it. Not again. Not now. Not even if Brady walked right out of her life and proved that she had been completely wrong about him.

She got out of the bed, dressing quickly in jeans and a loose cotton blouse that the policewoman had packed for her. Then she pulled a brush through her tangled curls, but she didn't twist her hair into a knot. She left it loose around her shoulders and didn't bother with makeup.

She heard water running in the bathroom, and without a glance at the closed door, she went out into Brady's living room and through to the kitchen.

She had to keep moving, to do something, anything, and she found herself looking in the cupboards to find coffee and the coffeepot. When coffee was on its way, she went into the living room, flipped on the television to a morning news show, then sat back.

She stared at the screen, not really looking, not really listening. Absentmindedly she twisted her wedding ring around and around. Then she looked down at it. Slowly she did what she'd been unable to do until now. She slipped it off, then closed her hand around the simple gold band. A part of her life was done, over with, and the ring symbolized that life.

She reached for her purse on the floor, slipped the ring in a side pocket, then caught sight of the computer printout. She lifted the top part of the stack, tucked her bare feet under her and rested the pages on her knees. She hated the slight unsteadiness in her hands when she began to flip through the printout, but had to make herself concentrate on something besides what had just happened. Had to hide from the fact that Brady had wanted to be rid of her before things had even begun.

Life wasn't all it was cracked up to be, but it was better than the alternative. She might have made a mistake with Brady, but something deep inside told her that nothing with him could truly be wrong. She wished she could let go, let Fate take its course, whether to keep Brady in her life or take him out of it. She wished she could accept either scenario, but she wasn't quite that trusting.

She knew Brady wasn't the way he saw himself. She saw the caring, the ability to help people and make a difference. But he didn't.

She focused on the papers in front of her while the television news droned on in the background. She skimmed each file, not even knowing what she was looking for. Maybe just a distraction. That was probably it.

"Coffee?" she heard Brady say.

When she looked up, he was coming into the living room, his hair damp from the shower, and, thankfully, he was slipping on a T-shirt, covering his bare chest. It was bad enough that she could literally smell the soapy freshness that clung to him and the astringent after-shave. She swallowed hard and looked down at the files on her lap. "It's probably ready by now."

He walked past her into the kitchen, and she heard him moving around, the clink of glass on glass; then the sofa shifted as he sat on the far end.

"How do you take it?"

"Black is fine," she murmured without looking away from the file in front of her.

She caught the movement as Brady put a mug near her on the coffee table, then felt the sofa shift as he reached for some papers on the floor between them.

"Find anything?"

"I don't even know what I'm looking for," she admitted, wondering how they could be talking so civilly when she felt as if the world had veered a hundred and eighty degrees off course.

"Anything that rings a bell, that seems out of place or maybe even familiar when it shouldn't."

She slanted him a look, unnerved to find him staring at her. When their gazes met, he looked away. So did she, back at the files. "Killen, Davis Evan. First degree homicide."

"Killen? I remember. He shot his girlfriend. He thought she'd been seeing another man, and he waited for her at her house, shot her five times, then sat on the stoop and waited for the police to come. Open and shut. He made a full confession. He's still inside."

"Yes, he's not eligible for parole for ten years." She flipped to the next page. "LaRusso, Stanley David. He—"

"—is dead. He committed suicide in prison."

She flipped the page on LaRusso. She saw the next name but didn't believe it. "Miles, DeForest Lee?"

She felt Brady shift again. "Our senatorial candidate. Open and shut. Self-defense."

"I had no idea. When . . . ?" She looked at the date of the killing. The day after she'd been in the accident. She hadn't paid attention to much back then. "You worked on this?"

"Yeah. He called the station to report a shooting. A man was dead."

She read further on the report. "John Delgado, 27, from Santa Barbara."

"Yeah, that's the guy. He was killed, so homicide took it. Jack and I got the call. It seems Delgado was a petty crook, drug pusher and user. He broke into Miles's house and got shot. One shot, through the heart. The guy had a gun but didn't fire it. It was open and shut, self-defense."

"What was he doing in Miles's house?"

"Breaking and entry, burglary. Miles lives in a mansion. Old money, from way back. He heard the guy, got the drop on him, and when the guy pulled his gun, Miles shot him."

"He's not running on a gun control platform, is he?"

"No, he's law and order all the way but anti gun control." She could feel him looking at her. "You really didn't know anything about it?"

"No, I didn't." She stared at the computer printout.

"It was on the news, in all the papers."

"And I was in the hospital," she muttered, reaching for her coffee and gulping the hot liquid so quickly it scalded her throat. She coughed, then sat back with the mug in her hand. "There are three months where I don't remember much, except—" She cut off her words, not about to tell him that the one stunning memory in that time was his voice, his caring, his saving her life.

He didn't pursue it. Instead, he reached for a sheet of paper that had been tucked in with the printout. "I got a list of the pros." He scanned it. "None is supposed to be close to Santa Barbara right now." He tossed the paper onto the coffee table and got up, then went out into the kitchen. "How about some toast or..." She heard the refrigerator open. "...peanut butter on bread...or cold pizza?"

She looked at the kitchen, at Brady, his head stuck in the refrigerator. If he only knew what he was capable of feeling, of being. But she couldn't convince him. "No, no thanks. Coffee's fine."

He straightened, closed the refrigerator door and ran both hands through his hair. Tension was in every line of his lean body, the tension she was feeling, too. He turned to her, and their eyes met, but at the same time the phone rang. Automatically she started to reach for it, but Brady moved quickly, coming over to stop her hand before it could make contact with the receiver.

His grip was tight, just this side of pain. "Never do that. No one knows you're here except Elaine and the captain. And that's the way it has to be."

She stared up at him, tears coming from nowhere to cloud her vision. She looked away quickly, wishing her emotions weren't so close to the surface. She didn't speak when Brady lifted the receiver.

"Yes?"

It took him a moment to focus on the voice on the phone, a voice that spoke slowly, carefully. "Is this Detective Knight?"

"Who wants to know?"

"Dr. Kincaid. I'm on staff at Santa Barbara Memorial." Not the baby, Brady found himself wishing, not now.

"Yes, what is it?"

"Your partner, Jack Wills—"

"What?" Brady asked abruptly. "What's going on?"

"Detective Knight, your partner came out of his coma. He's weak but stable, and with the respirator tubes out, he can speak. He wants to talk to you as soon as you can get here."

Brady felt such relief that it left him giddy for a moment. Then he found his voice. "I'll be right there. And, doctor?"

"Yes?"

"Thank you for calling. Tell Jack I'm on my way."

He put down the receiver and turned to Jayne. "Jack's regained consciousness, and he wants to talk to me right away."

Sudden relief lit her face, and a slow smile lingered in her eyes. "Oh, God, that's wonderful. That's terrific!" She stood. "Just let me get my shoes on and I'll—"

"You'll stay here," he said with more abruptness than he intended. He needed the break, to get away for a few moments. "You're safe. No one knows you're here, and I won't be gone for long."

She stood very still. "No, I need to go to the hospital, too." The smile was gone now. "I need to see Rocky."

Not that, not now. But he didn't know what to say to fight her. Finally he gave in. "All right, but let's hurry up and get out of here."

Jayne had a pair of running shoes on and was at the door by the time he had retrieved his holstered gun and his car keys. Without a word, he opened the door, stepped out into the brightness of the sunny morning first, then, seeing it was clear, motioned her to follow.

He slipped on his dark glasses and led the way down to the Camaro. Silently he got in, waited for Jayne to settle, then started the engine and drove off.

Impatient with the morning traffic he encountered as soon as he turned onto the main street, Brady hit the siren and attached the flashing emergency light. As the way opened for him, he hurried toward the hospital.

In record time he was pulling into the parking lot and slipping into an empty slot right by the entrance. Jayne was out of the Camaro as quickly as he was, and together they ran up the steps and through the lobby to the elevators. He hit the fourth floor button first. He had to see that Jayne was safe before he left her.

On the fourth floor, Jayne hurried ahead of him to a nurse nearby. He could hear them talking, discussing the babies; then he walked up to them.

Interrupting, he asked Jayne, "Where can you stay while I go up to Jack?"

Jayne looked at the nurse. "Can I hold Rocky for a while?"

"No, I don't think so, but Mandy's going to a foster home this afternoon. How about holding her for a while?"

"Fine. I'd love to." She looked at Brady. "I'll be in the Forest Room as soon as I get a cover-up."

"I can't leave you here," he said, impatient to see Jack but knowing he shouldn't leave Jayne.

"I'll be fine."

"I'm due for a break," Paula said, turning to Jayne. "I can sit in the Forest Room while you feed Mandy."

"That's fine, isn't it?" she asked Brady.

"Get her a cover-up," he said to Paula, and as the woman in white hurried off, he turned to Jayne. "I don't like this, but—"

"You need to talk to Jack. Go up and see him. Find out what he knows, and maybe this nightmare will be finished and done. I'll be all right."

He hated the nervousness in his stomach, the excitement because maybe he could really find the assailant now that Jack was conscious. But even more he hated the feeling that he was afraid to leave Jayne for any reason. As Paula came back with the plastic-wrapped white cotton garment, he made a decision. "All right. I'll send an officer down to be with you as soon as I get up to Jack's room. Don't leave the Forest Room for any reason." He hesitated, barely covering the need in him to touch her. Instead, he moved back a bit. "For any reason."

"I understand," she said softly as she took the packet from Paula.

He walked with the two women to the Forest Room, his hands balled tightly into fists in his pockets. Then he moved past the two women and pushed the door open, but he didn't go in. He looked to make sure the room was empty, then stood back and let the women pass.

He found himself holding his breath as Jayne passed him, then exhaling when she was safely inside the room. "I'll be back as soon as I can. You stay put," he said and left without giving her a chance to say anything.

He hurried down the hall to the elevators, saw that all three cars were on their way down and stared at the indicators as if he could coax them back to the fourth floor. After a few seconds he muttered a curse and headed for the door marked Stairs. He hurried up the stairs two at a time.

When he opened the door on the fifth floor, he stared out into the corridor, then hurried down it, past the empty nurses' station and farther along the hall. The policeman stationed at the decoy room was a man Brady didn't recognize, so he kept going.

At Jack's room he hesitated, looked both ways, then opened the door and went inside. But he stopped dead when he saw that the bed was empty, neatly made and with no sign that Jack had been there except for a monitor standing silent.

He stepped back out into the hall, checked the room number in case he had picked the wrong one, then hurried down the hall to the cop. "Where's Jack Wills?" he asked abruptly.

The man glanced at him. "Who wants to know?"

Brady tugged his badge out of his pocket and flipped the holder open. "Where is he?"

"They changed rooms, sir. He's all the way at the end, the last one on the right, 580."

Brady muttered his thanks. As he hurried back down the corridor, he wondered why the doctor hadn't told him about the change. At 580, he knocked softly before pushing the door back.

The officer in the chair by the door was on his feet before Brady had the door open, his hand on the gun at his side. "Oh, it's you," he said, then sank back down.

Brady did little more than nod before turning to the bed. He knew as soon as he saw Jack that something was wrong, terribly wrong. The respirator was still on, the monitor beeping softly in the background, and Jack was very still.

Brady turned to the cop. "What's going on here? I was told that Jack was out of the coma, that he wanted to talk to me."

The man shook his head. "Who told you that?"

"A doctor. Dr. Kincaid."

"Never heard of him. I might have missed him, but no Dr. Kincaid's been in here since I've been here." He looked at Jack, his expression strained. "And he hasn't moved, let

alone come out of it. We had to talk his wife into going
home for a while. She's been here ever since they brought
him in, and he—''

Brady didn't let the man finish. He suddenly understood, and he was already out the door into the hall. He'd
been pulled out into the open and he'd pulled Jayne with
him. He ran down the corridor, past the nurses' station to
the elevators. He caught the doors of the nearest one just
as they were closing and pulled them back. He lunged inside, startling the old couple who were already there, and
hit the button for the fourth floor.

The car slid silently downward, and all Brady could hear
was the beating of his own heart in his ears. Jayne. God,
he felt sick. He'd been taken in. Drawn away. He should
have made her stay at the apartment.

But he'd only been gone a few minutes. Not enough
time, he thought; then, as the doors slid open, he forced
himself to face the truth: a second was enough time to fire
a gun.

He took off at a dead run for the Forest Room. Then,
pulling his gun free of the holster, he pushed the door
slowly back until he had a clear view of the room in front
of him.

''What the hell?'' the only occupant said, and Brady
recognized the voice at the same time that he recognized
the man—Appleton. He was standing in the middle of the
room, a sleeping baby held awkwardly in his arms. His
eyes behind his glasses were huge and directed at Brady's
gun.

''Where is she?'' Brady demanded.

''Listen, I've had enough of this. I came back to try and
figure out if I could do this and—''

Brady moved closer. ''*You* listen. Where is Mrs. Spencer?''

"Gone. A man came in, said something to her, then she handed me the baby and left. She said, 'Just hold her for a minute until the nurse comes.' Then she took off. Just like that."

"What man?"

"I don't know. A doctor, I think. He didn't introduce himself before she handed me this baby, and—"

"When did she leave?"

"A few minutes ago."

"Where was she going?"

"I don't know," Appleton all but yelled. "But put that gun away."

Brady closed his eyes for a fleeting moment. The killer had Jayne. And he didn't know where to begin to look for her. "The other nurse that was in here, where is she?"

"She left as soon as I arrived. She said since Mrs. Spencer had company, she'd get back to the floor." Appleton looked startled when Mandy let out a whimper. "I'm not staying here, Detective. This place is crazy. I'm leaving. Take this . . . this . . ."

"Baby, Mr. Appleton, she's a baby," Brady muttered. "And a nurse will be here soon."

"I can't—"

"You damn well can!" Brady bit out. "Or you'll answer to me."

Then he hurried out into the corridor as he put his gun back in his holster. Nothing looked out of place. No one seemed to be looking at him, but before he could decide what to do next, a voice came over the speaker. "Detective Knight, Detective Brady Knight, please report to any nurses' station for a phone call."

He turned and sprinted down the hall to the nurses' station and felt relieved to see Paula there. "Where's Jayne?"

he demanded as he came to a stop, his hands gripping the front of the desk.

She frowned. "In the Forest Room with Mr. Appleton." She held out the phone to him. "You've been paged."

He took the receiver from her. "Detective Knight," he said, hoping it was Burkhart or someone else from the department.

"You did good, Detective. Brought yourself and the woman, now listen and listen good," said the same voice that had pretended to be Dr. Kincaid. "You've got exactly three minutes to get on the last elevator, number three. It's the only one that goes to the top floor, where they're doing construction. When you get there, step off, take out your gun so I can see it and let the elevator doors close. No backup, no one with you, no police at all...except you. I'll know if you contact anyone."

"Who the hell...?"

"Three minutes, then she'd dead."

"Listen to me. I'm not stepping out of the elevator unless I see Jayne and she's not harmed."

"Three minutes starting right...now." The phone clicked in his ear.

Chapter 13

Brady took off at a run for the elevators. He pushed the Up button, and the doors of the last elevator opened almost immediately. As he stepped inside, he looked at the single occupant, a young man in a T-shirt and jeans.

It took Brady a second to recognize Officer Neibauer. "What are you doing here?" Brady asked.

"Just seeing how things are going, sir."

Thank heavens the rookie was so involved in the department. "Where are you getting off?"

The doors shut, and the elevator started upward. "Five."

"Have you got your piece with you?"

"No, I'm off duty and I left my gun in—"

"Never mind. Just listen to me and do what I say without asking questions."

The rookie nodded, and Brady spoke quickly. "When you get off, call Burkhart and tell him the suspect is on the top floor of the hospital where the construction is going on. He's armed. He's got a hostage, and I'm going up. I need backup but without noise—no sirens, no lights. Tell him to wait until he gets a signal from me to show himself."

Neibauer looked more and more intent as Brady spoke to him. "What signal, sir?"

"Any gunshot."

The elevator stopped, but Brady held the Door Closed button for a second. "Don't say anything to anyone before you talk to Burkhart, and *don't* use a public telephone."

"Yes, sir," the rookie said. Then the doors slid back. As he went past Brady into the corridor, he said softly, "We'll be right behind you."

Brady hoped so. The doors closed again on the sight of Neibauer's retreating back; then the car started upward. Every nerve in his body was painfully alive. His focus was crystal clear. He had to get Jayne, no matter what it cost him, and get her out alive.

He watched the lights flash off and on as the floors passed, and he found himself accepting something in that instant that he had never accepted before. There was a rhyme and reason to this existence. Fate, or destiny, had a part to play. There was something beyond himself, the same something that had brought Jayne into his life and brought him to her when she had almost killed herself. The same something that had made him love her from the first, even if he'd never realized it until now.

The same power that had put Neibauer on the elevator and Appleton in the Forest Room. Maybe, just maybe...

The elevator stopped. Brady took a breath as the doors began to slide open at the eighth floor. For a fleeting instant he prayed fervently that Jayne would survive whatever was going to happen; then he forced himself to stay calm and look ahead.

Jayne was no more than twenty feet from him in the middle of the shadowy construction area. The only light was what filtered in from the outside through the unfinished windows. Drop cloths, stacks of drywall, tubs of paint, and power tools were everywhere. Jayne stood very still, her hands clutched in front of her, her hair loose and wild around her pale face.

Then Brady saw the man behind her, a shadowy figure with a baseball cap pulled low and a gun pressed to Jayne's temple.

"Jayne, are you all right?" he called out, one hand holding the elevator doors open, the other itching to reach for his gun.

She nodded in a jerky motion, her tongue darting out to touch her lips. "I'm sorry. He made me come with him," she gasped. "He was going to hurt the baby. I'm so sorry..."

He couldn't believe she was apologizing. "Forget it."

"You made it easy. She couldn't stay away from the kids and you couldn't stay away from your partner."

Brady looked at her abductor. "This is your show. What now?"

"Get out. Let the doors close, then put your gun in the open paint bucket to your right."

Brady did exactly as he was told.

"Careful," the man said when Brady started to remove his gun. "Finger and thumb."

Brady pulled the gun out of the holster, never taking his eyes off Jayne while he extended his arm to his right and let go of the gun. He heard a dull splash, then a gurgle as it sank into the thick paint.

"What do you want?" he asked, trying to buy time until Burkhart could get his men in position.

"To get this over and done with. I'm not getting paid for this mess."

Paid? His hunch had been right. The man was a professional. He'd been brought here to do a job, and Jack and Jayne had both gotten in his way. But who had brought him here? Brady began to talk, hoping to draw the killer out and keep the inevitable at bay.

"He didn't pay you enough for this, did he?" he said.

"No, he didn't," the man muttered. "Especially since both your partner and you figured it out." He pushed Jayne closer to Brady. "A real mess."

"Yeah, Jack caught on before I did." He took a guess. "I don't bother with closed cases. That's Jack's obsession."

"He should have left this one alone. Maybe he gets off on bringing people down." The man actually laughed. "Everyone does, one way or another."

"No, you've got it wrong. Jack hated what he had to do. He didn't want to mess up people's lives. But he's honest, and he hates loose ends."

"I can relate to that," the man said, jerking Jayne more tightly back against him. "It's down to this, isn't it? You two dead, along with your partner, in exchange for Miles getting to be senator without anyone knowing about his drug problem or his past. I wonder if the man's worth the trouble."

Miles? Brady hoped his face didn't show shock. He would never have guessed that DeForest Miles had done anything illegal beyond getting an occasional speeding ticket. Now he knew. The breaking and entry, the dead man in Miles's home. Drugs. Things began to click. "You didn't take out Delgado, did you?"

He laughed at that. "Hell, no. Miles did his own dirty work then and passed it off as a burglary. And it worked, for a while."

Brady realized that the man didn't want to create a scene. He wanted to take care of Jayne and himself without anyone knowing so he could get to Jack. If anyone found Brady and Jayne dead before the killer could complete his work, Jack would be untouchable. That was Brady's one trump card, and he was going to play it. He kept talking. "If you didn't hit Delgado for Miles...?" He let his voice trail off with the unfinished question while he moved a bit closer, narrowing the gap between himself and Jayne and the hit man.

"I came in after that, when someone else came into the picture. It was all the luck of the draw, the flip of a coin, that I happened to be available."

No, Brady could see the threads of the lives of all the people involved. No flip of the coin could make something like this come together.

The killer shook his head. "Delgado could just as easily have been working alone and it would have been over when Miles shot him. Or his brother could have been denied parole last month and never come back here to try and shake down Miles."

"It looks like everyone involved got the short end of the stick, even you." Brady narrowed his eyes. "Do you have a name?"

The man studied him intently and Brady realized his eyes were dark, not pale. He'd even thought to wear contacts. "I guess you should know who's taking you out. King. That's my professional ID."

It made deadly sense to Brady now. Blackmail and a man to clean up the resulting mess, a man who would kill both him and Jayne without batting an eye. But he wasn't about to make it easy for King, to go meekly or let Jayne go easily. He took another half step forward, cutting the distance to about six feet.

He was close enough to hear Jayne's ragged breathing, and it was all he could do to stay put and not look right at her, but he didn't take his eyes off King. Now he could see the pale eyes and the absence of fire there, just grim determination.

"Once this is over, I'll finish the job on your partner, then I'm out of here," King said.

And you can't let this be messy or noisy, Brady thought. A break for the good guys. Now all he had to do was get the gun.

"I'll pretend I never heard of DeForest Miles...until he gets to be president." King laughed at that, and Brady saw his chance to act as the gun lowered just a fraction of an inch.

He lunged forward, striking the gun with the heel of his hand and sending it sailing across the littered floor. He sensed Jayne swinging free to her right; then she was out of sight, and Brady grasped the man and yelled, "Jayne, get the gun!"

In the split second after Jayne saw Brady lunging at King, she realized what he was doing and jerked free from the man's hold. She heard Brady yelling at her to get the gun, and she twisted around just in time to see it land in a heap of drop cloths.

Brady was struggling with King, rolling on the floor, knocking over empty paint containers and crashing into an open tool chest, sending the loose tools flying everywhere. She ran to where the gun had landed, dropping to her hands and knees, pushing frantically at the jumble of paint-stiffened cloths to find it.

All the while she could hear the sounds of the struggle, the crashes, the scuffling, the muttered curses. And the louder they got, the more frantically she clawed at the cloths. Then she felt something hard and cold, and she closed her hand over the grip of the gun and tugged it free.

She lurched to her feet, running back to where Brady and the killer were rolling amid the debris and pointed the gun at the two men. She felt for the trigger with her finger and gasped, "I've got it, Brady. I've got the gun."

But before she could do anything, the killer rolled away from Brady, jerking toward her, his body hitting her legs with such force that she lost her balance and went flying backward. The gun flew from her hand, and the next second she hit the littered floor so hard that she could feel the air rushing out of her lungs.

Wildly she struggled to get up, trying to suck in air as she grasped the side of a stack of drywall and finally pulled herself to her feet. King was so close that she could hear his grunt as he dropped to his haunches and grasped the gun. She knew he was going to turn, that he was going to shoot her, but before it could happen, a hand was closing over her arm and jerking her sideways.

Brady had a vicelike hold on her, pulling her across the floor, and she stumbled over her own feet for a second, then broke into a run with him, around a newly constructed corner.

He never stopped and never let go of her as they raced past the litter, going by framed-in cubicles that looked as if they were meant to be offices someday.

Brady kept running, taking Jayne with him through the clutter until they came to a solid, cement block barrier. He turned, and she could hear the sound of running feet somewhere close by. King was behind them, and there was no escape in front of them.

Jayne took painful gulps of air into her lungs and looked at Brady. She didn't have a chance to ask what they were going to do before he pulled her against him and whispered in her ear, "You and I are going to survive." His lips were so close that she could feel them brush her ear. "Do what I say, no questions asked. All right?"

She nodded; then Brady motioned toward a plastic-covered opening in the wall that showed daylight. "There," he said and pulled her toward it.

When Jayne got closer, she realized that the opening was an unfinished part of the back wall that led to nothing but the sky above and the city far below. She didn't understand until Brady let go of her, grabbed both sides of the rough opening and pulled himself up and out. For an instant she thought he was going to jump; then she saw him touch something solid and turn as he ducked to look back and beckon her on.

She inched closer and saw that he was standing on a ledge that was no more than a foot wide. "Out here," he said, his hand held out to her.

She couldn't move. "I . . . I can't."

Brady glanced behind her at the same time that she heard a sliding sound, then sharp footsteps. King was coming for them. "You have to," Brady whispered. "Now!"

She knew that she did have to, or she would die right there. She looked at Brady, at the grim determination etched deeply into his face. No, she didn't want to die. She took a deep breath, then reached for him with one hand and grasped the rough brick on her left with her other.

The next instant she was on the ledge, and all she could do was stare down eight floors to the sheer hillside the hospital was built on, where the land careened into a vast canyon that led out to the sea more than three miles away.

The wind whipped around her, and the world swam in front of her eyes. She couldn't draw any air into her lungs. Then Brady's voice was there, everywhere, soft, coaxing, insistent, seeping into her. The way it had been two years ago.

"Jayne, come on. You can do it. You have to do it." He squeezed her hand. "We have to do it. We can't stop now. We have to make it. We'll find another way in and get to the stairs or the elevator."

And Jayne knew she would make it. She knew as certainly as she had two years ago that this man knew what he was talking about. She found the ability to breathe, to make her feet slide slowly along the narrow ledge to her left. And she held tightly to Brady, who was close behind her.

After a few more steps he whispered, "A ladder. It must go up to the roof."

She barely turned her head, just enough to see the glint of metal in the morning sunlight. Then Brady was shifting, actually passing her, and she never took a breath until he was on the other side. "Grab the ladder and climb," he said close to her right ear.

It was all she could do to stretch out her hand. Then she felt the cold metal, wrapped her fingers tightly around it and went closer.

"Hurry," he said, so close to her that she could feel his heat against her side.

She managed to twist, and then she was holding the ladder with both hands. She felt her legs give way; then she steadied herself and began to climb. It seemed to take an eternity before she felt the handrails curl at the top of the safety ladder; then she took two more steps and almost fell forward onto the flat roof.

She steadied herself, and suddenly Brady was there, reaching for her hand again, then pulling her with him away from the ladder to the shelter of one of the many sheet metal air vents that soared eight feet above the roof. He stopped when they were safely out of sight, and then they both leaned back against the solid support.

Jayne closed her eyes for a fleeting moment; then she felt Brady move. When she opened her eyes, she saw him looking around the edge of the vent. "Damn it, I can't see where the stairs are. They have to be here. There has to be a way in."

"Can't we just stay up here until he leaves?"

He turned to her, his eyes narrowed against the glare of the sun. "Sorry. He won't give up. He can't afford it."

"Don't you have something, a hidden gun or a knife?"

He shook his head. "On television I'd have a conveniently hidden derringer, but this is real life. My one and only gun is down there soaked in paint." He leaned back, his head resting against the dull metal.

This is real life. Jayne stared at him, the wind ruffling his sun-streaked hair, the way his jaw worked, and she felt his hand still holding tightly to hers. In that moment the loner cop, the man who didn't believe he could make a commitment to anyone, and the man she had made love with—the man she loved—blended completely. Brady Knight was Brady Knight. He might not know what he could be, but she did, and she loved him for what he was and what he would be. And she couldn't envision life without him.

Right then there was a sound, a scuffing noise, and Brady jerked straight. He carefully looked around the side of the vent again, then moved back closer to Jayne. "Here he comes," he whispered. "Don't move until I give you the go ahead, then you run that way." He motioned with his

free hand. "The way down must be over there somewhere. Find it and get the hell out of here."

Jayne stared at Brady. "And what are you going to do?"
she whispered unsteadily.

"Wait." He looked at her for a long moment. "And do
what I have to."

She saw him so clearly that it was almost painful. And
she felt a love that didn't need any rationalizations or reasons. It existed. It was as simple as that. In the short time
she'd known him, he'd become the core of her existence,
and she didn't want to live without him. "Brady," she said
softly, suddenly knowing that there was no reason not to
say the words that had only been in her heart up until now.
"Do you know I love you?"

Brady heard her words and felt something akin to real
pain radiate through his body. She loved him. Yes, he
knew it. He'd probably known it ever since the first time
she had touched him. Yet it shattered him to hear the
words said out loud. It made the concept real, very real.

And it shattered him to admit that he'd loved her from
the start, a love that had only deepened when they'd lain
together, when they'd known each other last night. Surely
she'd felt it in his touch, in his kiss, in his giving of himself to her.

He wanted to say the words himself, to throw caution to
the winds and open himself to what he knew she could give
him. He craved that release, hoping that if the words were
said, it might be possible for him to become the man she
wanted, the man she needed. And he knew one thing
clearly, that he would give his life to make her happy.

Then he heard the ladder jiggling as the killer climbed
to the roof, and he knew he might have to do just that.
And he knew he would. As corny as it sounded, he would

die if it meant Jayne would live. That was it. And that stopped him from saying what he wanted to say to her.

He couldn't do that to her, just to have her lose someone again. He couldn't tell her that he loved her more than life itself, then leave her.

"No you don't," he heard himself saying, hating the words even as he uttered them. But she had to go, and she couldn't look back. She had to leave him. He pulled his hand free. "It's the heat of the moment, the intensity of the situation. It certainly isn't love." He saw the pain he was inflicting, knowing it was nothing compared to what she would endure if he told her that he loved her, then died. "We've only known each other a few days. My God, that's not enough time to even tell if we like each other."

He saw the pain on her face and hated himself. Yet he knew he was right. "Forget everything but getting out of here." Then he forced himself to add, "I have. This is all that counts. Getting this guy. Now, get the hell out of here. And don't look back."

She seemed frozen for a heartbeat; then she hugged her arms around herself. Thank God there were no tears. He didn't know what he would have done if there had been tears. "You...you want to do this alone?" she whispered.

"The way I always have," he said quickly. "That's the way I want things."

He saw her swallow hard, then move a fraction of an inch away from him. "All right."

The hardest thing he'd ever had to do was to stop himself from reaching out to draw her back to him and hold her for one last moment. "Get out of here now. Quietly."

Before she could do or say anything else, Brady turned from her, knowing he had to block Jayne from his mind so he could concentrate on what had to be done.

She stayed very still. No tears. No words. He'd cut her off as neatly as a surgeon. Alone. He wanted to be alone. Her heart ached for what might have been. What could have been. She saw Brady inch closer to the edge of the vent; then he whispered, "Get out."

She moved back farther, then turned and started to run blindly in the direction he'd indicated. But before she got more than twenty feet, she heard Brady yell, "I'm over here!"

She stopped and turned, then moved toward the far side of the nearest air vent. She looked around it, but she couldn't see Brady anywhere. Then she caught a movement by the edge of the roof. King was there, right by the ladder, the gun in his hand. "You can't get away from here," he yelled.

"You *won't* get away from here," Brady yelled back.

Jayne watched as King started forward. "I've got the gun. We'll see who gets out of here first."

There was a rustling sound; then she saw Brady race from behind the vent, a blur of movement as he dove behind the next one, about ten feet away. King spun in that direction, his back to Jayne, his gun leveled at the metal barrier.

In that moment Jayne understood what Brady was doing. He was using himself for bait, drawing King's attention so she could get away. He'd done it again, risked his life for her. Yet he wouldn't let her be part of his life. She understood all too well how short-lived happiness could be, how unique it was to find real love in this world.

The odds were insurmountable that she would find it twice in one life, and yet she had. Maybe she couldn't be with Brady because he didn't want her, but she wasn't going to let him die up here. She quietly went to her left, keeping out of sight until she got within twenty feet of

King. Then she took a breath, stepped out into the open and stared at King's back. Her heart lurched in her chest, and she made herself say, "And *I'm* over here."

The killer had only half turned before Brady broke into the open and screamed, "No, Jayne, no," and ran at King.

The man turned at the same time that Jayne saw a flash of motion at the top of the ladder. Then the world was shattered with screams, guns exploding and a man in a T-shirt vaulting onto the roof.

Jayne screamed, "No, no!" as fire flared from the end of the killer's gun, an explosion ripped the world apart and Brady jerked as if hit in the stomach by a giant fist. Another explosion overlapped the first, and King seemed to arch back, his head lifted to the sky, his eyes closed, his arms thrown out to both sides as his gun sailed through the air.

Then Brady was pitching forward, striking the man in the chest, and both men fell flat.

Jayne heard someone screaming Brady's name; then she realized it was her and somehow found the ability to move. She ran, her feet feeling as if they were mired in thick mud, and it took an eternity to get to Brady and kneel by him. She tugged frantically at his arm until he rolled heavily toward her and his head lolled into her lap.

She paid no attention to the hit man lying completely still on his back, his eyes wide and staring lifelessly into the morning sky.

All she saw was Brady; all she felt was the heaviness of him and the heat of his blood as it spread on the whiteness of his T-shirt and soaked into her clothes. His blood.

"No, no," she sobbed. It couldn't end like this, not now, not this soon. She wanted years with him, a lifetime. Not days and minutes.

Then someone was over her, touching her shoulder. The man from the ladder spoke softly. "Ma'am," he said and gripped her arm, trying to lift her to her feet.

But she wrenched free, pulling Brady to her, knowing that she couldn't let him go. If she did, he could slip away forever. "No, no," she sobbed, brushing at his hair, feeling the cold clamminess of his skin under her fingers.

"Ma'am, please," the man over her said. "Help's coming. They'll be here any minute now. They'll take care of him."

Brady moaned, and his eyelids fluttered; then Jayne was looking into the unfocused blueness of his eyes. His tongue touched his lips, and he took a shuddering breath, whispering hoarsely, "I . . . I told you to leave."

His hand lifted, almost touched her cheek, but never made contact. With a shuddering sigh Brady closed his eyes, his hand fell to his stomach, and he slumped heavily against her once again.

Chapter 14

When Brady regained consciousness, he knew immediately where he was and what had happened.

He opened his eyes to a green and white hospital room, inhaled the scents peculiar to a hospital and felt the searing pain in his left shoulder as soon as he tried to move to get a better look at his surroundings.

Cautiously he turned his head to look to his right at the closed door, then to the left at the curtain-covered window. He didn't know whether it was day or night, or how long he'd been out.

The pain. He tried to look at his left shoulder, but all he could make out was a lot of white that looked like bandages. It hurt enough for him to have had a whole new shoulder reconstructed, he thought as he sank back against the pillows.

He could tell he was in a gown of some sort. His clothes were gone. And he wanted out of here. He wanted to find Jayne. He remembered everything, including the words he'd said to drive her away, to make her leave. But she hadn't.

He closed his eyes, the image of her yelling at King etched in his mind. She'd come back and tried to create her own diversion. He needed to see her, to make sure she was all right.

Everything came down to the most simplistic equation for him. He was alive. Jayne was alive. He loved Jayne, and despite everything that happened, he realized more fully what had just begun to form in his mind as the elevator had gone up to the top floor.

There *was* a plan, a master layout, for this life. And Jayne was part of the plan for him. He wanted her here, and he didn't want to be alone anymore. He knew that as surely as he knew he loved her. As surely as he knew that, no matter what, he would become whatever she wanted him to be, and he would make her happier than she'd ever been before.

Being on his own wasn't what he wanted now. It had been right for him for a long time, but not anymore, not since Jayne.

He heard the door open and he looked to his right, hoping it was her, but instead a man in white strode into the room. Balding, short and wearing glasses, the man came to the bed and looked down at Brady.

"So, you're awake, Detective," he said as he reached for Brady's wrist and held it between his fingers as he looked at his wristwatch. "Good, good."

"What happened to my shoulder?" Brady asked.

The man let go of Brady's hand and bent forward to touch the bandages. "You got shot, and the bullet went right through. You passed out because you lost a lot of blood and went into shock, but you're doing just fine now. You'll have to take it easy for a while."

Brady flinched when the man nudged at the pain in his shoulder, then watched the doctor stand back. "I want out of here now."

The doctor shook his head. "Sorry. You can't get up yet." He folded his arms across his chest. "Rest for now, and I'll send someone in to check on you in a little while."

Before Brady could ask where his clothes were or what happened, the doctor turned and walked out.

As soon as the door closed behind him, Brady tried to sit up by grasping the safety rail on the side of the bed, but he had no strength. With a sigh, he sank back against the cool linen. He would lie here and rest until he felt strong enough to get up; then he would put on some clothes and go find Jayne.

That one need filled him. He had to find Jayne. He had to see her.

He stared at the ceiling, trying to concentrate and make some sense of what had happened on the roof, what he had said, what she had said. Things ran around and around in his head, but he always came back to the pain he'd seen on her face when he'd tried to get her to leave him there.

His thoughts shied away from that moment and drifted back to the first time he'd seen Jayne walking toward him down the hospital corridor. That sense of the familiar about her, that aura of beauty in her looks and her soul. Jayne. Warmth, love, tenderness. Lying with her and knowing her.

The images began to blur as his pain began to overpower whatever medication they had given him. Agony seared through him, from his shoulder down his left arm and up into his neck, like fire burning into his brain.

"Sir?" someone to his right said.

Slowly he opened his eyes and turned to see Neibauer beside him, his face as earnest as ever. Where had he come from? Never mind. "Neibauer. Just the man I wanted to see."

"Oh?"

"What's going on? No one's told me anything except that my wound is going to heal."

The kid shook his head. "There's been a lot going on."

"First, what time is it?"

The rookie looked at his watch. "Six-fifteen."

"Morning or night?"

"Oh, night. You've been out for a while. Your partner's doing fine. He came out of his coma two or three hours ago. He's expected to make a complete recovery, just the way you are." He frowned as he glanced at Brady's shoulder. "I'm real sorry you got shot. I was trying to stay out of sight. Then, before I could do anything, you were running at the guy and he was shooting."

He had only swirling memories of that moment, of Jayne being there, holding him as he blacked out. He managed the main question. "Jayne. Is she all right?"

"Mrs. Spencer is just fine. She's a tough one, too."

"Where is she? Do you know?"

"Sure, she's downstairs with the babies. She hasn't left the hospital all day. She's been—"

Brady cut Neibauer off, not wanting to know any more about the babies. He couldn't even form a question about Rocky. "Thanks. I get the picture." At least he knew where to find her as soon as he could get out of here.

"Sir?"

"Yes?" he responded as he tensed the muscle in his damaged shoulder, to test how much pain it would produce if he tried to get up again.

"Can I ask you something?"

The pain wasn't as bad as he'd thought. "Sure."

"How many men have you killed?"

Brady blinked and looked at the kid. "Killed?"

"How many men have you shot in the line of duty?"

Brady understood. "He's dead, isn't he?"

"Yes, sir," Neibauer said flatly. "I didn't mean to kill him. I was just trying to wound him."

Brady closed his eyes for a fleeting moment, then looked back up at Neibauer. "A cop should never draw his gun unless he's prepared to use it." He touched dry lips with his tongue. "And you never get used to killing someone. Never."

"Did you . . . ?"

"Once. Just once. But if I'd had a gun up there, I wouldn't have hesitated to kill King."

"King?"

"The hit man."

"Oh, yeah. His real name was Ray Kingdom."

"And he's dead?"

"Yes, sir, he's dead."

"What about Miles?"

Neibauer shrugged sharply. "It's been all over the news all day. He's denying everything, but your partner's got him dead to right. Wills dug up a connection between Delgado and Miles before the breaking and entry. When he was looking into that night, he saw Miles with Kingdom, then followed Kingdom. He lost him for a while, and by the time he picked up his trails again, Kingdom had killed Delgado's brother. He called you while Kingdom was taking care of the body, but when he went back, Kingdom must have heard something or seen something and went after him. That's when you got there, when he shot him. He probably didn't even know he was a cop, just a loose end, a witness he couldn't afford to have running around."

Brady felt weary with the world and with the ugliness in it. The idea of getting away, of walking as far away from it all as he could, came to him. Then he knew he couldn't do that, no more than he could walk away from Jayne.

"Neibauer? Do you think Jayne is still with the babies?"

"Yes, sir. She's not about the leave the hospital."

"Do me a favor?"

"Of course, sir."

"Find me some clothes. Or find out what they did with mine."

As soon as the kid left the room, Brady began the slow torture of sitting up.

Jayne sat alone in the Forest Room in one of the easy chairs. The nurse had just taken the last baby back to the nursery, and she was too weary to move. Too much had happened in too short a time. She didn't know what to do; she only knew she didn't want to go home alone and remember.

She would only think about Brady, about the hour and a half while they operated on him, about sitting by the bed watching him, knowing he wouldn't know she was there. Hoping he would awaken, yet also hoping he wouldn't. She had only wanted the connection, to see him breathing, to know he was alive and would survive.

She had stared at him, his features paler than normal, yet eased by sleep. His hair had clung damply to his temples, and the white of the bandages that covered his shoulder, part of his chest, and his upper arm had looked stark against his tanned skin.

She'd finally left, coming down here to be with the babies, but her thoughts had been with Brady. His image was burned in her mind, and she wondered if that would be all she had to sustain her in the days ahead. She didn't know. But she ached inside for something that had been hers for so little time.

Without warning the door opened, and she turned.

Brady was standing there wearing mussed jeans and a green surgical top. For a minute she thought she had conjured up his image; then he moved into the room, slowly, cautiously, and she knew he was very real.

"So, I found you," he said in a vaguely hoarse voice.

"What are you doing here?" she asked, getting to her feet and fighting the urge to go to him, to take him in her arms.

The deep blueness of his eyes unnerved her almost as much as the extreme paleness of his skin. She had to stop herself from backing away from him when he took another step toward her.

She clasped her hands in front of her, nervously lacing and unlacing her fingers. "How do you feel?"

"Like I've been kicked by a mule," he muttered. He moved haltingly to the closest chair; then, very slowly, bracing himself with his right arm, he sank down into the cushions.

She watched him sit back, and for the hundredth time she wondered how she would be able to go her whole life knowing he was in the world, yet not seeing him, or touching him, or lying beside him.

He closed his eyes for a moment, then looked up at her from under heavy lids. "You don't look any the worse for wear."

Just where you can't see it, she wanted to say, but she didn't. "You're the one who was hurt. He shot you, and then that young policeman, he shot King. His name was really Kingdom, Ray Kingdom. And he's dead. That poor boy was so shocked that he killed the man, but he didn't have a choice. I told him that. And Kingdom was dead right away, and I thought . . .'' No, she wouldn't say that. She wouldn't tell him how she had felt as if *she* were dying when she held him, certain he would bleed to death before anyone came to help.

She kept talking fast, words falling over words. "He's dead, and DeForest Miles, he's being interrogated. He's denying everything, but he's not going to be able to keep it up. Jack's got proof. His wife told me he does. He knows what happened, all about the killings and the drugs and things.''

She was rambling, but she couldn't stop. "I . . . I never saw anyone like that man Kingdom. He was wearing brown contact lenses. He just wanted to kill. He could have killed everyone and just walked away. He didn't care about anything. He didn't—''

"How's Rocky?'' Brady asked abruptly, stopping her dead.

She stared down at him. "What?''

"Rocky? How is he? Neibauer said you were up with the babies and I thought . . .'' He exhaled and started to touch his damaged arm with his good hand, but he stopped and flinched. "Damn. You'd think he shot me with a cannon, the way it feels.''

"No, it was a .32 automatic.''

He lifted one brow in her direction. "Oh?''

She felt her face flood with heat. "I heard one of the policemen say that, Captain Burkhart, I think.''

"I thought you'd heard it on television.''

She felt off balance, not knowing what to do or say.

"Jayne, tell me about Rocky.''

She bit her lip. "Do you care?''

He hesitated, then spoke softly. "Yes.''

She moved away from the chairs to go to the windows, unable to deal with Brady's presence, or with what she could have sworn was his genuine concern about Rocky. She opened the drapes and looked out at the twilight, remembering yesterday's twilight. How she wished she could go back to that time, to live through it again, but just up to the point where she and Brady made love.

She licked her lips. "Rocky's surprised everyone, including me. He's actually getting better." Why were tears forming in her eyes now? "He's started to suck. He's taking food, just a little, but it's a start. He's so stubborn."

"So are you."

She closed her eyes for a minute and swiped at her cheeks. "I am?"

"I told you to get out of there, to head for the stairs. To leave me there."

She pressed a hand to her eyes. "So you could draw his fire?"

There was silence behind her for a long time; then Brady finally spoke again. "Yes."

Her hand dropped as she turned to him. "You admit that?"

"Yes," he said simply.

"It . . . it was your job."

He shook his head. "No, I did it for myself."

Through the blur of welling tears, she stared at Brady. "For yourself? You would have let him kill you so I could get away?"

He laughed, a harsh, short sound that ended on a soft cough. "I didn't intend to die. I told you before, I never have that intention when I'm involved in a case."

"But you could have died."

"Yes, I could have."

"And . . . ?"

"I didn't. I'm here, and so are you. And I came down here against doctor's orders to tell you that I lied to you."

She tasted the saltiness of tears on her lips. "You lied?"

"Yes."

"But isn't that a law of yours, to always tell the truth?" she managed in a tear-choked voice.

"Laws are made to be broken." He held out his good hand to her. "Come here."

She hesitated, uncertain whether she could bear to be that close to Brady, to actually feel his touch. "No, I . . . I have to go. I need to go to the nursery and see Rocky." She checked her watch. "It's almost time for his feeding, and I—"

"Jayne, be quiet and come to me," Brady said, his voice stronger all the time.

Jayne stood where she was and spoke the truth. "No, I can't."

"Don't you want to know what lie I told you?"

"No . . . yes . . ." She shook her head. "I don't know."

"When you said you loved me, I said it was the heat of the moment, the intensity of the situation. I said a few days wasn't enough time to even tell if we liked each other. That I wanted to be alone."

She couldn't stand hearing him reiterate what he'd said before. "I remember," she whispered.

"Well, I lied. I've known you long enough to know that I love you. I've loved you since you walked down the hall and thought I was Appleton."

The words hung in the space between them until she managed to ask, "You love me?"

"I've never told anyone that before and really meant it. I need you, Jayne Spencer. I really need you. I don't want to be alone anymore."

Jayne felt a burden lift so suddenly that she felt giddy and so light that she could have floated to Brady. She went to him, took his hand in both of hers and looked down at him. "Are you sure?"

"Don't."

"Don't what?" she asked softly.

"Don't question what I'm offering. Just take it. Accept that this was meant to be."

"As in Fate?" she whispered.

"As in Fate brought you to me, and I love you," he said.

She stared at him. "I . . . I want to hold you," she said, "and I don't know how to without hurting you."

"Like this," he said, gently pulling her down to his lap, then shifting until she was held firmly against him with his good arm.

The world had suddenly righted itself, and everything looked the way she had hoped it would.

"Say it, Jayne," Brady whispered against her hair.

She sat back just a bit so she could look him in the eyes. "Say what?"

His face was sober, the lines deep at his mouth and eyes. "Just say it," he said hoarsely.

She brushed at his hair, trailed a finger down his jaw to his throat, then rested it on the hollow there where the surgical top came to a V. His pulse beat rapidly against the tip of her finger. He was scared, and in a way that made her feel more sure of everything. He wanted this as much as she did.

"All right. I'll say it. I love you, Brady Knight. I love everything about you, and I don't care if I've known you three hours or three days or three years. I couldn't love you more."

She heard him release a harsh breath; then his good hand tangled in her hair and drew her to him. The kiss was fierce and hard, a bond that was as strong as tempered steel.

Breathlessly she drew back and looked at him. "I want whatever you want, whatever life you want."

"*Any* life I want?"

"Yes."

"All right." He rested his head against the back of the chair. "I see a life for us in that huge house of yours."

"We don't have to live—"

"Shh. This is my vision, remember. I see us in that house, and I see a child, a girl with amber eyes who looks just like you."

She couldn't believe what he was saying. "A child?"

"Yes, *your* child."

"But, Brady—"

"When you told me Rocky was getting better, you have no idea how happy and relieved I was. Jayne, if a child that isn't mine can mean that much to me, think how much *our* child would mean."

She couldn't believe her ears. She'd known there was a part of Brady he hadn't even recognized, but this was wonderful. She touched his chin with one finger. "Listen, if we only have one child and it's a girl, you won't have a son. That's important, Brady, a son with blond hair and blue eyes, and who knows, he could be really different, the way you are. He might want to be a cop, or maybe he'll want to get into land development and make his grandpa happy by taking over the A.K. Corporation. He might even—"

Brady cut her off with a satisfying kiss, then whispered, "We'll let him decide that on his own, and we can negotiate on the number of brothers and sisters the two of them will get later."

Jayne smiled at Brady. "Is that a law?"

He shifted, cursing the way his arm hurt when he moved, then whispered against her lips. "Actually, my newest law just came to me in the past few days. It's a law that we have to make the most of every minute we have together and to love each other forever."

Jayne gave her wholehearted approval of Brady's new law with a deep and lasting kiss.

Epilogue

Are you sure you want to do this, Brady?"

"Absolutely. I said you needed to broaden your horizons, have new experiences, and this is one experience I want to share with you, Jayne."

"Well, I'm not too—"

"Sure you are. The man at the sporting goods store said this sleeping bag is big enough for three people and warm enough to be used in Alaska. I think the two of us on the beach in Santa Barbara on New Year's Eve can survive."

Jayne took off her shoes and socks, then quickly got out of the cold ocean air by climbing into the huge plaid bag Brady had laid out by the flat rock. She scooted down until she was up to her chin in the down-filled bag. Then Brady had his shoes off and was in the bag with her.

"If you say so," she murmured.

"I say so," he said as he shifted until he was firmly against her side.

Jayne looked up at the clear winter sky overhead. The temperature had dipped to the low forties, but the heavens were so clear that she could see the constellations, and a crescent moon looked as if it was close enough for her to reach up and touch.

"I also say that the less clothes you wear when you're in a sleeping bag, the warmer you get."

She could feel him shift away from her and awkwardly manage to take off his shirt. He tossed it out of the bag and into the darkness behind him. Then his jeans were off and following the shirt, then his briefs. He raised himself on one elbow and looked down at Jayne by his side. "Your turn, love."

She smiled up at her husband of six hours. "Is this really the way you want to spend the first night of our honeymoon and New Year's Eve?"

"Absolutely. My two favorite things in this world are the ocean and you. You can't beat that combination for ringing in the New Year."

She felt his hand touch her breast, and even through the cotton of her blouse, the contact made her gasp. She would never get used to the effect this man had on her, the way he could look at her, or simply touch her, and her whole body responded.

He grazed his hand over her breast and found the buttons of her shirt. "First this," he breathed, dipping to plant a kiss on her forehead. The buttons were quickly undone, and she shifted to help him slip her shirt off; then he tossed it with the other clothes. "Next this," he whispered as, with an expert move, he put his hand under her back, unsnapped her bra and discarded the scrap of flimsy lace.

She held her breath, waiting for his touch, her breast swelling in anticipation, but instead she felt his hand move lower to the waistband of her corduroy slacks. With one motion he had the button unsnapped and the zipper undone.

Jayne reached down to push at them, pulling up her legs until she was free of the slacks and Brady had them out of the bag, tossing them behind him.

"And one last thing," he said, the words a vibration against her breasts when he moved closer, tugging at her panties and freeing her of them.

"There," he sighed. "Now we'll stay really warm."

She touched his face, her fingertips following the line of his jaw and coming to rest on his chin. "I feel warmer already, but what if the guard—"

"Taken care of. I paid him off."

"That's against—"

"—the law." He tasted her lips, his tongue tracing the line of her mouth; then he drew back, and she felt his hand on her heart. "I know, and this probably is, too."

"N—no," she whispered, barely able to form the word when he touched her like that. "Not when we're married."

"How about this?" he asked, his voice rough with desire as his hand circled her breast. "Or this?" he asked, taking her nipple between his fingers.

She mimicked him, spreading her hand on his chest, then running her fingers lightly over his muscles, feeling his nipple tighten on contact. "No, and neither is this," she said as her hand moved lower. "Or this." Finally, "Or...this."

Brady groaned, a deep passionate sound that echoed in Jayne's ears.

"Or this," she said.

"Where did you learn . . . ?"

"No questions," she murmured, her lips against his shoulder, her tongue touching the irregular scar the bullet wound had made. "Just take what there is. Accept what we have together."

He drew her to him in a hard, almost crushing hug. "We're meant to be together."

"Yes," she breathed against the heat of his chest, her eyes closed tightly to control the tears that suddenly threatened to fall, tears of pure happiness. "Yes, and the way Jack was meant to survive, and Rocky was meant to survive and be able to go home with his grandparents. It's all the way it should be. Perfect."

He drew back, one hand cupping her chin with heat and gentle strength. His shadowy gaze met hers. "Life isn't perfect, love, we know that, but we're going to come as close as any two people can."

"Another law?" she asked.

"No, a promise," he said.

Her tongue darted out to touch her lips. "Shouldn't we be looking for submarines?"

"No," he said, dipping his head to taste the sensitive spot just under her ear.

"But the races—"

"—are called off until I've had my fill of you. And that . . ." He tangled his fingers in her hair and gently pulled her head back until she was looking into his eyes. "That will take a lifetime, or longer."

She needed Brady more than she had ever thought it was possible to need another person. "A long, full lifetime," she whispered.

In the distance she could hear noisemakers and fireworks going off as the new year arrived. She circled Brady's neck with her arms. "Happy New Year."

"Yes, a very Happy New Year," Brady murmured and proceeded to show her just how happy it would be.

* * * * *

Double your reading pleasure this fall with two Award of Excellence titles written by two of your favorite authors.

Available in September

DUNCAN'S BRIDE
by Linda Howard
Silhouette Intimate Moments #349

Mail-order bride Madelyn Patterson was nothing like what Reese Duncan expected—and everything he needed.

Available in October

THE COWBOY'S LADY
by Debbie Macomber
Silhouette Special Edition #626

The Montana cowboy wanted a little lady at his beck and call—the "lady" in question saw things differently....

These titles have been selected to receive a special laurel—the Award of Excellence. Look for the distinctive emblem on the cover. It lets you know there's something truly wonderful inside! DUN-1

Silhouette Special Edition

Appearing in October
for a return engagement, Nora Roberts's
bestselling 1988 miniseries featuring

THE O'HURLEYS!
Nora Roberts

Book 1 THE LAST HONEST WOMAN *Abby's Story*
Book 2 DANCE TO THE PIPER *Maddy's Story*
Book 3 SKIN DEEP *Chantel's Story*

And making his debut in a brand-new title, a very special
leading man . . . Trace O'Hurley!

Book 4 WITHOUT A TRACE *Trace's Tale*

In 1988, Nora Roberts introduced THE O'HURLEYS!—a close-knit
family of entertainers whose early travels spanned the country. The
beautiful triplet sisters and their mysterious brother each experience
the triumphant joy and passion only true love can bring, in four books
you will remember long after the last pages are turned.

Don't miss this captivating miniseries in October—a special collec-
tor's edition available wherever paperbacks are sold.